For Lucy Fry, the Hatter to my Hare.

Ottilie Colter and the Master of Monsters
published in 2019 by
Hardie Grant Egmont
Ground Floor, Building 1, 658 Church Street
Richmond, Victoria 3121, Australia
www.hardiegrantegmont.com

 A catalogue record for this
book is available from the
National Library of Australia

Text copyright © 2019 Rhiannon Williams
Design copyright © 2019 Hardie Grant Egmont
Cover illustration by Maike Plenzke
Cover design by Jess Cruickshank
Typeset in Fournier MT Std 13/17pt by Eggplant Communications

Printed in Australia by McPherson's Printing Group,
Maryborough, Victoria.

1 3 5 7 9 10 8 6 4 2

The paper in this book is FSC® certified. FSC®
promotes environmentally responsible, socially
beneficial and economically viable management of
the world's forests.

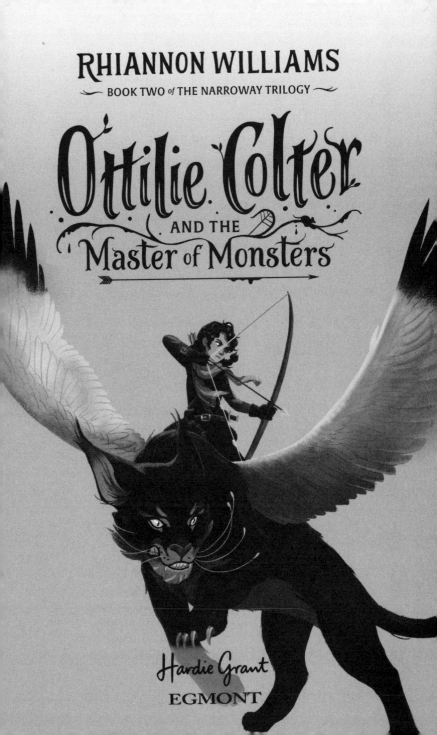

RHIANNON WILLIAMS

BOOK TWO *of* THE NARROWAY TRILOGY

Ottilie Colter

AND THE

Master of Monsters

Hardie Grant

EGMONT

Little Bird

Bill stood in a puddle. His eyelashes swept low, fluttering as he dreamed ...

A young girl was crouched in the corner of a shadowed space. Wisps of icy hair floated above her shoulders, and fading bruises coloured the backs of both hands, one of which rested at an odd angle.

Angry voices could be heard somewhere out of sight.

'How could you have kept this from me?' said a man's voice.

'I did not wish to speak of it!' a woman answered. 'If people heard ... if they knew ...' Her words were like the hissing and spitting of an angry cat. 'I couldn't face it. It felt like – like confirmation!'

'Of what?'

'That we are … that she is our punishment.'

'That was confirmed the day she was born,' said the man. 'Nothing for a decade and then this, a girl … That twisted creature is our curse. At least now she can be useful. We can put her to work.'

Inside the room, the girl's shoulders shook.

Bill's eyes opened. He considered his drowned feet and wondered how he had come to be there. All water was laced with memory. It tended to bring about funny dreams, which was just one of several reasons Bill didn't usually have snoozes in puddles.

He felt a scratching from his head. A downy ghostfinch was perched between his horns.

'Did you make me sleepwalk?' he said.

The bird didn't appear to respond. Instead, it pecked a fat green leafmite out of Bill's hair and swallowed it in one gulp.

Bill strained his mind, trying to remember the dream. He'd seen that girl again, the girl with the floating hair. The birds kept reminding him. He was sure he knew more – sometimes she was older – but he couldn't keep it straight.

Bill had never had so many memories about one person before. He wondered if it had something to do with his location. He had been living high up in the hollow of a tree on the edge of the River Hook for the past two seasons. He had picked the spot very carefully: it was safe, out of sight, with a perfect view of the duck hatch. He was waiting for someone. He still had her hair in a bag. He couldn't remember her name, or where she had gone, but he could remember her. She had said she would return, and Bill had been waiting ever since.

2

Leo's Remedy

Something screeched overhead. Ottilie tripped backwards, smacked into Maestro's side and bounced off him into the mud. Maestro swung around and bared his enormous fangs. His breath smelled of salted eel. Ottilie cringed, ignoring the impulse to dive sideways and curl to protect her underside. Showing fear only made Maestro worse.

'All right down there?' called Ned.

Ottilie scrunched her nose up. Ned was leaning over the fence, the ghost of a laugh lighting his face.

'What was that?' said Ottilie, clambering to her feet and scanning the skies.

'Just an owl, I think,' said Ned.

Ottilie's cheeks warmed. She squinted up at the boundary wall and could just see the silhouette of huntsmen against the pale sky. Of course it wasn't a dredretch. Fiory's huntsmen would have sounded the alarm or shot it down. That was their job. Fort Fiory was one of three stations in the Narroway, the slip of land between the Usklers, to the east, and the deserted Laklands, to the west. Huntsmen at the stations – Fiory, Arko and Richter – were charged with managing the dredretch threat, keeping the monsters out of the Usklers.

Ottilie should have known. Dredretches were not easily confused with ordinary beasts. Although the different dredretch species could vaguely resemble familiar creatures, they were a mockery of nature's design and, if they came close enough, caused a physical sickness that the huntsmen were trained to ward off.

Ottilie turned to Ned. 'Why are you down here?' she said, annoyed that he'd witnessed her moment of clumsiness.

Ned grinned. 'I was looking for Leo.'

Ottilie scowled at the mention of her guardian's name. It was Leo's fault she was there in the first place. 'He's not here,' she snapped.

Ned raised one of his dark eyebrows.

'Leo says he's not happy with my performance,' she quoted. 'He sent me to practise with Maestro by myself.'

'So why are you just standing with him in the paddock?' Ned said with a half-smile.

'Are you here to spy?'

He let out a bark of laughter.

Out of the corner of her eye Ottilie noticed Wrangler Kinney, the balding wingerslink master. He had undoubtedly been spying – hoping for a fresh excuse to mock her. Ottilie liked to think he was just bitter because none of the wingerslinks liked him. She had even seen Maestro trip him up with his tail when Kinney was passing by. The gold-toothed grouch walked around with a whip tucked into his belt and Ottilie knew it was the only reason the beasts obeyed him. She had never seen him use it, but the wingerslinks certainly seemed to know what it was for.

But it was more than that, Ottilie knew. The all-male Narroway Hunt had recruited her brother, Gully, not her. She might have cut off her hair and pretended to be Ott, Gully's older brother from the Swamp Hollows, but the ruse didn't last the year. When she was found out, Ottilie had feared being separated from Gully. But instead she had been consigned to the shovelies, the disgraced rank of former huntsmen, condemned to burying dredretch bones, until she saved Leo from the monstrous kappabak and was finally accepted as the first female member of the Narroway Hunt. But, after everything, that fear had never really gone away.

Her return to the Hunt had not been met with a warm welcome. It had been made very clear to her that many of the Fiory community resented Ottilie's position. Kinney was one of them. He loved to watch her fail – loved to comment, too – but Ned's presence was probably keeping him at a distance this morning.

'I tried to get the saddle on him but he kept throwing it off,' she said, scowling at the great silvery wingerslink. 'Then he bit me.'

Ned frowned. 'He actually bit you?'

'Yes. Well. No. He put his jaws over my arm and then let it go, but I got the message.'

Ned laughed again.

'Leo knew this would happen!' said Ottilie, giving Maestro a shove with her shoulder. 'He knew Maestro wouldn't let me anywhere near him by myself!'

'Probably.'

Ottilie growled. Maestro joined in, harmonising with her frustration. She elbowed him in the rump and he bared his teeth again. She stared him down, nearly losing herself in his huge, fire-wreathed eyes.

'Do you know where he is?' said Ned.

She blinked. 'Who? Leo? No. What do you need him for?'

'Voilies is looking for him. I figured you'd be the best person to ask.'

'Well, I wish I wasn't,' she grumbled.

Ned smiled. 'Only two seasons to go. Then you'll be rid of that one too.' He nodded at Maestro.

Although she had only just been permitted to hunt again, Ottilie's fledgling year was half gone. At winter's end she and her friends would undertake their order trials. After which Leo would no longer be her guardian and Ottilie, if she was made a flyer, would be assigned a wingerslink of her own.

'I can't wait.' She glanced at Maestro and felt immediately guilty. 'What does Voilies want with him, anyway? It's barely even light yet.' She waved her hand at the pink mist draping the dawn sky.

'He skipped out on his check-up this morning,' he said, with a trace of concern.

Nearly a month had passed since Leo had been cornered by the kappabak. Ottilie had found him just in time. Any longer and it might have been more than his leg that was crushed. The patchies were strictly monitoring his recovery. Maestro had come further much faster. Wingerslinks were remarkable healers, and the fur had already grown to cover the jagged scar in his side.

'Voilies needs a hobby. His obsession with Leo makes me gag,' said Ottilie, her words harsher than she intended.

Ned's brow creased. 'Are you all right? You don't sound like yourself.'

'I just got bitten by a wingerslink,' she said, looking away from him. She didn't want to talk about her bad mood, or what had caused it.

'And that's all?' he pressed.

It wasn't all. At breakfast that morning Igor Thrike had brushed against her, muttering something foul in her ear, and it wasn't the first time something like that had happened.

'It's early and Maestro bit me. That's it,' she said, forcing herself to look him in the eye. Ottilie had no desire to share the truth with Ned. She didn't want him thinking she couldn't handle herself, or that she needed protection.

➤————————————————

By lunchtime, Ottilie's mood had not improved and she found she couldn't face the dining room. It wasn't just Igor Thrike and Wrangler Kinney who bothered her; Maeve Moth and Gracie Moravec still took every opportunity to spit something nasty in her direction. The truth was, Ottilie was having difficulty sleeping and she found herself close to tears more often than she liked.

Determined not to be defeated by the day, she resolved to take a nap and start it over, but when she opened the door to her bedchamber it was immediately clear things were not going to go her way – Leo was leaning against her window.

Ottilie scowled across the room.

'Good afternoon to you too,' said Leo.

'What do you want?' she snapped, thinking of Maestro's jaws clamped over her arm.

Leo raised his eyebrows. 'You are in a bad mood.'

'What did Ned say to you?'

'Nothing,' said Leo, waving his hand. 'Just that you weren't having a good day.'

'And you thought you could make it better by breaking into my room?' she said, stomping inside and slumping onto her bed.

'Yes. Get dressed and come with me,' he said, moving towards the door. He refused to use his crutches any longer but still favoured his right leg as he walked.

'I am dressed.'

Leo made an impatient noise that reminded her of a whining dog. 'Get your hunting gear on, we're going out.'

'Why?'

'Because you're ranked seventy-sixth and I know where to find a knopo troop.'

Ottilie felt a flicker of excitement. Knopoes were an elusive, high-scoring dredretch. She had encountered a loner but never a troop. It was too tempting to resist.

The huntsmen were awarded points for every dredretch they felled. Some species, like jivvies, the bloodthirsty death crows, were worth as little as one point per fell. The highest-scoring dredretch on record was the ferocious kappabak, worth one hundred and fifty. At the end of the hunting year the huntsmen with the highest scores were named champions of their tier, a supreme honour.

Ottilie couldn't help but dream of becoming a champion. If she made champion, everyone would have to take her seriously. She would finally be considered a rightful member of the Narroway Hunt, and maybe the Hunt would allow other girls to join.

It was true that becoming champion of the fledgling tier was a near impossible dream. Over the last few weeks, she had improved her position quite quickly. But she had a long way to go. When Ottilie was made a huntsman again, they reset her score. She had to restart her fledge year two seasons behind everyone else, with a bottom-place ranking.

In the early days of Leo's recovery, Ottilie had taken the lead in their hunts. She scored more points per shift than ever before, improving her ranking of eighty-seventh to seventy-sixth. If Leo really knew where to find a knopo troop, she was sure she would make another leap in the rankings before this week was through.

Ottilie kept a close eye on Maestro's jaws as Leo tightened the girth on the double saddle. 'How can we even go out when we're not rostered on?'

'I got Rudolph Sacker to swap his shift for mine tomorrow,' said Leo, tucking in the strap.

'Well, this seems more like a treat for you than for me,' said Ottilie. 'I was going to take a nap.'

Leo snorted. 'You're miserable. I'm cheering you up.'

'Of course you think scoring points is the only way to cheer someone up.' She strangled her smile.

'It's not the only way,' he said, hoisting himself into the saddle. 'But it's the best way.'

Her smile broke free as she climbed up behind him. Slipping her feet into the stirrups, she braced as Maestro launched into the air. They settled into a smooth glide over the treetops and her worries pulled back, like a scarf streaming behind her. 'So where are these knopoes?'

'Jungle Bay on the north coast,' said Leo. 'There's a fair bit of Narroway between here and there and if we're lucky we'll see a lot of action.'

They were indeed lucky.

On their journey north they encountered a squail, six morgies, a nest of barbed toads, endless jivvies, a trick of flares and no less than twenty leaping ripperspitters – horrible rat-like dredretches with acidic saliva, which they used to spit in a huntsman's eyes.

Leo elbowed the last ripperspitter, sending it spiralling to the left, and Ottilie shot it clean through the head with an arrow. The rodent fizzled, its flesh bubbling and melting as it fell into the basin of bracken below.

Twilight draped the Uskler pines and the sickle moon glowed brighter in the dusky light. Leo guided Maestro down to land in a small clearing by a dried-up stream.

'It's getting late,' said Ottilie, pulling more arrows from the saddlebag.

Leo unbuckled his injured leg and slid down Maestro's side. He tossed her a knife to replace the one she'd lost inside a morgie's narrow jaw. Like reptilian terriers, morgies attacked from below, trying to tear foot from ankle. One of them had leapt and, to its peril, snapped just as Ottilie swung her knife: it ended up swallowing the blade whole.

Leo was grinning. 'You want to go home to bed?'

'Course not,' she said with a smile.

Jungle Bay was only a short flying distance from the clearing, but Leo decided Maestro should have a break before they took on the knopoes. The Hunt had had little success in tracking them. They were unpredictable, and seemed content to settle in all manner of landscapes: forest canopies, wetlands, alpine regions, and now Leo had found them in the coastal cliffs. Despite their adaptability, this was strange. There were two things they knew all dredretches couldn't stand: salt and rain. Coastal regions were a haven for natural beasts because dredretches disliked salty sea spray and tended to stick further inland.

Leo grabbed himself a dustplum, tossed one to Ottilie, and settled down on a half-rotted log. Maestro lay in front of him. His crystalline eyes slid shut, but he kept his head slightly raised, poised to act should the need arise.

They sat in silence for quite a while – probably because their hunt had run smoothly and Leo couldn't think of anything critical to say. Ottilie smiled to herself.

'See, I was right,' said Leo. 'I did improve your day! We haven't even got the knopoes yet and look at you, grinning like an idiot!'

'I am not grinning like an idi–' Ottilie froze. She could see something in the distance.

'What?' Leo stood up.

Ottilie raised her bow and aimed an arrow through a gap in the trees. 'Someone's watching us.'

❧ 3 ❧

The Sea Spears

The wind picked up, catching on the trees, whose shadows snatched like talons and teeth.

Leo moved to stand beside Ottilie, cutlass in hand. 'What do you mean someone?' he said, peering ahead.

The light from their glow sticks didn't reach beyond the clearing.

'I saw someone between the trees,' said Ottilie, her bow still raised. She had a horrible feeling that the mysterious hooded figure she had seen twice before was now watching them, only a few yards away.

'It's happened before,' she said. 'That day, with the kappabak.' She hadn't told Leo back then. She didn't know why she was telling him now. Maybe just because he was there to bear witness. People listened to Leo. If he reported the sighting, no-one would question it, or suspect he was just a frightened little girl.

Maestro stared ahead, his ears tipped forwards.

'He can see something,' said Leo, taking a step.

There was a flash – was it lightning? No. It was wrong: not bright but the opposite, a flash like blackness in the already night-heavy trees. Ottilie shook her head. She was just thinking she must have imagined it when there was a great swishing sound, followed by the swooping of wings and a bloodcurdling squawk to rival the call of a squail. They braced, but the creature didn't attack, and she heard the beating of its wings growing faint in the distance.

'It was just a dredretch,' said Leo, patting Maestro, who was growling quietly, ears flattened to his skull.

'I don't think it was – look at him, he's upset,' said Ottilie.

'He's not upset, are you, mate?' Leo rubbed the top of his head and frowned. Maestro relaxed at his touch. 'Unsettled maybe.' He looked at her. 'You saw someone that day?'

She nodded, still prickling with nerves. Her darting eyes found the husk of a stump to her left. Something drew her gaze, a single drip of thick black liquid trailing from a crack in the dried-out wood. It was hard to see, but it looked familiar, like the oily black gloop that dribbled down the leaves in the Withering Wood.

She frowned. That wasn't possible. The withering sickness spread outwards from the heart of the Withering Wood. It didn't show up in isolated patches. She shifted her weight to step closer, but then realised what it must have been. It was just dredretch blood. Someone had probably felled one nearby and the blood had spattered. Her fear was fuelling her imagination.

'Why didn't you tell me?'

'I don't know,' she said honestly. 'I didn't know what I could say and who I could trust. A lot was happening at once.'

She thought she caught a streak of hurt cross his face, but he turned away. 'Come on, you can go up front.'

'Why?' she asked, surprised. Ever since Leo's leg had improved, Ottilie had been relegated to the back of the saddle.

'Because I said I was taking you to hunt knopoes to cheer you up, so you can take the lead.' He paused, then turned back to Maestro. 'Fine – if you don't want to …' He moved to climb up front.

'No, I want to!' She hurried forwards and leapt into the saddle, bracing herself for adventure.

They flew north, towards Jungle Bay. Ottilie remembered her first glimpse of the sea. She and Leo had been flying through the mountains south of Fiory, and between the peaks she had seen it – an endless stretch of deepest blue, scattered with specks of sunlight. She remembered losing her breath and feeling very small, in the most wonderful way.

Ahead of them now, a hooked peninsula scooped Jungle Bay out of the darkened ocean, like a greedy arm of cliffs and caves. Maestro flew low over the giant dewy leaves and fat tree trunks. The trees, linked by thick vines, spread all the way down to the edge of the water, which mirrored the night sky.

Maestro touched down on a pad of damp rock, beneath the canopy.

'Hear that?' said Leo.

Ottilie couldn't hear anything beyond the gentle lapping of water against tree trunks.

'Jungle Bay used to be full of birds and frogs and insects. All the noisy things,' he said. 'I knew something new had moved in, because everything else has moved out.'

'Where are the knopoes?' She looked around, her pulse quickening.

'That's the really crazy part,' he said, pointing across the water. 'They're out there. Go slow, I'll show you why.'

Ottilie pulled her bow from her back and nudged Maestro into the air. Nearing the curve of the cape, she could just make out great columns of rock. Some stood independently, like ancient towers stretching up out of the sea. Others were still joined to the cliff in part, bridged by lines of jagged rock.

'We call them the Sea Spears,' said Leo. 'The knopoes are in the caves, on the cape just behind them.'

Approaching the caves, they were greeted with jarring hoots and ear-splitting screams. In the light of the glow sticks, Ottilie saw a knopo, twice the size of Wrangler Morse, lumbering out of a cave. It had matted fur and long, uneven fangs. Standing on its short legs, the knopo waved its elongated arms threateningly, and beat its melon-sized fists against the rock.

Circling, Ottilie glimpsed animal carcasses scattered around the edge of the cliff. Her breath caught and she felt a swoop of sorrow. She pointed to a rocky crag above the water, and the rotting skeleton of what might have been a large sea lion.

'How did that get up there?' said Leo, over the knopoes' screams.

'I think they must have dragged it,' she said. 'Look – they've been killing animals. There are so many!'

'Doesn't make sense,' he muttered.

Ottilie stared down at the remains of the coastal creatures and felt a burning behind her eyes. She nocked an arrow and aimed at the huge knopo. It lunged and the arrow bounced off the cliff wall. Three more appeared from the caves, all significantly smaller than the first. Fangs bared, they screamed like phantom apes.

Ottilie hit one, piercing its sloping shoulder. The knopo stumbled sideways, the beginnings of salt paralysis affecting its balance. She had missed the heart, but at least they knew the salt blades still worked.

There was a moment of stillness. Then they became frenzied, hooting and shrieking and dancing around — wilder, if possible, than before.

In an attempt to get closer to their attackers, one knopo leapt heedlessly onto the rocks that, like rows of teeth, stretched out to the Sea Spears. Leo shot it down and it plunged into the inky water with a great splash.

One by one the other knopoes leapt onto the rocks, clambering towards the Sea Spears. The first one to reach them hung off the edge, hooting and screaming. Maestro wove between the towering columns, tipping and tilting, dodging swinging arms and razor-sharp claws.

With an almighty shriek, a knopo sprang from its perch on the rock right above their heads. Maestro rolled so suddenly that Leo gasped. Both of them grabbed hold of the saddle, and Ottilie clenched her jaw so tight she hurt her teeth, as the knopo missed its mark and Maestro righted himself in the air.

She took a deep breath. Leo managed a shaky laugh, reaching forwards to ruffle the wingerslink's fur. Maestro made a rumbling noise in response and continued sweeping and soaring in spirals until Ottilie and Leo had shot every one of the foul monsters into the sea.

Their work done, Maestro landed on the cliff by the caves. There were carcasses everywhere, in varying stages of decomposition.

'They shouldn't have been here,' said Leo, his brow creasing. 'If they killed that sea lion …' He shook his head slowly. 'That thing would have been covered in salt. They shouldn't have been able to touch it.'

Ottilie shivered. 'They shouldn't have even wanted to try,' she said, staring sadly at the carcass of what might have been a mudcat. 'Voilies said dredretches don't bother with natural beasts. Not unless they threaten them, or get in their way …'

'That's normally true,' said Leo. 'And the salt blades still affected them …' He glanced at the curved scrap of light, high in the sky. 'We need to get back – we should report this.' He gestured at the carcasses.

Ottilie wasn't used to Leo looking worried. It made her feel unstable somehow, as if the cliff was rocking and cracking beneath them. She pushed Maestro into the air. They rose higher and higher until the trees were bristly shadows below. She let the flight calm her and, for a little while, felt there was no land or sea, no world beneath them, just wings and sky and starlight.

Fiory came into view, shining silver on the hilltop. Ottilie felt Maestro tense and hesitate. Moments later she heard the sounds that must have reached him first – a cacophony of bells ringing out from the station, the howls of the shepherds and, as they drew closer, the shouts from within.

4

Sleeper Come

Maestro landed in the upper grounds. A bespectacled boy dashed towards them, arms waving.

'There's a wyler!' Preddy cried. He clutched his ribs and panted, 'In the fort!'

Panic gripped Ottilie like cold hands in the dark.

'Where?' said Leo, leaping out of the saddle and kicking her in the leg.

'I don't know,' said Preddy. 'I just got in from patrol and Wrangler Furdles said … someone's hurt, and they've lost it. All of the elites on site are inside now, hunting it.'

'What do you mean they've lost it?' Leo barked.

'Who's hurt?' said Ottilie. Her thoughts were leaves in a windstorm: Gully wounded, Gully dead, Alba and

Skip … blood and venom and blackened fangs. How had a wyler got inside?

'A fourth tier, they've taken him to the infirmary. I think he's recovering,' said Preddy.

She swallowed her sigh of relief and rubbed her bruised calf. Leo merely grunted and charged off towards the lights.

Her fear told her to run to her bedchamber and bolt the door, but she wouldn't do that. She couldn't. Skip was her first steady thought. Gully knew how to handle a dredretch, Alba had Montie, untrained but armed with the instincts of a mother. Skip had no-one.

Steeling herself, Ottilie climbed down from the saddle and drew a long knife from her boot.

'Wrangler Morse said we're to stay clear,' said Preddy, staring wide-eyed at the knife. 'The elites –'

'Come on, Preddy.' She grabbed his arm.

Ottilie knew she couldn't hunt it. How could she track a wyler down the dim stone corridors with no crunching or rustling, no markings in the dirt? But Fort Fiory was full of unarmed custodians: girls that the Hunt refused to train, brought to the Narroway to serve the huntsmen and maintain the fort. Skip was a sculkie, an interior servant. Ottilie would head for their corridor, for Skip's bedchamber.

Everywhere she looked doors were shut tight. They tiptoed down each corridor, wary of drawing the wyler to them. Now and then they crossed paths with an elite, but no-one told them to go and hide. There were no wranglers to take orders from. Ottilie guessed they were locked in their chambers, under the impression they could do a dredretch no harm; like everyone else in the Narroway, they believed only an innocent – a child – could fell the monsters. Ottilie strongly suspected that wasn't the case. She and Alba had been reading, seeking answers, but they were yet to find any solid evidence that proved the rule of innocence true or false.

Leo was nowhere to be seen. She wondered where Gully and Scoot were. She had been so focused on her own mood that day, she didn't know what was going on with everyone else.

'Do you know where Gully is?' Ottilie whispered.

'What?' said Preddy. He leaned down, bending almost half over to get his ear closer to her mouth.

'Gully and Scoot, are they out or in?'

'Gully and Ned are on a night hunt, but they might have come back if they heard the bells. I think Scoot's in for the night.'

She didn't know which was safer, Scoot locked in his room or Gully out in the Narroway.

'They're probably fine,' Preddy murmured, more to himself, perhaps, than to Ottilie.

The silence pressed on her ears like deep water. With every step her nerves mounted and she found it a little more difficult to breathe. Fiory was supposed to be safe. There hadn't been an incident inside the boundary walls since the yickers in Floodwood, and that had been an anomaly – that was what Captain Lyre had assured them. Dredretches never got inside.

They reached the sculkies' corridor. Preddy was one step ahead of Ottilie when he lurched forwards and fell on his face. The crunch of his eyeglasses was like a boot to the teeth.

'Preddy!' Ottilie's heart skipped. Christopher Crow had lurched just like that.

'I'm all right,' he muttered, scrambling sideways. 'I tripped on something.' His voice was thin, his eyes fixed on the obstacle.

A feeble lamp hung by the sculkies' door, a little further down. Ottilie's gaze settled on the ground ahead. She could see a large shape just beyond the lamplight.

'Ahh!' Like a startled crab, Preddy scuttled further away. He kicked out with his foot and something rolled across the floor, clinking on the stone. Ottilie blinked, her insides squirming. It was a thumb – a huntsman's left thumb, with a flat bronze ring still clinging to the dismembered bone as if by magic.

The rings were their shields. Huntsmen still learning to ward off the dredretch sickness relied on those scraps of metal to keep their hearts beating when a dredretch was near. Her ribs pressed in. *Sleeper comes for none.* Those words were engraved inside all of their rings. She stared at the shiny piece of bronze to avoid seeing the truth. The sleeper had come. That ring belonged to a huntsman, and that huntsman was lying a few feet from where she crouched.

Wylers were smart. They went for the rings first. She had read that in a bestiary – or maybe Leo had told her. She couldn't remember.

Leo. Ottilie rocked on her feet, hot panic creeping up her neck. Could this be him, bested by a wyler?

No. The elites didn't wear their rings, didn't need them. This was a young huntsman. A fledge or a second tier. For one terrible breath she considered it might be Gully – but she knew it wasn't. Even from the corner of her eye she would know him.

Ottilie shook her head and forced her eyes to blink away from the severed thumb.

Preddy was leaning over the body. 'He's not a fledge,' he whispered. 'I don't know his name.'

'Are you all right?' She moved over to help him up and felt, strangely, as if she couldn't feel her legs.

'I don't know his name,' Preddy repeated.

'That's all right, Preddy, you were at Richter most of the –'

'Do you know his name?' he asked, desperation in his voice.

Ottilie clenched her jaw tight and looked down at the body. 'His name is Tommy,' she managed to whisper. He was a second-tier flyer. She didn't know his family name.

They weren't safe. They had to move. Ottilie scanned the corridor, noticing only vaguely that tears wet her cheeks. There was blood, but not nearly as much as there could have been. The wyler hadn't lingered.

'Come on, Preddy, we have to go. We have to make sure they're safe.' She pulled him to his feet. Her own knees quaked, but she kept hold of his arm and they steadied each other as they walked.

When they reached the door to Skip's bedchamber they paused, searching for any sign that the wyler was still in the vicinity. Ottilie caught Preddy's eye. Her fingers wrapped around the latch, but before she could lift it someone behind the door screamed.

The panic was like walking headfirst into an invisible wall. Dizzied but determined, Ottilie flung the door open. At least thirteen girls were inside, pressed into two corners of the bedchamber. They were all staring at a bed by the west wall.

'What happened?' said Preddy, to no-one in particular.

Skip's dark blonde head was poking up from behind Gracie Moravec. 'It's in here. No-one's hurt. We saw it by that bed, we think it's gone underneath.' She sounded calm – focused.

Preddy looked at the bed in horror. 'How did it ge–'

'Doesn't matter,' said Ottilie, readying her knife.

'One of us needs to sound the alarm,' he said. 'I wonder if anyone heard the scream.'

Ottilie wasn't thinking straight. 'You go, I've faced one before.'

Preddy sprinted from the room. Only when the beat of his boots had faded did it occur to her that one of the sculkies could have gone, leaving two armed huntsmen in the room instead of one. It was too late to do anything about it. They needed help, fast.

She felt someone move behind her.

'Give me a knife,' muttered Skip.

Ottilie passed her the one she was holding and pulled another from her belt. Skip stood beside her, knife at the ready.

What was it waiting for?

Ottilie didn't want to do anything that might trigger its attack. She would wait there, armed, standing between the wyler and the sculkies until help arrived. Preddy would reach a watchtower soon, and he might well come across an elite on the way. She was considering checking the wyler was still under the bed, weighing up whether meeting its eye might set it off, when there was a dull thud and the chink of metal on stone.

Ottilie whipped around. There was a flash of orange, and the flick of a dark tail disappearing under a bed by the window. Someone screamed again. A girl on the edge of the group was clutching her hand, blood seeping through her knuckles, her fingers grasping the stump where her thumb should be.

Ottilie felt her own blood drain at the sight of it. She had failed. She had already failed them.

'Get her out!' Skip barked. 'Get her away from it!'

There was nothing else to be done. The girl's ring had disappeared under one of the beds with the wyler and no-one could spare their own. Ottilie considered trying to ward off the sickness, but weakening herself was too dangerous – not that she had been of any help so far.

The girl fell to her knees, retching. A girl beside her bent down to help, but she did not take a step in any direction, too scared to separate from the pack.

'Get her out!' Skip said, again.

The girl went limp in her friend's arms, her pale hand falling to the ground like a lifeless squid. Her friend clutched it between her own, trying to slow the bleeding. It was clear that no-one was going to move, and in a couple of minutes that girl would be dead. Skip hurried over to the injured girl.

'Help me,' she said to the friend, and together they hoisted the girl to her feet and half-dragged her towards the door.

Ottilie was frozen, a strange lightness in her legs and lower back. She felt disconnected, unstable. How was she going to help them?

'Are you going to do something?' spat Maeve Moth. Her dark hair was loose and hung like a mourning veil, casting shadows on her face. From behind the thick strands Ottilie could see her bright eyes blazing.

'If I attack it, it'll start attacking you,' said Ottilie.

'It's already attacking us!' said Maeve.

Ottilie stared at the red pool on the ground and her fingers shook on the hilt of her knife.

Maeve growled in frustration. 'Kill it before it does that again!' She gestured wildly to the blood on the floor.

Ottilie did not move. Was she right to wait for help? Or was she just too scared to face it?

Something changed in the atmosphere. It was soft, but she could hear them coming, footsteps running in their direction. Help was on its way. The only problem was the wyler clearly sensed it too. Like a flaming arrow it shot out from under the bed, scattering the sculkies in all directions.

It was chaos. Some of them made it out of the room, knocking others to the floor as they stampeded. Maeve pulled the cutlass from the sheath across Ottilie's back and stood beside her just as Skip had done.

'Get onto the beds!' said Ottilie, trying to raise her voice above the clamour. She wanted a clear view of the floor.

As they shifted, Ottilie saw a shape slumped against the back wall. Mousy hair covered the girl's face, falling across her chest, where it mingled with blood and clumped together like marsh weed down the front of her nightdress.

Now she had really failed. Ottilie was there, in the room, and she had done nothing. But she couldn't think about that. She had to focus.

She saw a shadow shift to her left. Ottilie spun and dived, but the wyler was too quick. She glimpsed it skittering to the left and, anticipating its intention, she threw herself in front of Maeve, who had not jumped onto a bed.

Ottilie kicked out. Her boot met its horned skull and she grunted in pain as the wyler was thrown across the room. Dizzied by the kick, it slowed. Ignoring her throbbing foot, she nocked an arrow and fired, just a second too slow. The arrow hit the wall as the wyler shot under another bed.

The sculkies on top of that bed leapt onto another. They had gone silent.

Ottilie waved Maeve forwards and together they tipped the bed, shoving it to the side. The wyler shot out and pounced like a cat, scattering the sculkies on a nearby bed. Ottilie threw her bow to the side. It was too dangerous to be firing arrows with so many bodies everywhere.

The footsteps thundered. Igor Thrike raced into the room, followed by Bacon Skitter and Preddy. Bacon went straight for the wyler, which was perched on the bedframe. The wyler leapt at his face. Bacon ducked, creating a springboard for the wyler to leap across the room. Igor swung out with his hammer. He clipped it, managing to knock it off-course. The wyler rolled and righted itself. Ottilie slashed her knife, blade meeting flesh, but not deep enough. For a second the wyler disappeared. The room froze.

Maeve's low voice broke the silence. 'Gracie!'

The sculkies parted. Gracie Moravec was staring down at her forearm, a look of vague interest in her strange pale eyes, as ribbons of blood slithered from the teeth marks in her arm and dribbled onto the floor.

The wyler pounced at Maeve. It was slower now, leaking black blood across the room from where Ottilie's knife had slit its skin. Preddy dived in front of her, his cutlass slashing. There was a hiss and a thud and the wyler's horned head rolled across the floor to land at Gracie's feet. It remained whole for a moment before the flesh melted away, leaving only sticky bone and clumps of matted orange fur, which dulled to brown, then grey, then shrivelled to crispy black before their eyes.

5

The Dark Hours

'I don't think night-doubles apply if you're inside. Bad luck, Noel,' said Igor Thrike.

Ottilie looked him square in the eye and spat on the floor. She had never done such a thing, but the image of the sculkie being hoisted onto a stretcher, her chest in tatters, swam in her mind and it seemed the right gesture for the moment.

'Woah, Shovels, not very ladylike,' Igor sneered. 'Best put on an apron and clean that up.'

Ottilie ground her teeth but said nothing. She was distracted by Preddy. He was leaning against the wall, his pale face peppered with inky blood. He seemed sickly, and she was worried he'd been bitten or scratched. Wylers had nasty venom and their bite could be fatal. Bacon and Maeve had rushed Gracie down to the infirmary after the wyler had ripped into her arm.

Ottilie gripped Preddy's wrist. His eyes were hooded and heavy.

'Are you all right?' she said, as if coaxing an animal from its hiding place.

He didn't answer.

'Preddy, did you get hurt?' Her voice wobbled as she spoke.

He shook his head and swallowed. 'It's so different out there … hunting. It's different to this – protecting people, trying to save them.'

'You did save them,' she said. 'You stopped it hurting Maeve.'

'But that girl' – his eyes darted to the blood smeared against the wall – 'and the boy out in the hall.'

'You couldn't have done anything. You weren't even in the room when …' Ottilie couldn't finish the sentence. She had been in the room and done nothing. The chamber reeled, her vision clouded, but she snapped herself back. Preddy wasn't coping. She had to help him.

It occurred to her that Preddy had never seen anyone badly hurt by a dredretch. She remembered the shock of Christopher Crow's horrific death and took Preddy's hand in hers. She had nearly stifled the impulse, a habit from days past.

'But how did it get into the bedchamber?' said Wrangler Voilies' voice from the corridor.

Ottilie was more interested in finding out how it had got past the boundary walls. She looked to the doorway, as if Voilies would announce it upon entering the room.

Captain Lyre strode in, Wrangler Voilies just a step behind. Voilies was very pink in the face, and his skin looked shiny, as if he had been sweating nervously for hours. Captain Lyre looked much more composed. He was wearing his usual blue coat, and behind his neat black beard his mouth was a thin line, his normal cheery grin far from present.

'I can tell you how it got into the room,' said Maeve Moth, entering behind them. She looked to be in a terrible temper, which wasn't unusual, but Ottilie did wonder why she hadn't stayed in the infirmary with Gracie.

'You can?' said Wrangler Voilies, his voice pitching high and cutting out.

'Yes,' she said, eyes flashing. She didn't seem to be the slightest bit nervous about addressing a wrangler and a director. The directors were almost the highest authorities – only Conductor Edderfed, the Fiory Cardinal Conductor, ranked above them – and Captain Lyre was one of three Fiory directors. He went by Captain because he was captain of ceremonies – a title, Ottilie suspected, he may have given himself.

Captain Lyre fixed his gaze on Maeve. 'What happened?' he said evenly.

'Tommy came in to check on Fawn,' said Maeve. 'After he left we heard something out in the corridor, so Fawn opened the door to look. She found him on the floor and ran back and shut it, but that thing must have snuck in while it was open.' Her voice was heavy with accusation.

'Who is Faw—' began Wrangler Voilies.

'Fawn and Tommy Mogue are cousins,' said Captain Lyre, cutting him off. 'They were separated at a young age and reunited by chance here at Fiory.' His voice was calm, but his eyes were heavy.

Ottilie was taken aback — not because of the unlikely story, but because Captain Lyre knew such personal details about them. She had been under the impression that the directors, and many of the wranglers, thought themselves above knowing even the names of the custodians.

Ottilie glanced over to the corner where most of the uninjured girls were gathered. Montie Kit and the burly custodian chieftess, their supervisor, were talking with the girls. Montie's arm was around a girl with shaking shoulders. Ottilie couldn't see her face, but a tangle of coppery hair hung down her back.

Wrangler Voilies pursed his lips. 'Tommy shouldn't have been out of his room,' he said callously. 'The non-elites were instructed to stay out of the way.' His eyes fell upon Ottilie. He opened his mouth to speak but Maeve got in first.

'If they hadn't come, it would have been a massacre,' she said.

Ottilie couldn't believe her ears. Could Maeve Moth be standing up for her? Preddy had saved her life. She was undoubtedly speaking for him rather than for Ottilie.

'Indeed,' said Captain Lyre. 'I think in this instance they can be forgiven for disobeying orders.'

Ottilie could tell Wrangler Voilies did not agree, but it was clearly unacceptable for a wrangler to question a director. An unpleasant smile stretched his lips, as if pulled by two fish hooks. His tiny, watery eyes didn't leave her face and Ottilie had a feeling that had Preddy not been involved, Wrangler Voilies would have pushed much harder for punishment.

➤➤➤————————————————➤

Preddy's bedchamber was in one of the elite towers. Having spent the first part of the year at Fort Richter, Preddy had missed out on a fledgling room. His was just off the spiral staircase, and twice the size of Ottilie's.

Scoot was outraged by it – he insisted that Wrangler Voilies had assigned Preddy a better bedchamber because, in Scoot's words, he was 'a slimy old bootlicker'.

Knowing that there were plenty of other spare rooms in the fort, Ottilie was inclined to agree. Everyone knew Preddy came from a wealthy family and Voilies seemed to think that was something worth rewarding.

Ottilie took a deep breath. She was finding it difficult to form words. 'Drink,' she managed to say, pressing a cup of water into Preddy's clammy hands. He raised the cup and paused, as if he had forgotten what to do. Ottilie placed her hands over his and lifted the cup to his lips. He took a small sip and lowered it, his eyes unfocused.

In her concern, she found her voice. 'Are you sure you weren't hurt? Maybe I should get the patchies to check you over, just in case.'

He shook his head and said quietly, 'I think I just need to sleep.'

Ottilie waited on his bed while he scrubbed himself off in the washroom. Her head was spinning and every time she thought of the fallen sculkie and Tommy her heart seemed to stick mid-beat. Joely Wrecker, she realised – that was the girl's name. She felt ashamed for not remembering it earlier.

What was happening here? How had that wyler got in? And the knopoes by the sea, the dead animals, that creeper in the shadows – the hooded figure that always appeared before disaster struck. A witch? Ottilie had considered it before. The witches were supposed to be gone, dead and buried – or alive and buried, as some believed.

She shuddered but couldn't shake the thought. She and Alba suspected that a witch had hexed the king so that he couldn't defend his lands with armies of men. That was why the Narroway Hunt existed, why children were kidnapped and trained to hunt monsters.

She had wondered before if the same witch might be setting the monsters on them. Why? She couldn't even guess. But if a witch really was behind it, if that hooded figure had somehow snuck the wyler into the grounds, then this was surely just the beginning. But who was it? Who was the witch beneath the hood?

Ottilie's heart beat wildly. Her ribs seemed to press in around it, straining her breath. She lurched up and paced the room, counting her steps. An unwelcome image formed. Gracie Moravec. She'd had such a peculiar expression on her face after she'd been bitten. There had been no hint of fear or pain – just curiosity.

There was something not right about Gracie, unsettling, even fox-like. She never said much, but she put Ottilie on edge. She still remembered the time, months ago, that she had woken up to find Gracie staring at her, smiling in the dark.

Preddy emerged in his nightclothes with a little more colour in his cheeks. Ottilie found that she didn't want to leave him. In truth, she was scared of how she might feel on her own. Before she could consider her options the door swung open. Preddy jumped so violently he almost lost his footing. Ottilie took his elbow to steady him.

Scoot was standing in the doorway, an odd expression on his face. 'What are you doing in here?' he whispered, his eyes darting between Ottilie and Preddy.

'I'm ...' She wasn't sure what to say – looking after Preddy? That was what she was doing, but it seemed a strange thing to say. 'I'm just talking to Preddy.'

Scoot raised his eyebrows. She didn't understand his problem. Scoot was always in her room.

'What are you doing in here?' she said.

Scoot slid the door shut behind him. 'I heard Preddy snagged the wyler,' he said, a triumphant grin taking over his face.

'He did.'

'Nice one!' said Scoot, doing a celebratory jig across the room. As he approached, his grin faded and his movements slowed. 'You didn't get bit, did you, Preddy?'

'No, I'm fine.'

'You don't look fine,' said Scoot, narrowing his eyes.

'He's tired,' Ottilie said.

Scoot jumped onto the bed. 'Come on, give us the story. I heard Igor and Bacon were there – how'd you get in before the elites? They would have hated that!' He hooted with glee.

Preddy seemed on the verge of tears.

'Come on, Scoot, let him sleep,' said Ottilie quickly, pulling Scoot towards the door.

'What's wrong with him?' he said, taking no care to keep Preddy from hearing.

'He needs to rest. Come on.' She steered him out the door and shut it behind them.

'What are you two doing up here?'

Ottilie sighed and turned to face Leo, who was coming up the stairs, Ned just behind him. A familiar feeling settled in, a weight that reminded her of her old home in the Swamp Hollows and the people she had left behind: her mother, Freddie, and her neighbours, Old Moss and Mr Parch. She felt older and stretched thin, as if invisible ropes tethered her to the people she cared for.

'We were just talking to Preddy. Now we're going to bed,' she said wearily.

Something must have shown on her face because Ned said, 'Is he all right?'

'Why wouldn't he be?' said Leo. 'Tell him congratulations from me,' he added, grinning. 'For showing up Thrike.'

'He doesn't want your congratulations,' muttered Ottilie, her head spinning again.

'What was that, Ott?' said Leo, cupping his hand to his ear. 'I thought I got you out of your bad mood.'

'Two people died, mate,' said Ned, softly.

Beside her, Ottilie sensed Scoot stiffen. He hadn't known.

Something flickered across Leo's face, and his smile faltered. He hitched it back up. 'Well, thanks to Noel it wasn't more, that's all I'm saying.' His voice changed. 'Tell him well done,' he said, more seriously. 'He did good.'

6

Feathers

The next morning, Ottilie felt strange leaving the safety of her weapon-stocked bedchamber. For the first time she wondered if she should have armed herself for breakfast. She almost considered turning back for her cutlass, but something stopped her. What would people say if she arrived armed and in her daywear clothes? She was ashamed to admit it, but she couldn't face the judgement. She knew what they would think. That she was a frightened girl. That it was proof she was unfit to be a huntsman. That girls were cowardly and weak. Leo had once called her a weak little witch and Ottilie had never forgotten it.

Scoot was leaning across a table at the far end of the dining room. He was frowning and talking fast. Opposite him, Preddy looked pale but steady. He must have managed to get some sleep. Ottilie hadn't been so lucky. Every time she closed her eyes she pictured Joely Wrecker slumped against the wall.

A pall hung over the space. The clinks and scrapes of dishes seemed uncommonly loud and Ottilie realised it was because hardly anyone was talking. When she looked closely, she caught glimpses of swollen eyes and clenched jaws. She wondered if they were afraid. If one wyler could get in, then couldn't another?

It shouldn't have happened that way. Ottilie shouldn't have been the only armed and trained girl in that bedchamber. Was anyone else thinking the same? She wasn't sure what to do, but it was time to do something.

'Morning, Ott,' said Bayo Amadory, rising from a table to her left. Bayo was Scoot's guardian. He had very broad shoulders and a usually cheerful face with a crooked nose, which Ottilie suspected had been broken during a struggle with a dredretch.

This morning his smile was strained. She didn't know him very well, but he was always friendly, even back when she was a shovelie. 'I wanted to say well done, for last night. I heard what happened. You and Preddy really stepped up,' he said. His words were kind, but his voice was grave.

'Thank you,' Ottilie mumbled, looking at her boots. It was difficult to talk about. Silence fell between them and she felt a strange need to mention Tommy and Joely, as if discussing the night without mentioning them was somehow wrong – but what words were there to say?

She met Bayo's gaze and saw the same hopeless confusion. She wondered how many huntsmen they had lost in the three years Bayo had been at Fiory. When Christopher Crow had died, Captain Lyre had suggested that deaths were not at all common, but Ottilie didn't know how to ask anyone without trivialising the loss. Also, there was a very big part of her that didn't actually want to know.

Finally, Bayo said quietly, 'Horrible night.' He shook his head. 'The directorate's still trying to figure out how it got in. It's all really …' He couldn't seem to find the word. Giving up, he said, 'Did you hear about that bone singer?'

'No, what happened? Was someone hurt?' said Ottilie, her heart rattling. She didn't think she could cope if she heard one more person had been hurt.

'Apparently one of them had a sort of fit. It was before the attack. No-one seems to know what happened, if it had something to do with the wyler or what … But who knows what the bone singers get up to,' he said, with a forced shrug. 'I'm guessing he's all right now, but they keep to themselves, don't they? Anyway' – he clapped her on the shoulder with one large hand – 'praying for a normal day.' Bayo shot Scoot a stiff wave across the room, and strode out the door.

The bone singers were a mystery to everyone. They tracked the dredretch fells, marked the ranking walls, and performed some sort of ritual on the remains. Ottilie had worked with them a fair bit when she was a shovelie.

She remembered Bonnie and Nicolai humming and sprinkling glittering salt on the dredretch bones. She could only assume it was a ritual to make sure the dredretches stayed dead, although dead wasn't quite the right word; gone was perhaps better.

'Ottilie?' said a quiet voice.

She jumped. She'd been in a daze, forgotten to move. Gully was standing beside her.

'Morning,' she muttered, hardly knowing she said it.

His eyes darkened. 'I heard about last night. We came back when we heard the bells, then Ned let me stay and look for it with him, but we didn't find it.'

Ottilie just shook her head. She couldn't talk about it.

Gully nudged her shoulder with his head. 'Come on.' He steered her towards Preddy and Scoot.

She didn't eat. If it was possible to feel numb, fearful and achy all at once, that was what she felt.

At lunchtime they were called to the Moon Court. Captain Lyre spoke. He used words like 'tragedy' and 'heroic' but Ottilie hardly heard him. What reassurance could he offer? It had already happened.

The day was empty before her. Their training was cancelled to give them a bit of breathing space, but watches, hunts and patrols still had to go on. There were still dredretches out there and the Hunt could not ignore them, even though, as Captain Lyre put it, they were a fort in mourning.

She had seen this before, and the next day, as Ottilie watched the scattered feathers and bundles of moongrass light up the funeral pyres, her heart hardened and slowed. How had the wyler got in? Captain Lyre didn't address it. Was it because he didn't know? Bayo said the directorate was investigating it – had they not figured it out yet? Was Captain Lyre trying to avoid arousing suspicion and fear? Ottilie wanted to do something. This was wrong. Everything about it was wrong.

>>————————→

A rumour spread that the directorate was conducting private interviews with the huntsmen who had been on wall watch the night of the wyler attack. The news troubled Ottilie. Why all the secrecy? Why *private* interviews? Did they really believe that someone knew something about how the wyler got in and had not come forward? That someone inside Fiory was responsible for the attack? She thought again of the hooded witch in the shadows. Could it be someone she knew?

Tomorrow would be their first day back at training and Ottilie welcomed it. The prospect of her schedule filling up again made her feel steadier, and with that steadiness came the return of her appetite.

Ottilie was just about to join Gully and Ned at their table for dinner when something caught her eye. In the corner by the drinks station Gracie and Maeve were arguing. It was the first time Ottilie had seen Gracie since she had left the infirmary. She looked sallow and frail. Gracie had always seemed weightless, as if she could lift her feet and drift on a breeze, but she had changed somehow, as if a light wind would not pick her up but knock her down.

Opposite Gracie, Maeve was muttering furiously, gesturing at Gracie's bandaged arm. Gracie reached to pluck something small from Maeve's dark mane. Maeve swatted her hand away and Ottilie thought she saw something float to the ground. Maeve snapped at Gracie and marched away. After a moment, Gracie glided after her.

Ottilie waited for a breath or two, and then walked casually over to the drinks station. Reaching for a pitcher of water, she glanced at the floor. Resting on the stone was a single pale grey feather, about the length of her little toe. So Maeve Moth had a feather in her hair? It was strange, she supposed, but it didn't seem particularly important. She could have picked it up anywhere.

'Can I help you?'

Gracie appeared at her side. Her pale eyes found Ottilie's and a small, perfect smile appeared on her face. It was false – a slice of lemon stitched onto a scarecrow.

'I'm just getting some water,' said Ottilie, her neck stiffening.

'Here, let me help.' Gracie reached for the jug and Ottilie eyed her bandaged forearm. 'Nasty,' said Gracie.

'Sorry?'

'Teeth,' Gracie said, flashing her own again. She held out a cup. Ottilie took it, her fingers brushing Gracie's. She nearly flinched. Gracie's skin was hot, like stone under the midday sun.

'Enjoy,' Gracie sang, wandering away.

Ottilie looked at the water. It seemed fine, and Gracie surely couldn't have done anything to it with her standing right there. All the same, she wouldn't drink it. Every instinct told her to keep her distance from Gracie Moravec. Drinking from a cup she'd offered seemed downright stupid.

7

Hooves

Ottilie, Gully and Scoot strode across the dewy field in the direction of the stables. Having reached the second half of their fledgling year, they were to begin their next phase of training. To prepare for the order trials, they would be advancing their training on foot, and learning to ride and fly. They were divided according to their experience levels, so Preddy was exempt from horseback training and Ottilie, Gully and Scoot entered the stables without him.

'Welcome, come through, come through,' said a lively voice beyond the gate.

The horse mistress was the only female wrangler at Fort Fiory. She was fairly tall, with wild fiery hair and a small black eyepatch covering her right eye.

'I'm Wrangler Ritgrivvian,' she said, ushering them into a muddy yard at the centre of the stables. Her tone was gentle, reassuring, but it was like a swaying snake or a stretching cat: Ottilie could sense her strength. 'I like to get to know everyone by name and face.'

Her accent suggested an eastern origin. Leo's was similar and Ottilie wondered if she was from All Kings' Hill, like him.

Wrangler Ritgrivvian pulled a roll of parchment from her pocket. 'When I call your name, please raise your hand.'

Calling Ottilie's name, she paused for just a moment, her expression unreadable. Ottilie wasn't sure she would ever get used to this sort of thing. For months she had done everything possible to avoid being noticed, and now everyone knew her name – from their elusive Cardinal Conductor down to the most reclusive of shovelies. Ottilie Colter: the unwelcome huntsman.

Wrangler Ritgrivvian didn't waste any time. She and three stablehands moved through the group, sizing everyone up and pairing them with an appropriate steed. She chose Ottilie's horse herself. Billow was a hulking roan stallion, so tall that their pairing seemed strange.

She approached him cautiously, remembering that horses and wingerslinks didn't get on. Wingerslinks didn't get on with dogs, either, and since she'd begun flying with Leo, Fiory's shepherd pack had made their disdain for Maestro's scent very clear. It didn't seem to matter whether she had bathed, they could still smell him on her. Holding her hand out towards the stallion, Ottilie braced to withdraw. But if he could smell any hint of wingerslink, Billow didn't seem to mind. His large, gentle eyes regarded Ottilie with intelligent interest as she pressed her palm to his velvety neck.

'How many of you have been flying wingerslinks?' said Wrangler Ritgrivvian.

Ottilie and several others raised their hands.

'You will find that both an advantage and a disadvantage. While you have already prepared some of the muscles you will need to ride, wingerslinks and horses share little in common – your instincts may throw you off. But don't get too frustrated. We'll get there in the end. We always do,' she said, bracingly.

Billow nudged Ottilie in the back with his nose. She reached around to pat him, thinking that, so far, this was at least going better than her first meeting with Maestro.

As the lesson progressed, they began to trot. Ottilie was finding it difficult to balance. This was a new sensation – wingerslinks were never bouncy. Scoot was struggling ahead of her. His bay mare kept lurching between a walk and a canter, and both rider and horse were obviously frustrated. Ottilie was just getting into the rhythm of Billow's trot when Scoot's horse kicked out in front of them, flinging Scoot clean off. Billow swung sideways and if Ottilie had not been so used to an animal pitching her about, she might have joined Scoot on the ground.

Wrangler Ritgrivvian hurried over, calming Scoot's mare with a few soft words before pulling Scoot to his feet. 'Are you all right? Branter, isn't it?'

'Scoot,' he wheezed, clutching his side and eyeing the mare with bitter contempt. 'I'm fine. Fit as a firedrake.'

'You're letting your nerves win,' said Wrangler Ritgrivvian, looking him up and down. 'She can feel it.'

'I'm not nervous,' he snapped, his eyes darting towards Ottilie.

'You are, and with good reason,' she snapped back. 'She's a big beast with a mind of her own. But you must conquer it. If you don't relax, she won't either.'

Scoot grumbled and wiped a glob of mud off his cheek.

'And you, Ottilie?' Wrangler Ritgrivvian turned to her. 'Are you all right?'

'Yes, I'm fine,' said Ottilie, her heart still beating fast.

'You're a natural,' said Wrangler Ritgrivvian, with sunshine in her voice.

Ottilie glowed. She wasn't used to compliments, certainly not from wranglers. Since her return to the Hunt, many of the wranglers passed over her in training – ignoring her completely unless her form was so poor that they could make an example of her in front of the group.

'That's enough for today,' called Wrangler Ritgrivvian. She had a way of projecting her voice without raising it. Ottilie could understand why the horses liked her.

Scoot stomped his feet all the way back across the field. Ottilie knew he hated being the only one who had been unseated. She, on the other hand, was feeling brighter than she had in days. There was something about spending time with animals that made the world feel like a nicer place, if only for a little while.

She was just about to try to cheer Scoot up when Leo appeared.

'Ott – ugh, you stink of horse!'

Ottilie elbowed him. 'I do not.'

He sniffed in their direction. 'You all do.' He waved his hand at her. 'Maestro's going to hate that.'

'You can't smell anything,' she said, rolling her eyes. 'What do you want?'

He shrugged. 'I just wanted to know how it went.'

'It was good,' said Ottilie, feeling light.

Leo narrowed his eyes. 'Good?'

'She was great,' said Gully. 'Wrangler Ritgrivvian said she's a natural.'

'Don't be an idiot, Ott,' said Leo.

She laughed. 'What?'

'Don't let them see you performing in other disciplines. Do you want to be a flyer or not? Make sure you fall off a few times.' His eyes roved over Scoot's muddy uniform. 'He's got the right idea.'

Scoot looked like he was ready to hit Leo. Ottilie was surprised – that sort of comment would normally make Scoot laugh. She could imagine him claiming that he had fallen on purpose, that it was a clever ploy to ensure he stayed with the footmen.

Leo didn't seem to care. 'Come on,' he said, jerking his head towards the lower grounds. 'Let's go see Maestro. He can show you how he feels about you riding horses.' He marched off in the direction of the cliff stairs.

Ottilie made to farewell Gully and Scoot, but the expression on Scoot's face locked her tongue behind her teeth.

'You're not going with him?' said Scoot, his whole face taut with angry disbelief.

'I … yes? Why not?'

'We said we'd meet Preddy for lunch,' said Scoot accusingly.

Gully looked uncomfortable. His eyes flicked from Scoot to Ottilie to the back of Leo's head.

'I'll see him later,' said Ottilie, feeling annoyed. Gully and Scoot were still going. Preddy wouldn't be alone. Why shouldn't she go and see Maestro? If truth be told, bonding with another beast had made her feel a little guilty.

There was a long, awkward pause, which was broken by Leo's distant bark: 'Come on, Ott!'

In that moment Ottilie wanted nothing more than to get away from Scoot. Without a word, she turned her back and jogged up to Leo. Levelling with him, she increased her pace, her jog becoming a sprint. Leo charged after her, and they raced all the way to the gate at the edge of the cliff.

8

The Pack

As the days rolled by, Scoot seemed to forget his anger. Ottilie was so glad he was behaving normally again that she didn't raise the issue. In any event, she'd had little opportunity. With their new training arrangements, Ottilie was seeing far less of her friends. The only session they had all together was warding – and they spent the majority of that hour sitting silently with their eyes closed.

That afternoon, Gully, Preddy and Scoot were in the lower grounds for their beginners flying with Wrangler Kinney. Leo and Ned were using one of their rare afternoons off together to do some spear practice and Ottilie decided to tag along.

All three took turns sparring. Fighting each other wasn't the point of their training, but it was fun all the same. Ottilie particularly enjoyed watching Ned beat Leo. Ned, being a footman, had much more practice with fancy spear-work than Leo did. Spears could be a bit of a nuisance on the back of a wingerslink.

Ned's footwork was like a dance. He coiled and leapt, twirling his spear, tripping Leo off his feet and hovering the point over his heart. Leo glared at the blade. Ned laughed and flipped the spear, offering Leo the blunt end. Leo grasped it and Ned pulled him up.

'Stop smiling, Ott. You know he went easier on you?' said Leo, wiping the sweat from his brow.

Ottilie jumped down from her seat on the training-yard fence. 'But I'm just learning. You're supposed to be a champion,' she said with a grin.

'An injured champion,' he muttered, playing up his limp as he moved to stand beside her. 'Besides, Ned's been spearing things since he was old enough to grip – if he'd started the same time as me, it'd be a different story.'

'What do you mean, spearing things?' said Ottilie. She didn't know much about Ned's history. The huntsmen didn't tend to talk about their pasts, either because they came from unpleasant beginnings or quite the opposite. In both cases it seemed easier to choose to forget.

'Fish,' said Ned. 'I'm from Sunken Sweep, in the south. My aunt taught me to spearfish when I was young.'

Ottilie couldn't picture it. It was hard to imagine any of the huntsmen living somewhere else. 'Can we go again, Ned? I want to try that spin thing you did.'

Ned tossed her a spear. 'Here, I'll show you how –' He was interrupted by the bells. 'Is it five already?'

'We better hurry.' Leo grabbed the spear out of Ottilie's hand and jogged over to the weapons shed, his limp now magically improved.

She didn't know what they were talking about. 'Why? What's happening?'

'The meeting,' said Ned. 'Didn't you get the note? They were under our doors this morning.'

Ottilie felt a familiar sinking in her chest. She knew why she hadn't been given a note. Whoever was in charge of leaving them had undoubtedly skipped her door on purpose.

What could the meeting be about? Were they finally going to find out how the wyler had got past the walls?

They were only a few minutes late to the Moon Court. The directors, wranglers and bone singers were already there, waiting patiently as the huntsmen filed in, in varying states of grubbiness.

Ottilie hurried in with Leo and Ned. She could see Gully already seated with Preddy and Scoot. Scoot had an empty seat beside him, which she assumed was being saved for her. She moved towards it, but Dimitri Vosvolder dropped into it. Scoot glanced at Dimitri, and

Ottilie was sure he would ask him to move. But Scoot looked back at her, his eyes flicking to Leo and Ned, and turned his gaze forwards.

Ottilie felt a pinch of hurt. Leo and Ned took their seats in the elite rows, and she found an empty spot nearby. Was Scoot in a bad mood again? Why did he always seem to be directing his ire at her? She blinked, clearing her head. It was probably nothing.

'Good evening,' said an astonishingly deep voice from the centre of the courtyard.

Ottilie looked up to see Conductor Edderfed, his flyaway white hair combed unsuccessfully over his bald crown. This was a surprise: the cardinal conductor rarely addressed them. Captain Lyre always did the talking.

Tension thickened the air. Ottilie was sure that none of the other fledges had ever heard him speak. He usually just sat mutely on his throne – an ornamental figure looking down his large nose. But it seemed this meeting was serious enough to warrant his address, which made Ottilie very uneasy.

'We have called you here to discuss the worsening situation in the Narroway,' he said, every line on his face drawing into a frown.

She thought back to when the yickers had entered the grounds. Captain Lyre had done his utmost to convince the flighty fledges that this was not usual. It had been just before their fledgling trials, in the middle of the Hunt's attempt to bend them to the cause. Ottilie got the sense there would be none of that today.

'Since its inception,' continued Conductor Edderfed, 'the Narroway Hunt has seen a steady increase in dredretch numbers. You know, also, of the damaged land in the heart of our territory, the Withering Wood. This began with a single sick philowood tree, but the sickness has been creeping out in all directions, conquering new ground.'

Ottilie hadn't been near the Withering Wood since the day she and Leo had felled the kappabak. She liked to forget it when she could – but the thought of the sickness leaking out, ever nearer, crept into her thoughts in the night hours. They could destroy dredretches one at a time, but the withering sickness … She needed to find out more about it. Leo had suggested once that felling dredretches was the key to stopping it, but it seemed that no matter how many they dispatched, there were always more, slinking out of caves, lurking behind trees … it was endless. Someone was responsible for it – but who?

'However,' said Conductor Edderfed, 'our recent tragedy, along with unfavourable reports over these past months, has led us to believe that the danger is mounting at a greater pace than we were aware.

'We've had reports of stingers and spike-mites gathering in larger groups than ever recorded. A knopo troop was discovered hunting natural beasts and residing comfortably in a coastal region. Little over a month ago, a kappabak, a previously unknown dredretch of immense size, appeared for the first time, and in the last week we have had reports of wylers gathering in a large pack near the Red Canyon.'

Ottilie's ribs locked. A wyler pack? This was not good news.

Conductor Edderfed went on to insist that they watch for changes and irregular behaviour. Anything new or out of the ordinary had to be reported immediately, and the bone singers, with huntsmen as guards, would be given the task of monitoring the expansion of the Withering Wood.

He was linking everything. He had said nothing to suggest that the wyler attack was an isolated incident, or that the cause had been discovered and dealt with. This meant it could happen again – not just could, was likely to.

Ottilie couldn't focus. She saw Joely Wrecker, her blood-soaked hair dripping down her front, and shuddered. One wyler had done that – just one. She thought again of all the girls, unarmed and untrained. She imagined the bedchamber with ten wylers instead of one, and shattered the image as soon as she had the power. Wylers were supposed to be solitary. From what she'd read, they never so much as paired up.

She glanced at the back of Leo's head, wondering what he made of this new information. He didn't turn, but beside him Ned looked back at her. His jaw was set and his usually laughing eyes were cast in shadow.

Someone had to be behind all this. That hooded figure, and the witch who hexed the king, it was all connected. It had to be. She had to find out who the witch was.

She had been thinking about witches a lot – who they were and why they were gone. People didn't like talking about witches, or what was done to them, which, Ottilie was learning, was a sign that something was wrong.

For the first twelve years of her life, the only book she had access to was Mr Parch's *Our Walkable World*. It was how Old Moss had taught both Gully and Ottilie to read. Ottilie had read it so many times that random facts still clung to her memory like strands of old cobweb.

She was fairly sure they had started hunting and burying witches when the Roving Empire had control of the Usklers. The Usklerian royals had fled, and many of their people had gone with them. She had since learned, much to her surprise, that they'd escaped west to the Laklands, an old enemy of the Usklerian Kingdom. Alba, who was a distant descendant of the Lakland people, had told Ottilie a story …

'The Laklands and the Usklers were always fighting,' Alba had explained over a late-night cup of spiced saffi milk. The patchies stocked the milk to help calm distressed patients, but Alba's mother, Montie, kept a supply of it as well, considering the number of huntsmen who visited her kitchen when they were feeling vulnerable.

'But around a hundred and fifty years ago,' Alba continued, 'when the Roving Empire conquered the Usklers, the Laklanders offered many Usklerians refuge, even giving the royals land and positions in the court.

'Then, years later, when the Roving Empire lost its grip, the Laklanders helped the Usklerian royals take back their kingdom, on the condition that the Usklers would never attack the Laklands again.'

Before then, Ottilie had never heard this version of events. She had not known that the Usklers had promised to keep peace with the Laklands to repay their kindness.

'They kept the promise for a while.' Alba's face darkened. 'But when Viago the Vanquisher came to power, he decided he wanted to conquer the Laklands and take the land they had been granted in exile. So he broke the promise. They went to war and it lasted years, and eventually the Usklers flattened the Laklands.'

It was a horrible, bloody history. The Usklers had committed a great wrong and nobody talked about it. Ottilie wondered how many people even knew. The

Laklanders certainly did — those who had survived. But, landless, they had spread far and wide, few of them remaining in the Usklers, with good reason.

What exactly happened with the witches during that time, Ottilie didn't know. The Roving Empire had wanted them gone, and when the Usklerian royals were reinstated, it seemed they did too. The witch hunts continued until every last witch was supposedly locked in an iron coffin, deep beneath the ground.

Was it because witches were all bad? Was magic an evil, unnatural thing like the dredretches? Ottilie couldn't find anything in all her reading. But would people have allowed them to be buried alive if they were not evil? Surely not. Still, thinking about everything she had learned — about that broken promise, and all the senseless violence that followed — it seemed foolish to blindly trust that leaders knew what was right and wrong.

Ottilie looked up at Captain Lyre. He had told them on their first day that they had been specially recruited on a secret mission for the king. But where was Varrio Sol, King of the Usklers, grandson of the treacherous Viago the Vanquisher? East, in All Kings' Hill, across a fat channel of saltwater, where the dredretches could probably never reach him.

❧ 9 ❧

Wounds

'I've had it!' said Skip, flopping onto Ottilie's bed.

The custodians hadn't been invited to the meeting but Ottilie had filled Skip in later that night.

'What happened when that wyler got in? It went straight for us,' said Skip. 'We're defenceless because they won't let us defend ourselves!'

'I know.' Ottilie had been thinking about it too. There were hundreds of girls in the Narroway, tucked behind high walls with monsters beyond them. 'Everyone should be allowed to learn to fight them. Has anyone ever … I mean, besides what happened with me – has anyone ever asked?'

Skip scowled and crawled further up the bed. 'I

asked the custodian chieftess once, when I was much younger. She took the rod to the back of my hand for my insolence.'

Once, that might have surprised Ottilie, but after being locked in the burrows and put on trial in front of the directorate, she understood how dangerous disrupting the Hunt's rules could be.

'But what about Wrangler Ritgrivvian?' said Ottilie. 'They let her be a wrangler. Why is it different?'

'They let her be a wrangler because there's no-one better. I've heard she used to work for the king,' said Skip. 'But she had to claw her way up. She doesn't talk about it much – makes sense.'

'What do you mean?'

'Something went wrong,' Skip said, as if it were obvious. 'I don't know what, but I'd say that's how she ended up here.' Ottilie's confusion must have shown on her face because Skip added, 'You know … the eye-patch …' She raised her eyebrows.

'What about it?' Ottilie had just assumed that Wrangler Ritgrivvian was missing an eye, like Wrangler Furdles.

'It's crocodile skin, didn't you notice?'

She hadn't noticed, and she didn't understand the significance anyway.

'When an eyepatch is made of crocodile skin it means negligence,' explained Skip, cupping a hand over her eye. 'It's a punishment – supposed to humiliate. It's mostly for servants when something gets lost or broken, or someone under their care gets hurt. The length of time they have to wear it depends on how bad it was, and if it was really bad they take the eye too, and they have to wear the patch forever. I don't know what happened with Ramona, but she's been wearing that patch as long as I've been here.'

Ottilie had never heard about this. But, of course, no-one around the Brakkerswamp, where Ottilie grew up, had servants to punish. She wondered what had happened. Negligent wasn't a word she would have associated with the horse mistress.

'I've never asked her about it,' said Skip. 'It's not something you can just bring up.'

They were getting distracted. Whether Ramona Ritgrivvian had a right eye didn't matter. What mattered was convincing the Hunt to train girls.

'We need to ask again,' said Ottilie. 'Properly.'

Skip leapt off the bed, her face glowing. 'You'll help? You'll ask them?'

'Of course I will.'

'They may not take it well. We could get into a lot of trouble.'

Skip was right, it was dangerous. Many would say she was making trouble. Voilies would lash out, and some others of higher rank would too. She remembered the sallow-faced Director Yaist, the one member of the directorate who had voted that death be considered a punishment for her deception. He might even use it as an excuse to reopen that debate, to get rid of her once and for all.

But it was worth it. Things were clearer to her now. She couldn't let the fear of being cast out stop her from doing what was right. If she didn't do this, who would?

'People died,' she said firmly. 'Every girl in that room could have died. If there was ever a time to ask, it's now.'

They needed support. Although Ottilie was in a better position than Skip to ask the directorate, she was still just a fledgling, ranked in the bottom third, and considered by most a blot on the ranking wall. They would have to write their request and have it signed by as many elites as they could get. Surely after everything, Leo would help with this. A champion's support would have to make them consider it.

Ottilie was too wound up to sleep. She wanted to talk to her friends. Scoot's room was right next to hers, so he was her first stop. She knocked softly on his door.

'Who is it?' he called.

'It's Ottilie,' she whispered through the wood.

There was no response. Ottilie knocked again, a little louder.

He ignored her.

She frowned, feeling worried. Conductor Edderfed's speech had distracted her. She had forgotten that strange moment when Scoot hadn't saved her a seat. It was a small thing, but here, standing outside his door with silence from within, she felt the weight of it grow.

Invitation be damned – she tried the door, but it was bolted from the inside.

'Scoot, let me in!' she hissed.

'I'm sleeping.'

Even through the door she could hear the sullenness in his voice.

'I'm not going away. Let me in!' She rattled the latch. She heard the weight of his steps and the scrape of the bolt. The door flew open and Scoot stood there in his pale green nightclothes, glaring.

Ottilie shoved him aside and marched into the room. 'What is the matter with you?'

Scoot thrust the door shut and said nothing. He just stood there, jaw ticking and fingers twitching.

'Why are you mad at me?' she said, unable to hide the hurt.

'Because,' he said in a half-whisper.

'Because what?'

'Because you think you're too good for us!' he burst out.

'What?' Ottilie couldn't believe what she was hearing. She was one of the lowest-ranked fledges in the Narroway, and arguably the least popular person in Fort Fiory.

'You do!' said Scoot. 'You're never around anymore. You're always with the elites.'

'What elites?'

'Leo and Ned. We're not good enough for you,' said Scoot, turning away from her.

'I am not … I don't –'

'You're always with Leo!'

Ottilie moved around the room to face him, determined that he listen to her. 'Leo's my guardian. I have shifts with him nearly every day. You're with Bayo all the time too!'

Scoot still didn't look at her. 'I hunt with him, that's all. Same as Gully with Ned. He's still around … he's still our friend first!'

Ottilie was shaking with frustration. 'So am I! You're being stupid, Scoot. You just see Gully more because he's with the footmen too, so you do all the same training!' She took a step towards him, noticing a nasty set of puncture wounds high on his shoulder. 'Scoot, what's –' She reached out, but he jerked away.

'Fanged pobe got me, weeks ago!' he spat. 'You would know that if I ever saw you.'

Ottilie felt close to tears. 'That's not fair, your day clothes don't show –'

'Leo's the one who told them you're a girl! And you

just forgave him straight away. You don't care about ... about everything he did.' Scoot started pacing back and forth, his shoulders hunched so far forward it took inches off his height.

'I didn't just forgive him straight away.' Her hurt twisted into anger. 'And that's none of your business!'

'He doesn't even like you ... he thinks you're useless. Preddy told me, when he was his guardian and you were a shovelie, Leo said heaps of nasty stuff about you.'

'Stop it, Scoot!' It was like a punch in the gut. Though she wasn't overly surprised: Leo had said awful things to her face. She had expected him to say them behind her back as well.

'You're being pathetic,' said Scoot. 'You just follow him around ... you're like a lovesick whelp.'

She let out a bark of derisive laughter. 'I am not lovesick, and I do not follow him around.'

'You are and you do!' He was still pacing, moving further and further away from her. 'Everyone can see it.' He turned his back.

Ottilie clenched her fists. 'You wouldn't be saying that if you still thought I was a boy. I'm acting exactly the same.' With that, she stormed from the room, slamming his door behind her.

— 10 —

Wall Watch

Ottilie shuffled sideways, trying to get a bit of distance from Preddy. They were practising their footwork with Wrangler Voilies, and Preddy kept tripping over his own boots. The move they were learning would be used with a flail, but until they mastered it they simply held short sticks with no chain. It was lucky for Ottilie – if Preddy had been holding a flail, her skull would have acquired several dints that morning.

Preddy tripped again, his lanky legs leading him in completely the wrong direction.

'Enough,' called Wrangler Voilies, clapping his hands together with pursed lips. 'Take a short break.'

Wrangler Voilies was never one to criticise Preddy.

Coming from the wealthy outskirts of Wikric Town, Preddy had entered the Narroway with a basket of skills that the other fledges didn't possess. Not only was he educated and well spoken, but he had experience hunting – albeit natural beasts – and was already proficient at archery and horseback riding.

Voilies always favoured the most talented recruits. Gully had been a favourite of his from the first day, but Ottilie knew he had a particular liking for the huntsmen from wealthy families, like Leo and Preddy. This preference helped explain why he had always so disliked Scoot, who hailed from Wikric's slum tunnels and whose manners were nearly as rough as Gurt's, the bramblywine king of the Brakkerswamp.

Ottilie trudged over to retrieve her waterskin from the edge of the yard. She didn't want to think about Scoot. It gave her a dismal, sick feeling in her stomach. She hadn't talked to him since their argument the night before. In fact, she hadn't really talked to anyone. To avoid running into him she'd skipped breakfast that morning, which did nothing to improve her mood.

'He didn't mean it,' said Preddy quietly, over her shoulder.

Ottilie's chest felt tight. She took a gulp of water and didn't answer.

'I know you had a fight. Whatever he said – he didn't mean it. He's just …'

She turned and narrowed her eyes. 'Just what?' A lump formed in her throat, which only made her angrier.

Preddy nervously adjusted his eyeglasses. 'I think he's just jealous, and he's ... he's not very good at managing his feelings.'

Ottilie threw up her hands. 'Jealous of what? I'm ranked sixty-third –'

'Not of rankings or anything.' He paused for a moment, as if he wasn't sure he should say more. After a breath or two he added, 'He's jealous of Leo. Because you spend so much time with him, and not ... us.'

Ottilie couldn't believe what she was hearing. 'Leo's my guardian,' she said irritably. 'I've always spent this much time with him – except when I was a shovelie.'

If she really thought about it, though, it was possible she had been spending more time with Leo than she used to. Back before everything went wrong, before he betrayed her, Leo used to treat her more like a fledge. She remembered him complaining when he'd found Ned sitting with her and Gully at dinner. But since she'd come to his aid that day, he had treated her more like a friend, seeking her out in his free time, inviting her to practise with him and Ned. But she hadn't been neglecting her friends ... had she?

'Do you feel like I've been choosing him over you?' she asked, making a mental note to ask Gully.

A pink tinge bloomed on Preddy's cheeks. 'We're

all seeing less of each other now that training's split up. You're missed sometimes, that's all.'

'I'm sorry,' she said, her stomach twisting.

'You don't need to apologise. I wish I was better friends with my guardian. Everything's very serious with Jobe,' he added, with a slight grimace.

'But how come Scoot's having such a tantrum about it?'

Preddy's cheeks darkened to red. 'I think maybe Scoot sees you a bit differently now – now that he knows you're a girl.'

Ottilie tensed, resisting the impulse to stamp her foot. 'That's not fair!' she said through gritted teeth.

'No, I don't mean in a bad way. I mean in a … I think he thinks … or maybe he has a little bit of a fondness for you.'

'A fondness?' She didn't know what he was talking about.

Scarlet in the face, Preddy raised his eyebrows.

'Oh.' Ottilie finally caught on. 'Oh no. What? Why?'

'I … well … he –'

'No. We're not talking about it. Preddy! I wish you hadn't said that. It's not … I doubt …'

Wrangler Voilies clapped his hands. 'Back to work, everyone.'

'Let's never talk about this ever again,' she muttered.

'Agreed,' said Preddy.

That night, Leo and Ottilie stood alone, looking over the moonlit forest to the east. Leo hated wall watch. He always said it was his least favourite shift. At least on singer duty, when they guarded the bone singers, they were beyond the boundary walls.

He slumped over the parapets, moaning and groaning, and Ottilie gave him very little in response. She hadn't felt like talking to Leo since the horrible things Scoot had said the night before. None of it was new, but it had stirred up memories that she had been glad to put behind her.

A footman yanked the chain at the gate below, ringing the bell by her ear.

'Clear?' said Ottilie.

'Yep,' said Leo. He was supposed to be checking the area beyond the gate, making sure it was safe to open it. This would be their main duty for the night. The huntsmen on patrol rarely let anything close to the walls. Winged dredretches occasionally attacked, but they were usually large enough to mark from a distance. Jivvies were the worst. They were the smallest of the high-flyers and difficult to spot in the dark.

'Are you even looking?' she said, thinking of a wyler creeping through. Could that be how it happened – lazy wall-watchers? Strangely, she wished that were true.

But she was sure it wasn't. Wylers weren't like jivvies – their orange fur and bright eyes were hard to miss. Someone had snuck the wyler inside, probably the same someone who crept around the Narroway hooded and cloaked.

'Of course I am, Ott,' snapped Leo. 'It's clear.'

Ottilie waved the blue flag by the lantern. Below, the gates were raised and six footmen headed out into the Narroway.

They were stationed by the small and little-used east gate behind Floodwood, the patch of woodland where Christopher Crow had saved Ottilie and Scoot from the yickers all those months ago. Beyond the wall, Ottilie could see the Sol River; it looked like a silver serpent curling eastward, tossing moonlight off its scales.

They were positioned between two towers, one directly over the gate, and another, the loftiest tower along the border wall. Ottilie had never worked the east gate before and found herself wondering about that lonely tall tower. It couldn't be a watch station. It was too closed off and, as far as she knew, no huntsmen or wranglers were ever positioned there.

'What's that tower?' she asked, pointing.

Leo, who'd been slouching over the edge of the wall, looked up. 'Whistler,' he muttered, his jaw slack with boredom.

'Who?' said Ottilie, frowning.

'What's wrong with you today?'

'Nothing. What's wrong with you?'

'I hate wall watch,' he said. 'You know that.'

'Well, maybe I do too.'

Leo narrowed his eyes. 'I don't have the energy to cheer you up today, Ott. Snap out of it. We'll go and get some food from Mrs Kit as soon as we're done.'

Ottilie had only recently learned that Leo knew Montie. As it turned out, he had been visiting her kitchen since his first year at Fiory, and would habitually go and see her after his most hated shift.

'I don't need you to cheer me up,' she said, well aware that her tone suggested otherwise. 'You didn't answer my question. Who's in that tower?'

'The head bone singer,' said Leo as if it was the most boring question in the world. 'She goes by the name Whistler.'

'Whistler?' Ottilie couldn't picture her, but she thought perhaps Skip had mentioned her before.

'You wouldn't have met her. She splits her time between stations, and when she's here she keeps to herself. We call that the Bone Tower.' He gestured lazily to the building. 'Something's wrong with you,' he added.

'Just leave it, Leo, I'm fine.' She didn't want to talk to him about any of it: her fight with Scoot, her worries about the wyler, the risk of having unarmed, untrained girls in the Narroway.

'You're so moody,' he mocked.

'No more than you are! You've been sulking this whole shift.'

'For good reason, I hate –'

'Wall watch. I know!'

'So, what's wrong with you?' he demanded.

Ottilie turned to meet his eye. 'I'm going to ask the directorate to let the custodians train with us. You want to cheer me up – sign the letter.'

Leo gaped at her.

'And get the rest of the elites to sign it too,' she added.

'Sign what letter?' he said, still gaping.

'The letter we're writing to ask –'

'Petition.'

'What?'

'That's what it's called.'

'I don't care, Leo. Stop avoiding. Will you sign it?'

'I … no.'

'No?'

They were distracted. Too distracted. There was a great swishing of wings and a jivvie dived at Leo. She nocked an arrow and Leo reached for his mace but they were both too late. The jivvie's needle-sharp beak was less than an inch from his temple when a great, dark-feathered owl latched on to the dredretch and tore its head clean off. Circling and soaring to the east, the owl screeched and the remains of the jivvie slipped through its talons and disappeared into the Sol River.

The jivvie's flock broke the tree line. Ottilie swiftly rang the bells to alert the other wall watchers. Leo had already shot three jivvies down when she reached his side and took one more, before the remaining four were out of range. She and Leo watched as the huntsmen further along the wall dispatched the last of them.

They stood frozen for a moment. Silent. Ottilie wondered if Leo was feeling the same tug of shame. They hadn't been paying attention. They had been squabbling. Not only had Leo nearly been scalped by a jivvie, but they had almost allowed it to pass over them into the grounds. If it wasn't for that bird …

'Do owls normally help like that?'

'It can happen, other animals helping out there,' said Leo. 'It's rare. Something's happening in this place.' He gazed out over the trees. 'Stirring things up.' He glanced sideways at her. 'Everyone's acting crazy.'

◄ 11 ►

Secrets and Signatures

Before Ottilie had come to the Narroway, five hunts-men had been named champion of their tier. Only one of them wore Fiory colours – Leo – and Ottilie was determined to have his signature on her petition.

'Have you written it yet? I'll sign it,' said Gully.

He and Ottilie were bathing their horses after a gruelling riding lesson with Wrangler Ritgrivvian. It was an uncommonly warm autumn day. The afternoon sun lit the world with a fierce brilliance that did not match Ottilie's mood. In fact, all the squinting and sweating only increased the weight on her chest. Everything, she felt, was very difficult right now.

She had been feeling unstable ever since the wyler attack, and especially since Conductor Edderfed's speech. They were all on edge, more so than when the yickers had crept into Floodwood. Everyone was nervous, and everyone feared another breach.

But it was more than the wylers and the Withering Wood on Ottilie's mind. Scoot, still refusing to talk to her, had kept his distance and charged off the moment the bells had rung out, leaving his mount caked in sweat.

'No,' she said, turning back to Gully, 'it's not written.' She was planning to ask Alba to help write it. 'And thank you, but you're a fledge, and my brother. I really need elites, and I need Leo. His name will matter the most to them,' she said.

As soon as she spoke, Ottilie realised her words might be hurtful. She studied Gully's face, but he was nodding. He agreed with her.

Ottilie wished it were different. She wished that she were taken seriously as a huntsman. She resolved to work even harder. She would aim to get as close to becoming the fledgling champion as she could, and when she reached the third tier she would be one of the select elite. She was just going to have to make it happen. Then she would never need Leo's help again.

Scoot's accusation was still weighing on her. 'Gully, Scoot said I've been hanging around Leo and Ned more than him and Preddy.'

Gully just blinked at her, as if to say, what about it?

'He thinks I'm better friends with them now.' She didn't know how to put it. 'But I'm not. I mean, I don't mean to be.'

Gully shrugged. 'You're friends with everyone.'

Ottilie jumped. Billow had nudged her in the back and started rubbing his face against her shoulderblades. She laughed and pushed him off.

Wrangler Ritgrivvian called over to them, 'If you have some time, you can walk them in the sun – to help them dry off.'

Gully had to run in to change for a hunt, but Ottilie didn't have to patrol until later in the afternoon so she led both horses out across the grounds. Thankfully, Billow and Inch, Gully's little grey gelding, got on well enough and it was a peaceful stroll – just what she needed to calm her mind.

She hadn't even spoken to Leo since he'd refused to sign. She was so angry – this was their one chance. She and Skip were sure that if the directorate turned it down, they would not do so gently. There was a strong possibility they would be punished for daring to ask – that was why they needed to get it right.

How could Leo not understand how important this was? Ottilie shook out her shoulders. They would be patrolling soon, and she had to rise above it. Quarrels and grudges didn't have any place beyond the boundary walls. It was too dangerous.

Ottilie had lost track of her feet, wandering through the clover fields, Billow and Inch trailing serenely behind. They passed by the apiary and she wondered if the bees would bother the horses, but they seemed unruffled.

Ahead, Ned was on the path to the boundary wall. Ottilie experienced a strange swooping sensation as, spotting her, he doubled back. Feeling jittery, she moved in closer to Billow, pressing against his warm neck. What was wrong with her? She'd talked to Ned alone before – though, come to think of it, it was rare. When he'd found her in the lower grounds with Maestro, she'd been too grumpy to notice. But now, she found that she really noticed. What would they talk about without Gully or Leo? She suddenly couldn't remember any words.

Ned smiled at the horses. She remembered that he had spent his fledge year with the mounts but was placed with the footmen after his order trials.

'Don't let Leonard see you bonding,' he said, reaching to greet Billow.

To her great relief, Ottilie thought of a response. 'Do you miss them?' she asked, wondering if the same would happen to her. What if she was made a footman or a mount? She recoiled at the thought. She was a flyer. She had to be a flyer.

'Yes. But it's more fun on foot, closer to the action.' He flashed a grin. 'Is your brother around? We're supposed to be out the opal gate in a minute.' He tilted his head at the path through the herb gardens. Out of sight, there was a gate down the slope from Opal Tarn, the glittering mountain lake cradled between the peaks beyond the fort.

'He ran up to change. He should be here soon.' Calmed by his ease, Ottilie realised what a blessing it was to catch Ned without Leo. She seized the opportunity. 'Ned, I'm going to ask the dir–'

'I'll sign.' Noting her confusion, he added, 'Gully told me.'

She was taken aback. 'I ... thank you.'

He shrugged. 'I agree with you. Girls should be allowed to train here. There's no reason I can understand why they shouldn't ... I've thought about that a lot, ever since you first came here.'

A strange expression took hold of his face, something like guilt.

'It was just normal, the way things were,' he said. 'But when I saw you, I realised it didn't make any sense. But I should have realised that already. My aunt protected me and my brother from crocodiles and worse back home. Then I came here, and everything's so regimented – you have to focus on the dredretches, and soon enough you just stop asking questions.'

Ned's phrasing stuck in her head. 'What do you mean since I first came here?'

'Well, maybe not since you first came here,' said Ned, with a slight smile. 'But your trial, with the jivvies, definitely since then. I felt so stupid for not even thinking about it before – of course girls should hunt too.' His eyes glinted with amusement as her mouth fell open.

'You knew? From when? From the very beginning? How?'

Ottilie couldn't believe it. She had suspected that some people knew. She'd always felt that Maeve Moth sensed something amiss – although, that never made much sense, because surely if Maeve had known she would have given Ottilie up in an instant – but Ned, she had never had an inkling. He had never treated her any differently from the other fledges, never looked at her funny or …

'Do you remember when we brought you in and another fledge knocked you down in front of a shepherd?' said Ned.

She remembered the great black dog snarling in her face, and Ned pulling her by the elbow, out of its way. 'You knew then?'

'That was the closest I ever got to you,' he said. Ottilie thought his cheeks darkened a little. 'I thought it then,' he continued quickly. 'But I wasn't sure until I got Gully as my fledge.'

'He told you?' Ottilie didn't want to believe it. He wouldn't have, surely.

Ned laughed. 'No. He never told me, but he's not very subtle.'

'But you never told anyone ... Leo didn't know ... or I would have been in trouble much sooner.'

'You know, I think maybe Wrangler Morse guessed, but no, Leo had no idea. He's too self-centred, and you did a pretty good job of keeping your distance from everyone else.

'This place, Leo included ... arrogance can be blinding, I think. None of them would have guessed you were an imposter because they wouldn't want to believe a girl from the Swamp Hollows could fool them. And do well, too – you were ranked so high for so long. You should never have made it as far as you did. They didn't want to see it.'

Ottilie watched Billow and Inch grazing happily, her mind buzzing along with the bees. 'Ned, I need him to sign it,' she said. 'Could you talk to him? Will you tell him that you're going to sign?'

Ned didn't hesitate. 'I will. You can give it to me if you want. I'll talk to the other elites – get you some signatures.'

She felt a twinge of annoyance. Ned was being so helpful, so understanding. If only he was the champion and not Leo, things would be so much simpler.

<figure>⟶</figure>

Thankfully, Scoot was absent from the dining room when Ottilie arrived for a late lunch. She settled at a table in the corner on her own. Alba shot Ottilie a smile and nodded to suggest she'd be over in a minute. Thick braids bouncing, she disappeared with a stack of plates piled high in her arms.

Across the room, Gracie Moravec caught Ottilie's eye. Still recovering from the wyler bite, her usually golden skin was ashen. Ottilie was reminded of Bill, her old friend, the strange creature from the caves above the Brakkerswamp.

She wondered where he was now and slumped a little in her seat. She had always intended to return to the Swamp Hollows eventually, but if she stayed at Fiory until she was eighteen, would Bill still be there?

'She doesn't look well, does she,' said Alba, sliding into the chair opposite her.

Ottilie's head snapped up.

'Wyler venom is really bad,' Alba added. 'Should put an end to the rumours though …'

'What rumours?' Ottilie leaned closer, grateful for the distraction.

'People talk about Gracie. There's a rumour that she's —' She leaned in and mouthed, 'A witch.'

'What?' Ottilie had her own suspicions, but hearing that others felt the same was not welcome news. Skip called both Gracie and Maeve witches all the time, but

Ottilie had thought it was just name-calling. 'Why do people say that?'

'Just a lot of little things,' said Alba. 'But there was something that happened a couple of years ago. She and a girl called Yosha Moses both jumped from a really high branch of an Uskler pine. Yosha hit her head and was badly hurt. They had to send her away. But Gracie — she came out of it without any bumps or bruises that I could see.'

'That's horrible,' said Ottilie, trying her best not to picture the scene. 'But that doesn't mean she's a witch. She was probably just lucky.'

She didn't want it to be real. She imagined the figure lurking in the shadows, lifting the hood to reveal Gracie Moravec, smiling her false little smile. But then, Gracie was a victim of the attack. She couldn't have let that wyler in; it didn't make sense.

'I know, that's what I think,' said Alba. 'Looking at how sick she is, I doubt people will be saying that anymore. And, apart from all the horrible stuff, witches were known for healing, so it doesn't fit. I don't really think anyone actually believed it, anyway. They're just being nasty.'

'Why did they do it, that girl and Gracie? Why did they jump?' asked Ottilie, feeling sick.

'Well, that's another awful rumour,' said Alba, frowning. 'It was supposed to be more of a dare. Some people say Gracie talked Yosha into it, or used some sort of a spell to make her do it. But it's just silly gossip — people getting carried away. No-one seriously believes there are any witches left.'

Ottilie looked over at Gracie. Did she really believe Gracie was capable of hurting someone? The pranks in the sculkie quarters were one thing, but convincing a girl to risk her life … No matter how uncomfortable she was around Gracie, Ottilie couldn't believe she would do such a thing. Her eyes fell on the bandaged arm. 'Actually' – she turned back to Alba – 'I've been wanting to talk to you about the wyler attack.' She explained what she and Skip intended to do.

As Ottilie spoke, Alba paled.

'Didn't you go through enough of that already, Ottilie? Remember when they found you out and they locked you in the burrows with … with all the …'

'I remember,' she said, thinking of the dank burrows, and the flares sparking and trilling in the darkness. 'But it can't go on like this, Alba. It's getting worse here, everyone's saying it. Girls should be allowed to hunt dredretches too. They should be allowed to help. Wouldn't you want to?'

Alba didn't even hesitate before shaking her head. 'I don't want to go anywhere near them. I'm not the sort of person who … Isla's different from me. She wants to … that's fine.'

'But if they got into the fort again,' pressed Ottilie, 'you would want to be able to protect yourself. Surely?'

'Yes. Of course – that. But not … hunting. I'm not … it's not me. I'm good at other things. I can write it for you, though. I know what to put in.' Her eyes lit up. 'There are women from history who dressed up as men to join armies, just like you. And Seika Devil-Slayer, the princess who defeated the fendevil –'

'Who defeated the what?'

'Oh, Ottilie, you must know about it! You're from the Brakkerswamp.' Alba leaned across the table, eager to share.

'What's that got to do with anything?'

'Well, it was centuries and centuries ago, before the Roving Empire invaded, before everything … It's legend now,' said Alba. 'Didn't you ever hear about the monster that terrorised the west? They say it was like a giant firedrake with breath of blue flame that could melt iron.'

'Sure, I know about firedrakes but –'

'There was one in particular,' said Alba. 'Only it wasn't really a firedrake. They say it was twice the size and it seemed wrong somehow. Looking back, the scholars think it was a dredretch, but people at the time thought dredretches were a myth, so they never put two and two together. They called it the fendevil because it lurked in the western wetlands.'

'I didn't know,' said Ottilie. 'And a girl defeated it?' Her confidence grew. This was going to work!

'Seika Devil-Slayer — well, her proper name was Seika Sol. She was an ancient Usklerian king's daughter,' said Alba. 'She lured it westward all the way to the Narroway and over the Dawn Cliffs. The Sol River carried it through to the ocean and it never came back. That's why they named it the Sol River, it had some other name before.'

'Lured it over a cliff?' said Ottilie. 'But how? And she wouldn't have had a ring. How did she survive?'

'I don't know. It all happened so long ago. And stories get so mixed up over time.'

'Where do our rings come from?' Ottilie had never thought to ask before.

'Whistler,' said Alba. 'She makes them.'

'The head bone singer?' Ottilie supposed that made some sort of sense. But what were those strange things the bone singers could do? What mysterious magic did they wield? Were they mystics? They had to be, she supposed. But she'd always thought mystics were just glorified priests.

'Speaking of Whistler, will you help me with something?' said Alba with a mischievous smile.

'Anything,' said Ottilie.

Alba glanced around and leaned in. 'I want to get into the Bone Tower,' she whispered. 'To Whistler's library.'

Ottilie frowned. 'But haven't you been there before? I thought that's where you found the story about the hex.'

'No, this is Whistler's private tower,' said Alba. 'We could get in a lot of trouble, but I bet there's all sorts of amazing volumes up there! There might even be something that answers all our questions – about the hex on the king, and why the dredretches are here. I've tried to get in, but it's too difficult on my own. Will you help me?'

'Of course.' This was perfect! Ottilie was desperate to find out something, anything, that might explain why things were suddenly so much worse. She felt certain that finding out more about this mysterious witch would point them in the direction of who let the wyler inside.

'We'll have to be really careful.' Alba lowered her voice so much it almost cut out. 'But I have an idea how to get there unseen.'

Of course she did. Alba had admitted to sneaking books out of private libraries for years, and had managed to visit Ottilie in the burrows undetected. Her insides squirmed at the memory. If they were caught trying to break into the Bone Tower, would it be back to the burrows? Or worse?

They would have to risk it. The Hunt never told them anything. They were full of vague explanations and downright lies. If they wanted to find out anything about the witch and the dredretches, they were going to have to uncover it on their own.

12

Frost and Flame

Skip was the best at finding out what was happening and when. Whistler was leaving for Richter the following week and, according to Skip, was not expected back for a few days. When Ottilie told her of their plan, Skip insisted on coming along as well. Until then, Skip would help Alba with the petition.

Ottilie was glad to let them handle it, and happy to focus on hunting. She was desperate to catch up in the rankings. They all agreed that the more points she earned, the more likely it was that the directorate would take them seriously.

That morning, Ottilie was scheduled for a patrol with Leo. A little after dawn, she unlatched her shutters to assess the conditions. Beneath apricot clouds, the grounds were coated in frost. Already, the highest peaks beyond Fiory were draped in white capes, and she wondered if the smaller hills, where the fort perched, would see any snow – but winter was still a little while away. Still, she shivered and moved to close the shutters.

There was a gentle knock on her door and Alba slipped inside.

'Morning,' said Ottilie, yawning.

'Good morning.' Alba looked as if she had been up for hours. She held out a roll of parchment. 'I finished it late last night. We've been doing the breakfast, I only just managed to get away.'

Feeling instantly more awake, Ottilie scanned it quickly. Alba had left a large blank space at the end. She wondered if they would need so much room. The only names they had so far were Ned, Gully and Preddy. She assumed Scoot would sign too, but someone else was probably going to have to ask him. Despite Gully's and Preddy's endless attempts at reconciliation, she and Scoot still weren't speaking.

Ottilie threw her arms around Alba and kissed the side of her head. 'Thank you! This is perfect.'

They needed to be smart about this and keep it quiet. If the directorate found out too soon, they would have time to shut it down before reading Alba and Skip's marvellous words.

First, Ottilie would get it to Ned. She dressed quickly and snuck up to the elite towers. As she approached his door, her excitement faltered and she realised she was feeling more than a little nervous. Taking a big gulp of air, she knocked on the blue door.

'Just a minute,' he called from inside.

Realising the hand clutching the parchment was quite sweaty, she quickly swapped it and wiped her palm on her uniform. The door swung open. She could sense Ned's surprise, although he barely let it show.

'Ottilie,' he said with a smile. He was dressed to hunt, and his weapons cupboard was open. 'Come in.' He moved over to the cupboard and continued sorting through his knives. 'Sorry, I've got singer duty – have to head down in a minute.'

'No, that's fine, sorry I interrupted –'

'It's no problem,' he said, rather quickly.

Ottilie wondered if he might be a little nervous too. Thinking about nerves only made her feel more awkward so she quickly got to the point.

'I just wanted to give you this.' She held the roll of parchment out to him. 'You said you might be able to get some signatures.'

'Wow.' Ned looked it over. 'It's thorough. Did you write this?' He looked impressed.

Ottilie smiled. 'No. My handwriting doesn't look like that.'

He laughed. 'Mine doesn't either.' Rolling it back up, he said, 'I'll get you as many as I can.' He reached for a knife, his gaze lingering on the blade. 'The sooner we train everyone, the better.'

There was something in his expression that made Ottilie ask, 'How do you think the wyler got in?' Ned sheathed the blade and, before he could answer, she couldn't help but add, 'I think someone let it in.'

'I really hope that's not true,' he said gravely. 'I don't know how it happened, and the directorate's not telling us, which makes me think they don't either.'

She wanted to say that she was worried it was a witch, or to ask him if he thought witches even existed anymore, but she couldn't bring herself to say it. She remembered Leo scoffing when she had asked him if the bone singers were witches, as if believing they still existed was somehow childish. She realised she didn't want Ned to think of her that way, so instead she asked, 'Have you had a chance to talk to Leo?'

He frowned.

Ottilie's mood flattened. 'He still won't sign? Why?'

'He's full of stupid reasons,' said Ned. 'But I think he just likes the way things are. He's scared of change. This place serves him pretty well. He doesn't want to lose that.'

She clenched her fists. 'But there's already been change. I was a change, and he's happy with me being his fledge ... I mean, I think he is.'

Ned smiled. 'He is. Let me see how many signatures I can get, then I'll shove it under his nose and see what happens.'

Ottilie was too impatient for that. After a quick breakfast she hastened down to the lower grounds with purpose in her toes. She found Leo in Maestro's pen, brushing his coat.

'Morning,' he said cheerily, without looking at her.

'Good morning,' she said, her tone flat.

'You need to wake up.' His hand inched towards Maestro's water trough, but she got in first, splashing him in the face.

'Argh!' Leo lurched backwards, laughing.

Maestro, who caught some of the splash, swung around and bared his teeth at Ottilie.

'Sorry, Maestro,' she muttered, patting his side.

'Sorry, Maestro?' Leo scanned Ottilie's expression. 'You're mad at me again?'

Ottilie climbed the stepladder and hoisted the double saddle onto Maestro's broad back. She was well practised at doing it herself now, since Leo was still insisting she train with Maestro alone in her free time. She knew it was necessary. With the order trials approaching, she needed as much practice as she could get. If Maestro misbehaved, she might miss out on becoming a flyer.

'No. I'm not mad at you,' she snapped. 'I don't get to

be mad at you because we have to go out there and hunt monsters together.'

He flashed her a smug smile.

'Stop it, Leo. I need you to sign my petition.'

The smile slid off his face. 'This again. Now I'm getting it from Ned too. Give it a rest, will you.' He crouched down to buckle the saddle.

'Explain to me why you won't sign it,' said Ottilie evenly. 'Because I don't understand your problem.'

'Look,' he said, descending the ladder out of the pen. 'I don't want to put my name on it. They're not going to take it well, and I don't want to be involved.'

Her jaw dropped.

'What?' said Leo, looking up at her.

'That was honest,' she said, doing nothing to mask her disgust.

He shrugged. He was always honest, too honest sometimes. She climbed down to join him, and Maestro leapt over her head.

'They'll be angry,' he said.

'You're being pathetic,' said Ottilie, pulling up into the saddle.

Leo's face flushed, but they couldn't fight it out. A huntsman on the wall raised a blue flag and Maestro soared out over the boundary.

Icy air whipped Ottilie's face as Maestro tilted and swept them west, towards the Red Canyon. Their journey was smooth and eerily quiet.

'Where are they all?' she muttered. They should have happened across something by now.

'I don't know.' Leo sounded uneasy.

She remembered that smaller dredretches would clear the area when lycoats were near, and her back stiffened. Could something similar be happening here? The Red Canyon was the first place she had ever seen a wyler and, according to Conductor Edderfed, was also where the new pack had been sighted.

They were under strict instructions not to attack the wyler pack. The Hunt wanted to watch them – to try to understand why they had suddenly changed their patterns.

Ottilie could feel that Leo was on edge. Not only had they amassed no points on this patrol, but now they were about to enter a zone where they were forbidden from felling a high-scoring dredretch.

Something caught her eye to the left – a sickly myrtle tree. Ottilie gasped. Its mossy pelt, usually vibrant green, was dark and slimy, and its branches were blackened, the leaves drooping and dripping like the trees in the Withering Wood.

'Leo, look!' she said, grabbing his shoulder.

Maestro circled around and landed in front of the tree. He wasn't happy. The ground was sticky and he kept lifting his feet one after the other.

'But we're not anywhere near the Withering Wood!' said Leo.

She remembered the single black drip she had seen oozing from the stump on the way to Jungle Bay. Maybe it hadn't been dredretch blood after all.

Something was happening to the ground. Maestro huffed and growled, shuffling backwards as the damp, tacky soil sank in on itself, forming a small basin of rotting earth.

Ottilie looked around frantically, searching for any clue as to why this was happening. Her eyes fell on the carcass of a golden dog, smaller and sleeker than the shepherds. A driftdog – one of the few natural beasts still inhabiting the Narroway. There was a pack living near the mouth of Flaming River, but this one was much further inland and completely alone.

'Its heart's missing,' said Leo weakly.

It couldn't be possible. Dredretches didn't rip out animal hearts; they only did that to humans. But then dredretches weren't supposed to attack animals at all.

Ottilie twisted in the saddle, searching for any sign of the driftdog's heart, but saw nothing. 'Leo, I think its heart was eaten,' she said.

'What?'

'Look. It's nowhere around. They …' She gulped. 'They usually tear it up, right? There should be … be … bits of it.' She did not welcome the images that crowded her mind.

'Dredretches don't eat hearts. They don't eat anything,' said Leo stubbornly.

'Well, do you think something else did it?' she said. Ottilie wasn't sure if that was better or worse. She thought of that hooded witch and her gut twisted.

'I don't know. We need to look around,' he said, burying his hand in Maestro's fur.

Maestro, eager to be free of the festering soil, leapt into the air.

Before long, the Red Canyon was in sight, the shimmering river tinted red and glinting like flame far below. They swept down, level with the caves.

'Did you see that?' said Leo, stiffly.

Ottilie scanned the cliffs. She hadn't seen anything.

'A wyler?' Her pulse quickened.

'Too big ... wrong colour.'

Wylers were like the canyon, varying colours of fire. Maestro circled lower and Ottilie spotted a bushy tail, pure white, disappearing into a cave.

'What is that?' She was flipping back through her memories, trying to remember the bestiaries. Had she read about a white dredretch with a tail like that? She couldn't think of anything, but of course she hadn't read them all. Leo was an expert on the bestiaries and he didn't have an answer either.

Ottilie's shoulders bunched into knots. Something drew her attention, down by the river. They must have been there the whole time, their colours blending with the rocks and weeds, but the movement caught her eye. There were wylers below, at least ten.

Leo swore and nudged Maestro higher. It must have been instinct. She felt it herself, the impulse to flee. Those vile, vicious things were a nightmare on their own. Ten of them, a pack – it was unthinkable. Why was this happening? What, or who, had brought them together?

Fighting her instincts, Ottilie said, 'Go lower, Leo.' She had spotted it again, a streak of white. 'The white thing is down there.'

Maestro circled down and every wyler froze, like tiny rusted statues, their black horns tipped back, their flaming eyes staring. Ottilie shivered. Maestro touched down on a ledge just above the pack. Ottilie and Leo both raised their bows, warning them to stay away.

She saw it, the creature with the white bushy tail, weaving through the frozen pack, the only one moving. It was a wyler. There was no doubt. But it was bigger than them, the size of a young wolf, pure white with two black horns poking through its fur.

It wasn't just its appearance that was strange. There was a sense. It seemed more natural, more alive. Ottilie's instincts were thrown. She had the feeling that if she pierced its flesh, red blood would spill out onto her hands.

Something was wrong here. Ottilie needed to get to those books. She needed to learn more, to understand more. Where had these monsters really come from? What was causing these changes, this blending, this blurring of the lines?

13

The Haunted Stables

'We're doing it tonight,' said Ottilie, her voice hushed.

Whistler had left for Fort Richter three days before, but Ottilie had been scheduled for evening or overnight shifts every day, so they had wasted a good part of her absence.

'Finally,' said Skip, lacing her boots.

After breakfast, Ottilie had come to find Skip in the sculkie quarters. Maeve had greeted her with a look of disdain, followed by an even more familiar expression of suspicion. What Maeve had to be suspicious of now, Ottilie did not know. Her secret was out – there was nothing more to know. Of course, she was planning on breaking into the Bone Tower that night, but there was no way Maeve could have picked that up. Could she?

'Shovels,' Maeve had muttered, inclining her head as she passed.

'Witch,' Ottilie had muttered back. She didn't normally respond, but nerves were making her snappy.

Now, it was only Skip and two other sculkies in the bedchamber.

'We should wait until midnight, it's safer,' said Skip quietly, rising to her feet.

Ottilie managed a tense nod. After everything she had faced, she was surprised at her nerves. She just didn't like how much of their plan relied on luck.

She was about to be very late to her warding lesson and Skip was due to clean Captain Lyre's chambers, so they both headed for the door. She was lost in thought, imagining all the things that could go wrong, when Skip grabbed her arm and pulled her backwards.

'Watch out!'

Ottilie dropped her gaze to the floor. She had been about to step on a dead mouse.

'Another one?' Skip pulled one of the scrubbing brushes from the hooks in her belt and prodded at it.

'Ugh, Skip, don't do that,' said Ottilie, wrinkling her nose.

'You see smooshed dredretches all the time.' Skip laughed. 'This is nowhere near as disgusting.'

'But I don't poke them. Stop touching it. We should take it outside,' said Ottilie. 'What did you mean, another one?'

'It's the third dead mouse I've found in here in the last month,' said Skip. She pulled her orange headband off and used it to pick up the mouse, wrapping it carefully like a picnic lunch.

'Is there a rodent problem?' Ottilie's eyes flicked around the room. 'I haven't seen any around.' She didn't say what she was really thinking – another dead animal, in the room where the wyler had attacked. The thought made her shiver. But there hadn't been any more dredretches inside Fiory. Sometimes a dead mouse was just a dead mouse.

'Well, I don't see any live ones in here,' said Skip, frowning. 'They're always dead. Do you remember –'

'The one in my boot?' Months ago, they had thought either Maeve or Gracie had put a dead mouse in her shoe as a prank.

'Maybe Moravec got a taste for it,' said Skip, her mouth turned down. 'She's probably slaughtering them for fun.'

'But why would she just leave them lying around?'

'Because she's insane, Ottilie.'

The mystery of the dead mice would have to wait for another day. Ottilie had a rodent of a different kind to deal with. They had progressed to the next stage of their warding training, moving into the arena where their fledgling trials had been. It was the only place within the Fiory grounds where they were allowed to work with dredretches.

Perched on one of the large engraved blocks that Ottilie had dived behind during her trial was a small cage, and in it was a shank. It was about the size and shape of a ferret and was covered in yellow spines. The shank had curled itself into a wheel and was somersaulting in all directions, trying to break free of the cage to get at the fledglings sitting cross-legged below.

Wrangler Morse had them removing their rings for as long as they could manage it. Ottilie was struggling a great deal. She didn't feel any more capable of resisting the sickness than she had the first time that Captain Lyre had brought a jivvie into the room.

Sweating and frustrated, she stared down at the little bronze ring on the ground in front of her, trying to resist the urge to shove it back on her thumb. She couldn't help thinking it would be a whole lot easier to concentrate if the shank stopped battering against the cage. Of course, there were plenty of distractions like this beyond the walls, and Ottilie knew she was just going to have to get used to them.

The shank slammed into the cage once more. Ottilie's heart felt sluggish. She retched. Her breath grew short and finally her vision began to cloud. She realised that she must have pushed it too far this time. Her limbs went slack. She swayed and tried to send a signal to her hand to reach for the ring, but she couldn't move.

Distantly, she sensed herself flopping sideways, but then something changed. She felt a tingle sneaking up her arm. Someone pulled her back up to sitting. She squeezed her eyes and opened them. The bronze ring caught her gaze. Someone had slipped it back on her thumb.

It was Scoot. Struggling with warding as much as she was, Scoot must have put his ring back on earlier and noticed that she was in trouble.

'You all right?' There was no anger in his eyes.

Ottilie nodded, screwing up different bits of her face, trying to get the feeling back. 'Thanks, Scoot.' She struggled to shape the words. Her tongue felt numb, as if she'd been drinking icy water.

He smiled and Ottilie felt a knot loosen in her stomach. Was the fight over? Did something need to be said?

'Careful there, Ott!' said Wrangler Morse. His red beard was pulled into two braids that dangled in front of her face. 'Don't push yourself too hard.'

Gully and Preddy turned to look. Neither had put their ring back on, and they both seemed fine. Why was she so bad at this?

Wrangler Morse interpreted her expression correctly. 'You'll get there,' he said. 'It takes some longer than others. No telling why. There are better ways to risk your life than sitting near a caged shank,' he added, ruffling her hair. 'All right everyone, enough for today. Rings on.'

They used to walk out of their warding lessons feeling sleepy, perhaps a little bored, but very calm. Now the hour left them shaken and weak. Scoot drifted out by her side. Neither of them spoke, but neither did anyone else. No-one had the breath to spare. He glanced sideways at her and she at him: the fight was over.

Beneath a starry sky, Ottilie, Alba and Skip met outside the root cellar.

'What if Montie wakes up and finds you gone?' said Ottilie, following Alba inside. The temperature seemed to drop with every step she took. The air pricked at her skin like tiny needles and she hugged herself tightly, wishing she'd worn her gloves.

'It wouldn't be the first time,' said Alba, as Skip pulled the door shut. 'She'll just think I've snuck off to read – which is half true,' she said, smiling mischievously. 'Here, we need to move this.'

They hauled sacks of potatoes and other heavy vegetables out of the way. The work took the edge off the chill and Ottilie was grateful for it.

'This is the first door I ever found,' said Alba. 'There are secret tunnels and passages all over the place. I mightn't have found any of them if I hadn't accidentally rolled a yam under the shelf.' She got down on her stomach and slipped feet first under the lowest shelf. 'Follow me,' she said, her head disappearing.

Ottilie hesitated. She had never much liked small spaces. Back in the Swamp Hollows, Gully was always finding places like this and dragging her along – but no matter how often she tackled them, the fear never completely went away.

Skip seemed perfectly fine. Her face glowed with excitement as she disappeared beneath the shelf. This was clearly her idea of a good time.

Ottilie closed her eyes and thought of the kappabak. She remembered her feet dangling above its jaws. This was nothing compared with that. She just wished her nerves would listen to reason.

'Come on, Ottilie,' hissed Skip, from somewhere below.

Clamping down on her fear, she jumped to the ground and slid under the shelf. Shimmying backwards until her feet found the opening, she shuffled down, dangled off the edge and dropped.

It was uncomfortably dark. Ottilie fumbled in her pockets, finally locating the dry glow sticks and dropping them into a vial of water. Greenish light fizzed to life as she hung it around her neck.

'I don't think I've been in this one,' said Skip. 'Where does it come out?'

'This one?' said Ottilie. 'You know about the tunnels too?'

Skip shrugged. 'I don't know them as well as Alba.'

'All sorts of places,' said Alba to Skip. 'Most of the tunnels are linked, you just have to find the doors.'

'Not past the boundaries, though? Is it safe to keep these a secret?' Ottilie was thinking of the wyler. She had given up hope that the Hunt would discover how it got in. When the yickers had attacked in Floodwood, a crack had been found in the boundary wall almost immediately. But they had checked it since the wyler attack, and there was nothing wrong. The general consensus seemed to be that the wyler had crept through the gates behind a huntsman.

Ottilie did not believe it. There were too many eyes on those gates when they opened. Wylers were quick, but they weren't invisible. Someone had snuck it in. She didn't know how they had managed it, but if it was the hooded witch, a bit of magic would surely have been useful.

Alba interrupted her thoughts. 'I don't know any tunnels that cross the boundaries. This one only reaches as far as the old stables.'

'Why are there two sets of stables?' said Ottilie. She had jogged past the old stables before. They were a desolate complex of abandoned stalls and training yards, with a huge stone barn that looked almost churchlike.

'They decided to move the horses years ago, because the old stables were too near the boundary wall,' explained Skip. 'The horses sensed the dredretches and could never settle.'

'That's why people call it haunted,' added Alba. 'They say it's haunted by the spirits of horses that died of fright.'

They spoke in hushed tones. Ottilie was sure there was no way they would be overheard, but there was something about the air down there that warned her to keep quiet. She pressed her palm against the surface of the tunnel wall. By the greenish light of the glow sticks she could see rocks wedged in unusual formations, as if they were confused fragments of ancient sculptures. Withered roots slithered behind and between, and here and there little shadows scuttled, their features distorted by the imperfect light.

Ottilie found her mind wandering back to her first journey with Bill, through the Wikric tunnels. If it weren't for Bill she would never have found Gully.

If he hadn't broken into their hollow and guided her, however reluctantly, all the way to where the swamp picker held the recruits – Ottilie paused mid-thought, surprised by her own mind. Not recruits, pickings … kidnapped children. Was she already forgetting that the Narroway Hunt was in the business of kidnapping?

'This is it,' said Alba.

Ottilie twisted back to the present and shook out her hands as if she could flick off her nerves like water. Around the corner there was a steep stairway. At the top was where the danger lay. Once they were out in the open night, they risked being seen. Ottilie followed Alba up and helped her push open the trapdoor, which was partially sealed with mud.

The rumours were understandable. There was something about those abandoned stables. Whether the spirits of horses truly lingered in those decaying stalls, Ottilie couldn't know, but fear was very present, as if echoes of their terror hung in the air, like a fog she could feel but not see. It was no wonder people avoided the place.

They passed through the shadowed stalls and out into a yard. Ottilie could see the Bone Tower above. A midnight moon hung high, just a sliver in the black. She was about to suggest they head over as soon as possible, when something white caught the fringe of her gaze.

She didn't want to look. A ghost horse was not something she had a desire to see. A low growl greeted them from across the yard.

'What is that?' said Skip, her voice sharp.

The pale shape was moving towards them through the dark. It couldn't be a ghost. Ghosts didn't growl, did they? Well, certainly a ghost horse wouldn't growl. But then Ottilie remembered the white wyler. Her heart pounded and she reached for the knife sheathed at her back.

'She knows we're not supposed to be here,' said Alba nervously.

'Who?' said Skip.

'Hero,' said Ottilie with a sigh. The leopard shepherd.

Skip and Alba didn't seem to share her relief. Hero's teeth were bared and her growl deepened as she drew near, but Ottilie was so used to hostile felines that she didn't blink an eye.

'She shelters here sometimes,' said Alba breathlessly. 'I think she likes the solitude. It's right by the perimeter but the shepherds stay out. They don't like it.'

'She clearly wants us to leave,' said Skip. 'How are we going to get past?' She pointed up at the Bone Tower.

'I brought her some fish. It's salted, but she should be used to that.' Alba produced three fat chunks of fish wrapped in a large leaf from the pockets of her dress. Keeping her eyes fixed on Hero, she carefully held them out and inched towards the snarling leopard, as if she were walking on ice.

'Are you sure this will work?' asked Skip.

'I've given her eggs before. She should like this better,' said Alba.

She placed the chunks of fish on the ground and scurried back to stand beside Ottilie. Hero sniffed at the fish, growled and then, as if giving them leave to pass, lowered her whole body to the ground and ate it.

'Quick,' said Alba. 'But don't run.'

Skip powered ahead, in a jerky half-run. Ottilie followed, in less of a hurry, and Alba, probably calmed by her confidence, stayed close to her side.

14

The Bone Tower

There were huntsmen on the wall. Ottilie could see their silhouettes in the flickering torchlight high above. She hastily tucked away her glow sticks, and they tripped, bumped and stumbled all the way to the inner edge of the boundary wall.

Besides their encounter with Hero, none of the shepherds bothered them. A couple prowled past, monitoring the inner perimeter: just heavy shadows, crunching twigs in the night.

A stairway zigzagged up the face of the wall. Feeling her way up, Ottilie kept one shoulder pressed to the rough stone, avoiding the exposed edge. Finally, they reached the base of the tower and gathered close, hunching in a slice of shadow.

'Where's the window?' breathed Skip.

They had discussed this beforehand. Alba said that Whistler's door seemed to be locked, with no visible lock to pick. She assumed it was some bone singer trick. But there was a window above that she always left ajar.

Alba's eyes were anxious, but her mouth was set with determination. 'The other side,' she said, patting the rough stone of the cylindrical tower.

'But there are huntsmen patrolling on the other side,' said Skip.

Ottilie knew that stretch. It was the gap between the east gate and the Bone Tower, where she and Leo had been rescued by the owl.

'They'll stay down the other end, by the gate,' said Ottilie. 'As long as there isn't too much light, we should be fine.'

Her words seemed to reassure the others; she only wished her own nerves would settle as they crept around the edge to the lockless door. It was narrow and painted pale blue. Ottilie pressed her fingers against it and quickly withdrew them. It was like ice.

'Cold?' said Alba.

'What do you mean?' said Skip, stroking the door. 'Argh, it's like being burned, except –'

'The opposite,' said Ottilie.

Alba nodded. 'It's always like that.'

The window was small, too small for anyone bigger than Skip, who was the tallest of the three. It was a fair way above the door, just low enough for Alba to pull herself in when she stood on Skip's shoulders. Ottilie kept her eyes fixed anxiously on the silhouettes of the huntsmen, while holding her hand as high as she could, helping Alba balance.

Alba disappeared inside with a loud thump. Skip followed after with a little more grace, leaving Ottilie to climb up herself. It was no worse than the wall in the Wikric tunnels that Bill had helped her scale, but it took her a while to riddle it out. She was so lost in the task that she didn't sense anyone approaching.

'What are you doing?'

Ottilie lurched in shock, and nearly fell. She was caught so off-guard, she hadn't even recognised the voice. Turning her head slowly, she breathed a huge sigh of relief. It was Gully.

'Gully? What are y—'

'Wall watch,' he said, gesturing to a far-off figure by the east gate. 'We saw movement and Ned sent me to see what's going on. What *is* going on?'

Ottilie's eyes flicked over to Ned. 'We're breaking in to the Bone Tower,' she whispered.

Gully's eyes lit up. 'Why?' He didn't bother to lower his voice.

'To steal books.'

'Can I come?' he asked eagerly.

'No, Gully, you're on wall watch,' she said, grinning. 'Do you think you could lie to Ned?' Her smile faded quickly. 'Tell him we're a bunch of bone singers or something?'

Gully frowned. He had never liked lying, and had never been any good at it. It was too late anyway. Ned was coming over. Ottilie's pulse quickened. She'd just been caught breaking into a restricted building, but still, this hummingbird beat did seem fairly common around Ned.

'What are you doing?' His voice was reproachful, but there was an amused glint in his eyes.

Ottilie let herself drop to the ground and shook out her arms. 'Does it matter?' She wriggled her fingers, trying to get a bit of life back into her cramping joints.

Ned smiled. He didn't seem to be able to help it. His face was shaped for laughter. 'Yes.'

She weighed her options. She trusted Ned, but he'd been a huntsman for nearly three years and he was an elite. He hadn't told anyone she was a girl – that was something – and he'd been discreet about the petition. Ned wasn't like Leo. If he thought her reasons were good enough, he might not report her.

'We're borrowing books,' said Ottilie.

He raised an eyebrow. 'We?'

'Me, Alba Kit and Isla Skipper.'

Alba and Skip both stuck their heads out the window, looking sheepish.

'Why?' said Ned, supressing a smile.

'Because things are getting worse here, and there are too many secrets in this place,' she said, very quickly. 'I think the rule of innocence is a lie, and someone let that wyler inside, and we think some answers might be in Whistler's collection of books.'

Shadows gathered behind his eyes. 'You think the rule of innocence is a lie?' The tone of his voice suggested he might have considered it himself.

'Yes,' said Ottilie, 'but I don't have time to explain.'

His eyes searched hers. Finally, he seemed to make a decision. 'We'll give you a leg-up. But the watch changes soon, so be quick.'

Gully and Ned locked their arms together and Ottilie used them like a step ladder, gripping the wall for support. Ned, who was far taller than Gully, helped push her higher until she was able to scramble through the window and join her friends.

She pulled the glow sticks from her pocket, washing the circular room in greenish light. By a triangular hearth there were benches and shelves with pots and jars full of all manner of strange plants and powders. The room smelled of rotting parchment and dried herbs, and a thick layer of dust rested on every surface.

Skip turned to Ottilie. 'You think someone let that wyler inside?'

'Don't you?' said Ottilie.

Skip considered it for a moment.

'It could have been by accident,' said Alba.

'I think it was a witch,' said Ottilie.

'There are no witches anymore,' said Skip with a snort.

Ottilie opened her mouth to argue, but Alba got in first. 'That's why we're here – to find answers.' Gesturing to the room, she added, 'Come on, we don't have much time.'

The walls were lined with books of varying thickness and states of decay. Ottilie guessed that at least as many books were piled up on the floor, some open, some closed, some just covers with all their pages ripped out. Here and there a scroll peeked up through a mound, and by a spiral staircase Ottilie saw a bolted chest with loose sheets sticking out.

'I think we can take as many as we want,' said Skip with a grin. 'I don't think she'll notice they're gone.'

Alba had already begun to go through them, running her fingers along spines and flicking hungrily through their pages. Ottilie settled on a mildewed rug to do the same.

It didn't take long for Alba to gather a fairly extensive collection. Ottilie was having less luck. Many of the books didn't have titles and the writing was small and difficult to read.

'Look at this!' said Skip. She was holding up a medium-sized book with a dark, greenish cover. Its pages looked like they had been soaked in the blackest tea.

'What's it called?' said Ottilie, forgetting for a moment that Skip couldn't read very well.

Skip ran her fingers over the cover. 'There's no words on the front. But it's creepy – and so heavy! Feel it.' She tossed it to Ottilie.

Skip was right. The book was smaller than many of the others but it seemed to weigh three times more than it should. She opened it to the middle and saw a drawing of what looked like a woman being shoved into a coffin by a host of bodiless arms. She snapped it shut and passed it to Alba.

Alba had a quick look through, her eyes growing wider by the second. 'It's about witches!' she said, adding it to the pile of books she had collected.

Ottilie felt jittery with excitement. This might be just the book they needed!

There was a ghastly screech somewhere far off and the gentle night-bells tolled.

'That's the shift change,' she said. 'We have to go.'

Alba gathered the pile in her arms.

Ottilie turned for the door, but something froze her in place. In the darkened spiral stairway was the outline of a figure, sitting, watching them in silence, the whites of her eyes unnaturally bright in the dark.

15

Whistler

Ottilie gasped, shock locking her bones.

'Ottilie, what?' Skip spun around and jumped a foot in the air.

Alba didn't make a noise. She simply shuffled closer to Ottilie's side.

The bright-eyed shadow rose from her perch on the stairs and stepped into the light. She was not a graceful figure. She was bony, her shoulders seemed a little lopsided, and she made rather a lot of noise as she walked.

Ottilie had never seen her before. She seemed to be in her middle years, but it was difficult to place. Her hair was silver and her eyes were a stormy grey to match. Her face was sharp and angled, and there was something birdlike about her eyes.

'Ottilie Colter.' Her voice was sharp, but amused, and her face unreadable. 'I've been looking forward to meeting you.'

Who was this? Ottilie glanced questioningly at Skip, who inclined her head in response. Ottilie understood – Whistler. It didn't surprise her that Whistler knew who she was. Everyone knew who she was. But Whistler was supposed to be at Richter. Where had she come from? How long had she been in the room?

'Here to steal my books, I see,' she said, waving her purple sleeves in Alba's direction.

Alba immediately dropped the stack of books she was holding. One of them bounced and hit Ottilie in the foot. Ottilie smothered a cry and hopped sideways, keeping her eyes on Whistler.

They were done for. Surely Whistler would report them to the directorate. What was going to happen now? Would all three of them be spending the night in the burrows?

Whistler just stood there, gazing at them. Stationary, she seemed elegant for a moment – only a moment.

'Drinks?' she said abruptly, swinging one arm in an exaggerated gesture of offer.

Ottilie didn't know what to say. Alba seemed incapable of speech. But somewhere to her left Ottilie heard Skip say, 'Yes, please.'

Whistler sprang into action. With much clattering and clunking, she gathered four dusty cups and a pitcher from the shelves by the hearth. 'Sit, sit,' she demanded, waving her arms about.

Ottilie and Alba squished into a single armchair. Beside them, Skip carefully removed the assortment of oddments from the ottoman and settled on it.

'Lillywater,' Whistler muttered, placing the tray down. 'Acceptable?'

'Yes,' squeaked Alba, surprising Ottilie.

She looked warily at the pitcher.

'Not the poison kind,' said Whistler, with a half-smile. As she began to pour, Ottilie noticed that she did not pull back the long purple sleeves that covered her hands. She seemed well-practised at handling objects through the fabric, and it did not appear to hinder her movement.

Whistler passed Ottilie a cup.

'Thank you,' she said, without lifting it to her lips. It didn't seem wise to accept a drink from a stranger, and a strange stranger at that. But Whistler was an important member of the Hunt. She was the head bone singer. Even so, Ottilie didn't drink.

'So, who else have I caught in my web?' Whistler wrung her hands. 'Isla Skipper, sculkie, and Alba Kit, kitchenhand and daughter of third cook, Montie Kit, wearer of fine scarves.'

Alba and Skip both seemed surprised that Whistler knew who they were. Ottilie wondered if there was anyone in the Narroway that Whistler didn't know.

'Pleased to meet you,' Whistler said, ducking her head in an odd sort of bow. 'They call me Whistler.' She sat down in the remaining armchair, not bothering to clear the objects it held. 'So you're here for my books. Why? What do you want to know?'

None of them answered.

'Let's be lions not mice,' she said, loudly.

Ottilie didn't know what to do. Could they tell her the truth? She couldn't think of a single lie.

'Parrots at least. Come on, girls, speak.'

Ottilie glanced at Skip. Her jaw was shut tight.

'We want to know more about this place,' said Alba, her words almost inaudible. 'Why there are dredretches here.'

Ottilie settled with a silent sigh. It wasn't a lie. It just wasn't the whole truth.

Whistler smiled. 'Knowledge seekers. No need to break in and rob me, girls. Although I appreciate the effort. But in the future, just ask.' She shrugged. 'The dredretches are here because of the Laklands.'

'We know that bit,' said Ottilie impatiently. Captain Lyre had told them that much on their first day at Fiory. 'Why are they even in the Laklands? Where did they come from? Is it something to do with the war?' By all accounts, the dredretch presence in the far west seemed to originate sometime after the war between the Usklers and the Laklands a hundred years ago.

Whistler seemed amused by Ottilie's curtness. She straightened up in her chair. 'The dredretches are in the Laklands because of the broken promise.'

'Oh,' said Alba, her eyes wide.

'What?' said Skip, looking between Alba and Whistler.

'Go on, then,' said Whistler. 'You know the story?'

'It's complicated …' Alba began. Her words seemed to shiver with nerves. She glanced at Whistler, who gestured for her to continue.

Ottilie thought she knew what Alba was going to say. She gave her an encouraging smile, and Alba quickly recounted the story she had told Ottilie a while ago, about how the Usklerians had broken their promise never to attack the Laklands.

'But what's that got to do with dredretches?' said Skip.

Alba didn't seem to know. She looked to Whistler for help.

'They feed on death and human wickedness,' said Ottilie. Where had she heard that before? Old Moss, back in the Swamp Hollows, perhaps.

'Have you ever heard the tale of the Vanquisher's bane?' said Whistler.

'No,' said Alba.

'They like to keep it quiet,' said Whistler. 'But still, the story is known by some. They say that when the Usklerian king – Viago the Vanquisher, history named him ...' At this, her voice grew very cold. 'They say when he broke that promise and invaded the Laklands, he was punished. The land that he had conquered became uninhabitable and, like the land, his wife was condemned to birthing only monsters.'

'What do you mean?' Ottilie leaned in, eager to hear more.

'Why do you think the land was uninhabitable? Because dredretches started sprouting from the soil,' said Whistler coolly. 'There weren't many at first, but no-one knew how to fight them. People were dropping to the ground left, right and centre, some without ever laying eyes on the monsters. Before long the entire kingdom was abandoned.'

'But what do you mean, the queen gave birth to monsters?' said Ottilie, still thinking of dredretches.

'For a while the queen was considered barren,' said Whistler. 'Then finally, ten years after the end of the Lakland war, she fell pregnant. But it was a girl – who, of course, could not be an heir to the throne.'

'But that's not a monster!' said Skip.

'Agreed,' said Whistler, with a wry smile. 'But they say she was unnatural somehow. Nothing on dredretches, but it wasn't the ideal result of a long-awaited royal pregnancy. Most considered it further proof of punishment. Of course, then a perfectly healthy son followed some years later – and the bane was linked evermore with daughters of the royal line.'

'When you say unnatural, do you mean she was a witch?' said Ottilie.

Whistler smiled. 'They had many names for her; the clawed witch was one.'

'Clawed?' said Alba, frowning. 'Why?'

'A number of reasons …' said Whistler. 'Some say she was a fiorn.'

Ottilie remembered the cave paintings in the Swamp Hollows of the monstrous creatures with gaping mouths and feathery crowns – halfway between a bird and a human.

'Others said it was because she was a twisted, cruel thing that Viago the Vanquisher would set upon his prisoners.'

'But what was true?' asked Alba.

Whistler's eyes flashed. 'Truth is subjective. In the years since the witch purge, many females have been named as such, particularly the undesirable or feared. Few, if any, were true witches.'

Ottilie had so many more questions. She wanted to ask about the rule of innocence, but she was wary. Asking this was admitting to distrusting the Hunt. That didn't seem like a good idea, considering Whistler's position within it.

'Why are there more dredretches now?' said Skip. 'Why is the Withering Wood spreading?'

'They've been growing in numbers since the beginning,' said Whistler.

'They're saying it's quicker now,' said Ottilie, carefully. 'There are new ones the Hunt's never seen, and the others are acting strange.' She pictured the dead driftdog and tensed in her seat. 'The wylers have made a pack and …' She was unsure if she should mention that she thought someone had let the wyler inside.

'This is all true,' said Whistler, offering no explanation.

Ottilie couldn't resist. 'Could a witch be controlling the dredretches? Gathering them together and making them attack?'

Whistler fixed her eyes upon Ottilie. 'Let me give you some advice. These are good questions, but dangerous. If the Hunt begins to suspect witchcraft is involved, every female in the Narroway will be in grave danger. Historically, witch hunts do not result in the punishment of the guilty. I advise you to keep those questions to yourself for the good of every girl at Fiory.'

Ottilie swallowed. She had always been hesitant about asking questions and sharing information with

133

the Hunt. But she had not realised how dangerous the word 'witch' could be.

'Enough,' said Whistler. 'It's late, and I have things to do.'

Ottilie wanted to press her for more, but it didn't seem wise. They had been caught breaking into her tower, after all, and it appeared they were not going to be punished for it – she didn't want to push her luck.

'I'm afraid I can't let you leave with all of those.' Whistler gestured to the big pile of books Alba had dropped on the floor.

Ottilie's eyes flicked to the green witch book, disappointment burning up her insides.

'However, I will allow you to take one.' Whistler riffled through the volumes on her shelf. 'This one should quench your knowledge thirst.' She dropped the book into Alba's lap and ushered them up, wading through the mess over to the pale blue door. There was no bolt or handle on the inside either. She knocked jerkily with her elbow. There was a clicking sound and the door swung open with a creak.

She herded them through and pulled it mostly closed. 'Watch out for the big cat.' A purple sleeve swung out through the gap in the door, pointing in the direction of the haunted stables. 'She's finished her fish.'

The door clicked shut and Ottilie thought she saw a faint mist puff out from under it – that or a cloud of dust.

Alba held the book under the torchlight. Ottilie squinted at the faded lettering.

'What does it say?' said Skip.

'Sol,' said Ottilie.

'The royal family?' Skip asked.

Sol was the royal family's name – their current king was Varrio Sol. 'Maybe it's got information about the hex?' said Ottilie, her hope rekindling.

Alba frowned, flipping through it. 'We didn't ask her about the hex, and I doubt it will be in here. It's just a family tree and facts.'

Ottilie's shoulders slumped. 'She must have just given you the most harmless book she had.'

'Doesn't matter,' Skip whispered, patting her jacket.

'What did you do?' A smile crept onto Ottilie's face.

Skip opened her jacket, revealing the top of an old greenish book. 'I stole the one about witches.'

☙ 16 ☙

The Flaming Tapestry

For the next week Ottilie barely laid eyes on Alba. She had locked herself away with the two books, determined to find answers. Ottilie returned her own focus to hunting. She was now sitting in fifty-first place. It wasn't enough!

She was determined to do better. Not just to improve her ranking, but for other, more dire reasons. Not only had she and Leo found another isolated patch of the withering sickness – this time further east, not far from the Arko zone – but that morning they had flown over the Withering Wood, and the growth was clear. If the sickness began to spread from other spots too, the Narroway would be a festering, blackened waste in no time.

Ottilie couldn't help feeling that their work was achieving nothing. The whole situation put her in a hopeless mood, which was somewhat lifted when Ned knocked on her door that afternoon. He had the petition in his hand. The room brightened.

'It was less than I hoped,' he said, holding out the parchment for her to see. Including Ned, only six elites had signed. 'You know, I think a lot of them agreed with me, they just –'

'Didn't want their name on it.' Ottilie frowned. If taken badly, this would essentially be a list of troublemakers – rebels. She knew the elites must be scared the Hunt would react negatively and they would fall out of favour with the directorate. But it was so much safer for the boys than the girls. They were unlikely to throw huntsmen in the burrows or banish them from the Narroway just for marking their name.

The boys probably feared that they would be docked points, consigned permanently to wall watch and singer duty or, worse, the shovelies. She also understood, from personal experience, that those things were not as trivial as they seemed.

The elites had been at Fiory a lot longer than she had. The Narroway Hunt was their family, their whole life. Scoring points was the driving force behind their day's work – it was how they marked their achievements.

But this was so much bigger than that. It was worth the risk; how could they not see? The more huntsmen that signed, the more likely the directorate would agree, and the less likely they would all be punished.

Ottilie didn't know how she felt. Six was better than nothing, and six elites at that. Her friends signed it that afternoon. Scoot, possibly trying to make up for their fight, was overly enthusiastic and smudged the ink across the page, covering Gully and Preddy's names, so they both had to sign again.

Ottilie tried once more with Leo. She found him napping in his room. They weren't ideal circumstances. Not only was he annoyed at being interrupted, but he seemed embarrassed to have been caught resting. He liked to maintain the illusion of invulnerability. Predictably, he refused once again, and the whole thing ended with Leo throwing a pillow hard at her face and Ottilie calling him spineless and slamming the door.

Skip had far better luck with the custodians. After the wyler attack, many of them were enthusiastic about learning to defend themselves against the dredretches, and willing to risk the consequences of marking their name.

Ottilie was not an elite – she couldn't just ask for an audience with the directorate. Her plan was to pass the petition to Wrangler Morse, the wrangler she trusted most, and ask him to take it higher. She was hoping to catch him in the training yards and was just cutting through the grove when Gracie and Maeve appeared.

A mouldy dustplum squelched beneath her boot. Ottilie stiffened and stopped. This could not be good.

'Hello?' she said.

Gracie smiled her cold little smile, and Ottilie found herself thinking of Yosha Moses, the girl who had jumped from the tree.

Gracie was looking a little better, she thought. Still pale, but more yellow than grey. Ottilie's eyes darted to Gracie's arm but the scar from the wyler bite was hidden beneath her sleeve.

Ottilie was surprised to see that Maeve, on the other hand, looked awful. Her dark hair was matted, and she had purple smudges under eyes. It looked like she hadn't slept in days. What was going on with those two?

'Are you doing it today?' Maeve demanded.

'What?' She felt shaky and wasn't sure why.

'Don't play dumb, you're taking the petition to the directorate today?' pressed Maeve, flicking hair away from her strangely fraught face.

'How did you … yes. Why?' Ottilie regarded her with wide eyes. Maeve seemed angry. Her mood radiated from her in a way that Ottilie had never felt before.

'We'd like to sign, please,' said Gracie with her usual false sweetness, her mouth quirking up.

'You … really?' Ottilie had not expected this.

'Of course,' Maeve snapped, glowering. 'Isla didn't even ask us.'

Ottilie wasn't surprised. They had only asked people they trusted and Ottilie considered these girls two of the least trustworthy people at Fort Fiory. She held out the petition with narrowed eyes. What if they tore it up? Or ran off and took it to Wrangler Voilies? But then Ottilie remembered Maeve on the night of the wyler attack. She had been fearless — and angry. It did make sense that she wanted to sign.

'I've only got this with me,' said Ottilie, pulling a stick of charcoal from her pocket.

'That'll do fine,' said Maeve, scratching Ottilie's hand as she snatched it.

Ottilie blinked. She had the oddest sensation of wind sweeping across her face, but the day was perfectly still.

>———————————>

The petition was out of Ottilie's hands for only half a day before they had their answer.

'Insubordination!' spat Wrangler Voilies, his face the colour of rotting meat.

Wrangler Morse had promised to pass on the petition to Captain Lyre — after that, Ottilie didn't know what had happened. She could only guess that the directorate had rejected their request and sent Voilies to deal with them.

He had called everyone who had signed to a small chamber, well out of the way of the rest of the fort.

They wanted to keep it quiet, thought Ottilie, keep it contained. She swallowed the lump in her throat. This was not the moment for tears. Gully stood beside her, gripping her wrist hard.

'It is a disgrace!' hissed Voilies.

Ottilie felt Gully twitch. Skip was on her other side, hard-faced, with fire in her eyes.

'A devious attempt to undermine our operation.'

Heat began creeping up Ottilie's neck. Her disappointment morphed into anger and she ground her teeth and fixed her eyes on the tapestry hanging behind Voilies.

'Sneaking. Manipulation. I've thought for years that there should be no women allowed in the fort at all. A noxious distraction! But there are jobs that need to be done. Ingratitude, that's what this is!'

Skip cracked her knuckles, and Ottilie quickly linked her arm – more a gesture of restraint than support.

'My elites … I am deeply disappointed.' His gaze lingered on Ned.

She studied his face. How did he feel about this? Was he regretting helping her? His shoulders were square and his brow furrowed in quiet defiance – it didn't seem so.

'The custodian chieftess has been informed. She is rightly outraged. Every custodian in this room is to report to her chambers the moment this meeting is over.'

A tiny fraction of the weight lifted off Ottilie's shoulders. The custodian chieftess was going to handle the girls, not the directorate. They would be punished, she was sure, but not locked up, not sent away.

'And as for the huntsmen,' said Voilies with a dangerous hiss. 'You are all on probation, and if I hear a word about this again you can pull on a shovelie suit, because I WILL NOT HAVE IT! This is the natural order, and I will not have it disrupted!' he said, sending spit flying in their faces.

'These are dangerous times. If you girls are concerned about your safety you should focus on your jobs. Keep the fort in order, keep the huntsmen comfortable and well fed, so that they are in the best condition to go out and do the job that you are not capable of doing. We will protect you. There is no need for you to learn to protect yourselves.'

His eyes fell upon Ottilie and strange white patches blossomed on his dark red cheeks. He had not targeted her specifically, so that must have meant that Wrangler Morse had not named her as the instigator. Even so, he would never accept her as a huntsman, and any fool could see that the question of training girls had not been raised before a girl had infiltrated the Hunt. Ottilie would have to be very careful. People would be looking for a way to silence her.

Voilies was still rambling on and on. 'An attempt to destabilise the natural order is an act of rebellion!'

There was a loud bang. The tapestry directly behind Wrangler Voilies fell to the ground and burst into flame. He shrieked and hopped sideways.

For a moment everyone froze, then the two closest, Bayo and Alba, hurried forwards, ripped another tapestry from the wall, and smothered the fire. It sparked and licked, catching on one of Alba's braids. She flicked it like a bothersome fly and kept stamping until there was only smoke.

Wrangler Voilies was clutching his heart, breathing hard. His eyes darted accusingly around the room. But none of them had caused it. How could they? A fire like that, from nothing? Not even bone singers could pull a trick like that. The tapestry must have caught on a candle when it fell. But still Wrangler Voilies observed them, mouth gaping, his eyes darting manically from girl to girl.

'Witchcraft,' he hissed, his eyes rolling back. 'WITCHES!'

Ottilie's heart sped to a gallop. Her gaze found Gracie. She was utterly calm, her face absurdly peaceful. Once again, Ottilie pictured Gracie under the hood. But she had been bitten, Ottilie reminded herself. It couldn't be her. Beside Gracie, Maeve was white as salt, her eyes wide with fright and fixed on the embers sparking and drifting from the smoking tapestry.

17

Hush

The custodians were quiet. Even those who'd had nothing to do with the petition kept their heads down and their mouths shut. Ottilie spotted bandaged hands and bruised cheeks. Any signs of behaviour that the Hunt deemed inappropriate – questions, spirited talk, gathering in groups – were met with punishment. Penalties ranged from scolding and skipped meals to … well … Ottilie had heard threats about locking 'malefactors' in the burrows, but she was not sure if anyone was following through.

'Why aren't they punishing us?' asked Scoot, as he and Ottilie left the dining room.

'Because they're too scared,' she said. 'They need us – the huntsmen.' She remembered the look Voilies had given her when they were called in for reprimanding. He wanted her gone. She knew that. But, for now, her connections were keeping her safe. Gully, the Hunt's star fledgling, was her brother. Ned and five other elites had signed the same petition, and Leo, their only champion, was her guardian. He had turned on her before, but he was the one who had begged her back into the fold. They probably didn't trust that he would betray her again – but of course, his name hadn't been on the petition. That wouldn't have gone unnoticed. Ottilie knew she would have to watch her back.

Her interactions with Leo since the business with the petition had been chilly at best. She hadn't raised the topic because she was furious with him and didn't think she could stomach an 'I told you so'.

Leo, to her surprise, was sensible enough not to bring it up. He was simply pretending nothing had happened, meeting her frostiness with smiles, which only made her angrier. If he had signed, it might have made all the difference! Now it was too late, and they would never know.

Scoot was in the middle of a sentence that Ottilie wasn't paying attention to, when someone grabbed her arm and wrenched her sideways, pulling her into an empty broom cupboard.

'Ottilie!' Scoot hammered on the door.

Her heart thundered, the tight space pressing in.

A dim lantern rested on an empty shelf and in the amber light Ottilie saw Maeve, pulling hard on the inside of the door to keep Scoot from opening it.

Strangely, Ottilie's breathing eased, and she found herself feeling more curious than afraid. What was this, another prank? Was Maeve trying to frighten her?

'Get him to shut up,' Maeve hissed.

'Well, let me out, then.'

Maeve didn't budge.

'Or at least let him in!' she snapped.

'Fine.' Maeve kicked the door open, sending Scoot sprawling.

Ottilie felt a great tug towards the wide, high-ceilinged corridor beyond, but her curiosity kept her captive.

'Get in, quick,' said Maeve.

Scoot got to his feet, his jaw jutting out. 'What the –'

'Just get in,' said Maeve sharply.

'Fine … fine …' Scoot threw up his arms and entered the cupboard. 'Crazy,' he muttered.

Ottilie looked Maeve up and down. She looked so dreadful that, despite everything, Ottilie couldn't help but feel concerned for her. She leaned closer, intending to ask what Maeve wanted, but the words came out differently. 'Are you all right?'

It might have been the fractured light, but Maeve's cheeks seemed hollower than Ottilie remembered and there were scrapes and cuts all up her arms. She found herself thinking of Gracie, and the girl who had jumped from the tree. She might not be the hooded witch, but that didn't mean she wasn't capable of doing someone harm.

Scoot grabbed Maeve's arm and twisted it to the light. 'Did they do this to you?'

Maeve shook her head.

'Did Gracie?' said Ottilie, quietly.

Maeve tugged her arm back. 'What? No! Are you crazy?'

'We're not the ones pulling people into cupboards,' said Scoot.

'I just wanted to talk to you.'

'In a cupboard?' said Scoot.

'Yes, in a cupboard. It's not safe to talk out there, not to her.' She nodded at Ottilie with narrowed eyes. 'They're watching us, all of us that signed, but particularly you.'

Ottilie had guessed as much.

'I want to know what we're doing,' said Maeve, desperation thinning her voice.

Scoot snorted. 'We're standing in a cupbo–'

'What's the next step?' Maeve interrupted. 'What are we going to do now?'

'I … there is no next step,' said Ottilie, hopelessness weighting her words. 'They said no, and now they're … it's not safe to do anything now.'

Not now that Voilies is going on about witches, Ottilie thought. She didn't say it; she had begun to fear ever uttering the word 'witch'.

'I want to train in secret,' said Maeve, her eyes stretched wide. 'I want you to teach me.'

It made sense after the wyler attack, but Ottilie couldn't help but wonder if Maeve wanted to learn to defend herself against someone else. The thought made her stomach churn.

She really did want to help but ... 'I can't teach anyone,' said Ottilie, shaking her head. 'I'm only learning myself.'

The lantern flickered and sparked. Scoot jumped and leaned away from it. 'What was –'

Maeve threw her hand over his mouth. Someone was passing.

They moved away.

'Argh!' Maeve drew her hand back. Scoot had his teeth bared. He had clearly bitten her.

'You're an animal!' spat Maeve.

'I'm an animal? Have you looked at yourself lately?'

Ottilie elbowed him. 'Maeve, this isn't smart. We have to go. I'll ... I'll think about it.'

— 18 —

The Tipped Barrow

Later that day, Ottilie visited Alba in the root cellar. She was settled on a grain bag with a woollen blanket wrapped around her like a cocoon. 'It's slow going,' she said. 'It doesn't look like a big book, but every page I turn, it's like I get nowhere.' She tapped the spine, the tips of her fingers poking through the ends of her chunky gloves. 'I don't know if it's because it's really dense, or because the book is spell'd.'

Ottilie frowned and leaned away. 'Why would a book be spell'd?' she whispered.

'I don't know,' said Alba, stroking its cover. 'It's about witches, and not the kind of things you normally read – about how they were evil and they ate their babies.'

'I have never read that,' said Ottilie, with a grimace. She wished they were having this conversation somewhere else, preferably in a wide-open space beneath a cheerful sun.

'Well, trust me, it's out there,' said Alba. 'But this one … I think it was written by witches. Did you know they were sort of growers first – "keepers of the land". Then they learned that they could heal people, like they could heal plants and animals, and then … well, that's about as far as I've got. The writing is really small and I have to keep stopping to look up words I don't know, but I think it's more than that. I think it's a much bigger book than it pretends to be.'

Ottilie blinked at the book and crinkled her nose. 'What do you think Whistler will do if she finds it missing? She'll know it was us.'

'I don't know. She didn't punish us for breaking in. I think she quite liked it. "Lions not mice", remember.'

Ottilie picked up the other book, the one Whistler had given them. She traced a finger over the lettering on the cover. Sol. Everything kept coming back to the royal family. Centuries ago, the young princess, Seika Devil-Slayer, had felled the first dredretch, then a hundred years ago, Viago the Vanquisher had broken the promise and caused the dredretches to infest the Laklands, and now their current king, Varrio Sol, had created the Narroway Hunt. And Whistler had given them this book – what did it all mean?

The door to the root cellar flew open. 'What do you two think you are doing!' said Montie.

Alba jumped to her feet, masking the book from view. 'We're just talking, Mum.'

'Just talking? Secretly in the root cellar?' Montie's eyes were sharp as daggers. 'Ottilie, dear one, I've told you, you can't come down here for a while. Alba's name was on that petition – if they catch her talking to you like this –'

'Why would they catch us?' said Alba. 'Why would they come in here?'

Montie sighed, her eyes heavy. 'You know very well that they're watching all of you. Our … my position is not secure here, Alba, and they don't allow people they consider untrustworthy to just go back to the Usklers! Who knows what they would do with us.'

Not for the first time, Ottilie wondered why Montie had come to the Narroway. What had driven her to bring her daughter to such a place? Her eyes traced Montie's face. Ottilie had never asked about the burns slinking down from under her scarf, twisting the skin on the left side of her face.

'I'm sorry,' she said, and she really meant it. The last thing she wanted to do was cause trouble for Montie and Alba.

Montie's eyes softened. 'It's all right. I love that you visit us, I do, but you both need to settle for a while. No creeping around – not until things calm down.'

Ottilie needed to stretch her legs. She felt as if she had spent half of her afternoon off crouching in store cupboards. The sun was setting over the trees and the grounds were bathed in fiery light. Deciding to make the most of it, she looped the pond and wandered further across the fields.

Bayo Amadory passed, crossing paths with a sculkie with coppery hair and fairly large ears. Ottilie recognised her immediately. She was infamous. It was Fawn Mogue, the girl who had accidentally let the wyler into the sculkies' bedchamber.

Fawn was pushing a barrow loaded with shiny red apples from the grove. Hitting uneven ground, the barrow wobbled and a few apples tumbled onto the grass.

Ottilie watched Bayo retrieve them for her and was just about to go after the last rolling apple herself when she caught a flash of orange in the corner of her eye.

Her mind said it must have been the sun, but her gut stopped her in her tracks. Bayo and Fawn paused too. Fawn touched her temple. It looked as if she, like Ottilie, was sensing the ghost of a headache.

In the distance, a shepherd howled.

Ottilie's heart froze as she spotted another flash of orange – a bushy tail. She swallowed. She and Bayo were both unarmed.

'Run!' Ottilie cried. 'The wall!' It was closest and there would be armed huntsmen up there.

Fawn released the barrow. It tipped and apples rolled underfoot as they sprinted. Ottilie tripped. Bayo and Fawn ran back to help her up, and the wyler pounced out of nowhere. Ottilie grabbed the only weapon she could find, pelting the dredretch with apples. One after the other, she missed, but dodging kept it busy.

Ottilie heard shouts, howls and thundering hooves. The wyler leapt at Fawn.

'Your ring!' cried Bayo.

Fawn lifted her left arm high and kicked out. The wyler tore across her leg with its claws. Ottilie hit it hard with an apple and it fell back. Bayo grabbed Fawn, helping her to her feet and then shifting to stand between her and the wyler, apple in hand, his broad shoulders masking Fawn from view.

Ottilie could see Leo running towards them, bow raised, but he was too far away. Further still, the dark shadows of shepherds streaked through the dimming light. The hoof beats were louder and Billow thundered into view, Ramona Ritgrivvian on his back, her red hair flying.

She was a wrangler – she had no weapons, but Billow reared and stamped. The wyler dodged and leapt back. It bent to spring: Billow, the biggest threat, was its new target. The wyler leapt high. Billow lunged sideways and kicked hard.

She heard bone crack and the wyler hit the ground with a thump. It didn't fall to pieces. That meant it could heal. She took a step towards it. The wyler got shakily to its feet and she could almost see the bones of its spine clicking back into place. Its fiery eyes met hers. There was a whoosh and a nasty sticking sound as Leo's arrow flew past her ear and pierced its horned skull.

Ottilie watched him approach. The shepherds overtook him, hackles raised, teeth bared. One of them leapt forward and sniffed at the bones. Ramona dismounted and Ottilie could hear her checking on Fawn, who stood trembling, fat trails of blood snaking down her leg. Ottilie didn't move. She looked Leo right in the eyes. He was pale.

'Congratulations. Thirty points,' she said coldly.

➤ 19 ➤

Fish for Hero

Seizing the opportunity to escape, Leo ran to report what had happened. Bayo wanted to help Fawn to the infirmary, but Wrangler Ritgrivvian insisted that she and Ottilie would do it, so he accompanied Leo instead.

Fawn hadn't been bitten. It was unlikely that she'd been infected with the venom that had made Gracie so sick, but the scratches on her leg cut deep and she was thoroughly shaken.

'The old stables,' Wrangler Ritgrivvian muttered, taking Fawn's arm.

'What?' whispered Ottilie, taking the other arm.

She had never seen Wrangler Ritgrivvian's eyepatch up close before. Skip was right. The surface was rough and scaly-looking. It was crocodile skin. But what was beneath it? Was it just a hollow socket stitched over, like Wrangler Furdles's? What had she done to earn such a punishment?

'That's where we can teach them,' Wrangler Ritgrivvian explained.

Between them, Fawn looked as confused as Ottilie felt.

'I heard about the petition. They talked to all the wranglers, told us to watch you. It's the only way — they'll never train girls, but we can.'

Ottilie didn't know what to say.

'Meet me at the old stables tomorrow night, tenth bell. Bring anyone you can trust, but stagger it, don't come in a group.'

Ottilie's heart leapt. 'I know a secret way.'

'Good.' Wrangler Ritgrivvian turned to Fawn, who was regarding them both with wide eyes. 'You'll be better by tomorrow, Fawn,' she said, as if her words would make it so. 'You must come too.'

She nodded, still looking a little confused.

Once Fawn was settled in the infirmary, Ottilie realised how hungry she was. She stepped out into the twilit lavender field, intending to jog all the way to the dining room. But someone was waiting for her, pacing back and forth outside the door.

'What do you want, Leo?'

He stopped pacing but shifted his weight from foot to foot. Ottilie rarely saw him so withdrawn. He seemed unsure of what to say. Impatient, she marched past him.

He jogged up to meet her. 'I should have signed.'

She stopped.

'But it wouldn't have made a difference.'

She charged on ahead.

'Ott. They would have said no either way.'

'You don't know that!' she said through gritted teeth.

'I do. I'm sure. You saw how they reacted. My name –'

She wanted to shake him. 'You're their champion!'

'It wouldn't have mattered.'

'It might have! And look what's happening here. They won't let the girls train, and they're still getting inside – it's going to happen again! And Fawn –' She gestured back to the infirmary. 'She could have died.'

'So could you,' he said quietly. 'You were unarmed.'

'And that's the last time I will be,' she said, her hand sweeping the side where her cutlass should have been. It was sheer luck that an armed huntsman was nearby. Leo had only had a bow because he was doing target practice. 'If the wylers are getting in, it's not safe.'

'I think someone's letting them in,' said Leo, crossing his arms tight across his chest.

Her stomach lurched. 'You do?' Despite her own suspicions, a small part of her still hoped she was wrong.

'Two in the grounds in autumn alone, all of them gathering together, that weird white one … the missing heart … something's going on. I think someone in here is behind it,' he said, distress stilting his speech.

'Me too,' she whispered, stepping closer to him. 'Leo, we have to tell them about the person we saw. That day we hunted the knopoes.'

'I didn't see anyone –'

'They were there – Maestro saw them, and I told you it's not the first time.' Heeding Whistler's advice, Ottilie didn't say she thought it was a witch. 'Can't you just trust me?' she said, gripping his sleeve.

'I do trust you.'

'We have to tell them. You have to. They'll take it seriously coming from you.'

He nodded and took a deep breath. 'It's not safe in here, you're right. We should be armed all the time. And they need to learn … the girls … they should be armed too.'

Ottilie grabbed his shoulders and shook him hard.

He shoved her off. 'What is wrong with you?'

'I told you this! I said we need to let them train. Why are you so SLOW!' She lunged at him and he dodged.

'Don't shake me again!'

'You're going to help me,' she said, firmly. She needed more than Ramona. The Hunt assigned them guardians for a reason. The wranglers didn't know what it was really like out there – what it was like to face those monsters.

He opened his mouth to object, but she didn't give him the chance. Leo was her guardian and she wanted him with her on this. 'You're going to help me teach them.'

>———————————————→

The guilt of going against her word to Montie was almost enough to keep Alba out of it, but this was too important. She needed to learn to defend herself and Ottilie needed the use of the tunnel. Thankfully, there was more than one entrance – Ottilie highly doubted all fifteen of them could pass through the root cellar without drawing Montie's attention.

It turned out Alba and Skip weren't the only custodians with knowledge of the tunnels. Several of the sculkies, including Fawn, knew about one or two, which made organising their gathering fairly simple.

They spread the word, passing out instructions for different groups to use different entry points to the tunnel, and asking anyone who had easy access to fish to please bring a little for Hero.

Ottilie would have liked for there to be more than fifteen girls, but they had to be cautious. They could only tell those they considered wholly trustworthy. Of course, Ottilie broke that rule when she invited Maeve Moth. She just couldn't bring herself to leave her out. Maeve was so desperate to learn, and it had been her idea in the first place.

Wrangler Ritgrivvian was already waiting for them by the entrance to the stone barn. Billow was tethered to a gate nearby. He did not seem at all happy to be there. The hulking roan stallion snorted and stamped, wide eyes roving over things that Ottilie could not see.

Wrangler Ritgrivvian followed Ottilie's gaze. 'I often walk them around the grounds in the evening. Bringing him looks less suspicious.'

Ottilie moved towards Billow, but he wasn't in the mood to be greeted.

'Alba,' said Ottilie. 'Do you know Wrangler Ritgr—'

'Ramona, please,' she cut in. 'And yes, I watched Alba grow up, and I know Skip, of course.' She shot Skip a familiar smile. Ramona had been giving Skip secret riding lessons for years, and Ottilie knew she still let her ride around the grounds under the pretence of exercising the horses.

In groups of twos and threes, girls started appearing from the trapdoor inside the stalls. Gracie and Maeve were the last to arrive. Ottilie's shoulders bunched at the sight of them, the hairs on the back of her neck prickling. She told herself again that Gracie could not be the witch … or Maeve – for the first time she pictured

Maeve under the hood. But she was the one who had wanted to train, so it couldn't be her either.

'What are they doing here?' spat Skip.

'Maeve wanted to come.' Ottilie forced her voice to sound casual. 'I guess she told Gracie. They won't tell anyone,' she said, willing it to be true.

'They better not,' said Skip, cracking her knuckles.

'I have a feeling they're good at keeping secrets,' said Ottilie, watching them approach. Gracie was looking healthy again. Her fair hair shone and the golden tone had returned to her complexion. Despite her slight frame, she seemed strong.

Maeve looked the opposite. She was drawn, her dark hair matted and lank, and she seemed thoroughly sleep-deprived. It was as if Gracie had somehow stolen her strength.

There was only one person missing. Ottilie hadn't told Leo about the tunnels. He didn't need to know, not yet. Out of all of them, he was the least likely to be watched or questioned about wandering the grounds after dark. He often trained on his own well into the night, everyone knew that.

'He's not going to come,' said Skip, her attention still fixed on Gracie.

Perhaps she was right. There had been other offers of help – Gully, Preddy and Scoot were eager, but they were fledges, like her. Besides, she didn't need them all tonight. The smaller their number, the better, for now. Scoot seemed ready to throw his dinner against the wall when she said Leo would be helping instead. But, clearly wanting to avoid another fight, he'd managed to restrain himself.

Ottilie wanted a huntsman more experienced than her, someone who knew how to teach. Leo was her guardian, her partner and, despite everything, her friend – she wanted him by her side. She wanted to give him a chance to make up for his mistakes, because she really wanted to trust him.

Her only fear was that he would report them. And with each passing moment the fear grew stronger. Would he do that to her again? She honestly didn't know.

'Someone's coming,' hissed Maeve.

They fell silent, pressing themselves into shadows. Ottilie backed into a dangling cobweb. Swallowing her gasp, she tried to brush away the sticky threads without drawing the newcomer's eye.

Hero prowled into the light, a fresh silver fish clamped between her jaws. She was making a throaty rumbling sound, almost like purring.

Leo was just behind her, a bundle in his arms.

'It's all right,' said Ottilie, and she and Ramona moved to greet him.

Leo lay the bundle at her feet and unrolled it. Salt-forged knives – enough for all of them.

He looked between Ottilie and Ramona. 'I thought we should start with these. It's the only thing they'll be able to conceal on their bodies. Until things ... until things change around here.'

✒ 20 ✒

A Secret Blade

As they'd discussed, Leo had reported Ottilie's sighting of the hooded figure to the directorate. A few days later, Captain Lyre himself asked for an account of things, and Ottilie was called to his chambers after a particularly productive hunt that hoisted her up to thirty-eighth on the ranking wall.

Captain Lyre had fresh flowers everywhere: on the desk, by the window, hanging from hooks on the walls. Aside from the flowers, the only other feature of the room was an ancient painting of a brown duck behind the door.

'So, more secrets,' he said, with a smile.

Ottilie's mind raced. Did he know about their training sessions? Is that why he had asked to see her?

'Why didn't you report it sooner?' He twirled a long finger around the tip of his black beard.

She let out a shaky breath of relief. He was talking only about what she had seen. But she still didn't know how to answer. She hadn't said anything because she didn't trust the Hunt. That was the truth.

'I didn't know what – who – it was. I didn't know if the Hunt knew, or whether they were supposed to. I don't know. I worried about speaking up after … after everything.' It wasn't a lie.

'You listen to me, Ottilie,' he said, leaning across his desk. 'You can always come to me. About anything.' His brown eyes crinkled. He seemed so warm, so genuine. Ottilie felt a pinch of resentment.

'Our petition, did you … what did you do with it?'

Captain Lyre's face was unreadable. 'I passed it on to Conductor Edderfed,' he said evenly.

'Was there a vote?'

He shook his head.

'Did he even read it?'

'I don't know, Ottilie. But' – he met her eyes – 'you mustn't draw attention to yourself. Recent events, strange occurrences and this person you saw … they're talking witchcraft.' He raised an eyebrow. 'We must all prepare for the worst.' He paused, looking her right in the eye. 'But be careful.'

He knew.

'There have been several more reports of dead animals since you and Leonard found the driftdog,' he said gravely. 'We've examined them and concluded that something has indeed been eating hearts.'

Ottilie's insides churned. It was one thing to suspect it, but quite another to find out it was real.

'But how?' she asked. 'They never eat anything – now they're attacking animals and eating hearts. Why?'

She remembered the carcasses at Jungle Bay. They had been so decayed, and it was too dark to see properly, but it was possible that their hearts had been eaten too.

Captain Lyre's eyes darkened. 'The legends speak of a creature the ancients called a bloodbeast – it began as a dredretch but became something other, something that feasted on hearts. Legends are reliably unspecific, so we can't be sure if they ate animals or humans or both. We don't know where that name came from, or indeed anything more about them,' he said. 'But if they are here in the Narroway, I would imagine that your mysterious lurker is involved somehow. Now' – he leaned back in his chair – 'I need anything you can tell me ... stature, height, did you get a sense of age?'

She picked fruitlessly through her memories. The figure was often too far away to get an accurate sense of height, and Ottilie was either in the dark, overcome with dredretch sickness or in mortal peril during every encounter.

Captain Lyre entwined his spidery fingers and frowned. She couldn't help but feel she had disappointed him. Finally, he dismissed her and she was reaching for the door, but something stopped her. Captain Lyre's cane rested in a stand to her right. The silver bird head had come loose and she caught sight of a sharp edge beneath. The cane sheathed a blade with a familiar subtle gleam. If Captain Lyre was under the impression that he couldn't harm dredretches, why was he armed with a salt-forged weapon?

Clearly, she was not the only one who questioned the rule of innocence. But Captain Lyre himself peddled the story. Why did he go along with it? Ottilie walked away feeling more confused than ever. Still, the meeting had made one thing clear. Training in secret was the right thing to do.

In a fortnight, fifteen girls grew to twenty-three, then thirty-one, then forty. There were sculkies, gardeners, stablehands, beekeepers and many more. The Hunt kept them busy, and not everyone was available on the same nights. This was for the best, Ottilie decided. So many could not meet regularly without rousing suspicion and their numbers were only increasing. The training sessions happened three times a week. When

Ottilie and Leo were unavailable, Ned and Gully took over, then Scoot and Bayo.

Ramona was almost always there. 'This is more important than anything,' she said, as they prepared for that night's session. Her red hair was braided away from her face, and her eyes shadowed. 'Something's happening here, and we need to be ready for it, all of us.'

'They're talking about witches,' said Ottilie, lowering her voice. 'Did you know that?'

Ramona's frown deepened. 'Nothing's been said to us specifically, not about witchcraft, but Voilies has been blathering on about it ever since that tapestry caught fire.' She picked up a spear. 'Come on, we should start.'

The cavernous barn had space enough for all of them and it was a large group that night; luckily Preddy had come along to help. They kept their glow sticks buried between old grain bags and rotting bales of hay, cautious of the light slipping through cracks and catching the eyes of the wall watchers by the east gate. They were far enough away that Ottilie wasn't worried about sound carrying, but lights were easy to spot from a distance.

The stables seemed less spooky now. It was as if with every lively, hopeful new member of their squad, the living had begun to outnumber the dead. Despite winter's arrival, the air around the stables no longer chilled to the bone, and the eerie mist that hovered perpetually in the yard seemed merely a glimmering moonlit veil. Even Hero, who had initially put many of the girls on edge, had become a welcome, almost comforting, presence. She had taken to curling up in the corner of the barn, snacking on her fish or sleeping soundly as they trained.

Ramona had managed to salvage some untipped spears and Ottilie and Leo had got their hands on some clubs. The bows, cutlasses and other salt weapons were precious, and difficult to remove without anyone noticing. Emergency weapon stores had been set up all around the fort after the second wyler attack, but they were located in busy areas and Ottilie was loath to leave them understocked. Still, they managed to swipe a small knife for every new recruit to keep on them.

'We're going to have to divide into two,' said Ramona. 'Spears with me and Noel, clubs with Leo and Ottilie.'

Ottilie moved through their group, offering help when she knew the fix, and learning herself when she didn't.

'Don't let your shoulder lift like that,' barked Leo. 'It has to come from here.' He jabbed Skip in the stomach with his club.

Skip knocked his club away. She looked ready to punch him. For a moment, Ottilie considered holding her back, but Skip simply gritted her teeth and practised the move again.

Over on the other side of the barn, Ottilie saw Ramona pacing between spears, offering gentle yet firm advice. When it came to teaching, she and Leo couldn't have been more different.

'Clubs are the easiest,' said Leo, louder than necessary. 'Learn how to swing with enough force and you can stop most smaller dredretches with one hit.'

'It's a good thing to learn,' Ottilie added. 'Because once you know how to do it, you can use anything heavy you can get your hands on.'

'I was just about to say that, Ott,' Leo muttered.

'Well, now you don't have to, Leo,' she muttered back.

Beside her, Alba chuckled. Leo clenched his jaw and crossed the group to criticise Fawn.

Preddy wandered over to them. 'Look.' He pointed back to Gracie Moravec. Ottilie turned. Gracie had detached herself from Ramona's group and was practising throwing her knife into a bale of hay, hitting the same spot over and over with freakish accuracy.

'She must have used one before,' he said, looking impressed and a little afraid.

'And used it a lot,' said Ottilie, feeling very disturbed. 'I can't do that. Skip,' she whispered, beckoning her over. 'What do you know about Gracie's background?'

Skip glared over at Gracie. 'They say she's a Laklander.'

'But that doesn't mean anything,' said Ottilie, glancing sideways at Alba.

'They always say that about fair-haired people,' said Preddy, running his hand over his own wheat-gold hair. 'My mother hated that about me ... I was the only one of my brothers. Some of them had it when they were young, but it darkened. Not mine, though.'

She felt the sudden urge to give Preddy a hug. He never said much about his parents, but when he did, it wasn't good.

Skip wasn't paying him any attention. 'I heard a rumour that she had to come here because she was on the run,' she said darkly.

'But isn't that sort of the same reason you came here?' said Ottilie.

'Maybe,' said Skip, shrugging irritably. 'For stealing some pearls and a bit of cheese.'

'A whole chest of pearls, I heard.' Preddy smiled.

'How did you know that? Who's talking about me?'

'Probably the same people who are talking about her,' said Ottilie, pointing at Gracie. 'What else do you know?'

'Well, I heard she had a habit of laming horses – but that wasn't the worst. They say she tried to push a boy off a cliff near Scarpy Village.'

Ottilie felt a strange jolt. 'She's from Scarpy Village?'
She knew Scarpy Village. It was north of the Swamp
Hollows, near the mouth of the River Hook.

'Somewhere around there,' said Skip.

Preddy paled. 'Do you think it's true?'

'No way to know,' said Skip. 'She doesn't exactly talk
much. Where's her evil twin? That witch loves to talk.'

'We shouldn't call her a witch, Skip,' said Ottilie. She
felt guilty for ever using it now that they were all under
suspicion.

She looked around – Maeve wasn't there. In fact,
Ottilie couldn't remember the last time she'd seen her.
She watched Gracie tossing the knife over and over, and
a cold pricking crawled over her skin.

← 21 →

The Spy

Gracie Moravec reached for Ottilie's plate.

'Finished with this?' she asked sweetly. The sculkies didn't usually clear plates until after the huntsmen left the table. Gracie seemed to know she unsettled Ottilie – and enjoyed doing it. 'Will you be there tonight, Captain?'

'Really,' said Ottilie flatly. 'Captain? Not Shovels?'

'I never called you Shovels.'

'To my face,' said Ottilie. 'I'm not your captain.'

'Sure you are. Captain Colter, commander of the sculkie army,' she said with a cat's smile.

Ottilie didn't understand the joke. Gracie herself was a sculkie, and she had never missed a training session. She was mocking herself.

'What do you want, Gracie?'

'Your plate,' she said with a tinkling laugh.

Ottilie realised she was still holding on to it. Releasing it, she said, 'Where's Maeve?' She watched closely for a reaction.

'She's assigned to the library today.' Gracie calmly took the plate and turned away.

'What was that about?' said Gully, approaching with a pitcher of apple juice. Gully rarely ate at breakfast time.

'Skip's right. We can't trust her,' said Ottilie, staring at the back of Gracie's head. Her pale tresses seemed to float a little off her shoulders, just as her feet seemed to float a little from the ground. There had always been something spectral about her.

'But she already knows about everything,' said Gully, with a shrug. 'And she's been coming along. She's good too, have you seen her with a knife?'

She watched Gracie drifting away. She had that knife on her somewhere, concealed in her uniform. Ottilie had thought it such a good idea to arm them all, give them weapons to use against the dredretches, but knives could cut people too, and knowing that Gracie Moravec was carrying one around made Ottilie very nervous.

Ottilie and Gully were on their way to the arena for warding when she got a strange feeling and slowed.

'What?' Gully turned back towards her.

'I just want to check on something.' She started jogging towards the library. It had been bothering her since breakfast – Ottilie hadn't laid eyes on Maeve in a week. She wanted to see for herself that she was unharmed.

Gully caught up with her. 'We'll be late,' he said, somewhat gleefully.

They descended the stairway into the library and looped through the stacks.

'What are we looking for?' said Gully.

'Maeve,' said Ottilie, offering no further explanation.

They rounded the corner and Ottilie saw two legs stretched out on the ground, illuminated by a lantern.

'Maeve,' she said in a carrying whisper.

'What? Ottilie?' The girl got to her feet, holding the lantern aloft. It wasn't Maeve. It was Alba.

'What are you two doing here?' she said, a little breathlessly. 'I was just about to come and find you. I found something in here – about dredretches!' She held the green book into the light.

'What is that?' Gully reached for the book.

'A book about witches. Careful, it's old.'

'I don't think you should be reading this here, Alba,' said Gully, his brow furrowed. 'You don't want to get caught with a witch book.'

Ottilie stared at him. Listening to Gully advise someone to be cautious was very strange. 'What did you read?' she asked.

'Well, for starters, witches were experimenting with salt weapons long before the Narroway Hunt ever existed, even before the Lakland War! After Seika Devil-Slayer defeated the fendevil the witches starting investigating how she did it, and that was how they found out about salt – but most of their knowledge was lost in the witch purge.'

'The witch purge?' said Gully.

'When the Roving Empire had control of the Usklers they hunted all the witches,' said Alba, speaking so quickly Ottilie was impressed the words were clear.

'Is there anything in there about how she defeated the fendevil?' said Ottilie.

'Not that I've found,' said Alba, chewing her lip. 'But there is an explanation of what dredretches are – where they come from. It says that they're creatures from down below, from the underworld, and that evil – acts of violence or when people do bad things – sings to them, calling them to the surface, guiding their way up.'

Ottilie had heard that before, from Old Moss or Mr Parch, she wasn't sure which. She imagined a kappabak bursting through the stone floor beneath her feet. 'Is there anything else?' she asked, blinking away the horror. 'Why are they talking about dredretches in a book about witches?'

'Because,' said Alba, 'the book says dredretches can be summoned and even controlled by a witch!'

She knew it! This was what she had suspected all along.

'But the book condemns it,' said Alba. 'Says it corrupts witches' spirits and infects their power. Witchcraft is supposed to be a natural art – but this sort of thing destroys them, makes them less alive, less human – and more powerful.'

Ottilie's breath grew short. The confirmation that one person was responsible for all this horror was devastating. 'Do you think that the dredretches in the Laklands – that a witch brought them there?' she asked, hoping the answer was no.

Alba swallowed. 'After everything we've learned, and talking to Whistler, that story about the broken promise, I think the dredretches came to the Laklands because of all the terrible things that happened in the war. But since then, in the Narroway, I don't know ...'

Gully gripped Ottilie's wrist.

She turned to him. His eyes were cold, serious. He was warning her not to react. She skimmed the space discreetly, listening hard. Alba didn't seem to have noticed anything, but Ottilie sensed it: someone was nearby – spying.

She heard soft footsteps, someone carefully backing away. She glanced at Gully. He nodded, and they both dashed in opposite directions, looping around the aisle, trapping the spy between them.

Ottilie got there first.

'Get off me,' Maeve hissed.

Ottilie pulled her into the light.

Maeve looked truly terrible. Her hands shook as she shoved Ottilie away. She looked so frail that Ottilie released her, scared of breaking her.

'Maeve, are you all right?' she asked, forgetting about the spying.

'What's wrong with you?' said Gully.

'I'm fine,' Maeve snapped. 'Better before you manhandled me!' She glared at Ottilie.

Several books slid back from the shelf next to them and Alba's face appeared in the gap. 'Why were you listening to us?' she demanded.

'I wasn't listening to you. I was dusting,' she said, lamely raising her feather duster and sweeping it over a row of books. 'I'm working in here today.' Her tone was not at all convincing.

'You were listening,' said Gully.

The nearest lantern sputtered and sparked. Maeve recoiled and dropped the feather duster, her eyes wide. Then, so slightly that Ottilie couldn't be sure it was happening, the air around them shifted, like a cool breeze through a window. She thought she glimpsed a swirl of dust sweep by the lantern.

'We shouldn't be gathered here like this,' said Maeve, her voice hoarse. 'If they catch us it will look suspicious. So, unless you're going to chain me to the shelf, I'm leaving.'

As she hurried away, Ottilie noticed a dark feather sticking out of her matted hair.

'She's right,' she said. 'And Gully's right, Alba – don't read that book anywhere you can get caught.'

For Alba's sake, Ottilie didn't want to be seen with her. So she and Gully left the library first.

'Did you see the lantern?' said Gully, sounding more excited than alarmed. 'And the tapestry ... you don't think –' He didn't leave a moment for her to answer. 'If I had to pick anyone to be a witch, it would be her.'

Ottilie knew what he meant, but it didn't seem possible. Maeve a witch? Controlling the dredretches? Summoning the kappabak – the monster that had nearly killed Leo? Maeve had always seemed to like Leo well enough. Ottilie couldn't imagine her wanting to hurt him. And the wyler in the sculkie quarters – it had killed Joely Wrecker and bitten Maeve's best friend. Maeve had been so angry about it; she wanted to learn to fight. It didn't make sense.

⇒ 22 ⇐

Ambush

The next morning, Ottilie was on her way to the lower grounds when Alba and Skip hurried after her, down the icy path.

She scanned the frosted gardens to see if anyone was watching. 'We can't talk in the open, you know that,' she said when they reached her. But up close, she saw the raw panic on their faces. Her breath caught. What was it? More animals with their hearts missing? Another wyler in the grounds? Someone injured … or worse?

'Someone stole it,' Skip spat, her neck visibly taut.

'The book,' said Alba, with tears in her eyes.

Ottilie's chest tightened.

'Someone took it,' said Alba. 'I was hiding it in the root cellar. And when I went to get it early this morning it was gone!'

She tried to muster her nerves. 'But who ... Maeve?'

'She's the only one, other than us and Gully, who knows about it,' said Alba, hugging herself in the cold.

'It's her, Ottilie,' said Skip, with venom on her tongue. 'I know it. She's the witch. Her or Gracie Moravec. Maeve could have taken it for her.'

'We don't know that, Skip.' She was trying to stop Skip from acting rashly, but Ottilie knew it must have been Maeve.

'We should report it!' said Skip. 'They're looking for witches. It's them. I know it. I knew they were evil. I could smell it!'

'Skip, stop it,' said Ottilie. 'Listen to yourself. We can't report it. Then they'll find out we stole the book from Whistler. And we can't just accuse ... it's so serious ... we can't accuse anyone without real proof.' After everything that she had been through, it would take a lot for Ottilie to report someone to the directorate – and with all this talk of witches, it would be even worse now than it had been for Ottilie.

'What should we do, Ottilie?' asked Alba, her voice pleading.

'I ... I don't know. I have to go, I've got a hunt. We'll just talk to her. We have to ask her why she took it ...

try to get it back. But, please, just wait for me. I'll be back around midday. Don't do anything yet.'

She had to put it all aside for now. She certainly couldn't tell Leo about any of it – for all she knew, he would run straight to the directorate to report the entire thing, including their break-in. She did her best to act normally as they saddled Maestro and soared out over the peaks beyond the fort.

***

In only a couple of hours, they had already felled six yotes – like nasty, winged mountain goats – and four highland morgies, paler in scale colour than the lowland kind. Now they were on the trail of a cinder snake in the icy caves behind Opal Tarn.

Cinder snakes were monstrous serpents with sharp-edged scales that leaked sizzling acid, which could corrode stone. It was an easy trail to follow, but a perilous path to walk on foot. Maestro waited for them out in the open air, while Ottilie and Leo wandered the track with caution in their tread.

The enormous red snake was curled up inside a narrow cavern. Ottilie raised her bow and was about to take the shot when Leo's foot slipped and he stumbled with a scuffle and a gasp. The snake raised its sleepy head. Opening its cavernous jaw, it hissed and shot at them like a spear.

Leo, determined to salvage his dignity, knocked Ottilie's arm so that her arrow flew off sideways, hitting the cave wall. He raised his own bow, landing his shot squarely between the serpent's eyes.

'Leo!' growled Ottilie, as the cinder snake fell, sizzling and crumbling a few yards from where they stood. 'That was mine!'

'You probably would have missed,' he said.

Ottilie was about to reply but something stopped her. Far away, back through the maze of tunnels, she could hear Maestro's cry. She and Leo didn't say a word; they both turned and sprinted back through the caves, leaping over pools of acid, slipping and stumbling on ice and collapsed rock.

They burst out into the sunlight to find Maestro stalking back and forth, tossing his head.

'What's wrong?' said Leo, hurrying over to the distressed wingerslink.

Then Ottilie heard it, a dreadful cry – a song of agony, sorrow and terror.

Leo leapt up into the saddle and held out his arm. Ottilie gripped it and swung up behind him. Maestro launched into the air and circled the peak. Ottilie could see Opal Tarn below, crystalline blue and gleaming in the sunlight, the alpine plants glittering with frost at its edges.

Something was wrong – moving flashes of orange, and pools of ruby red. There were wylers, at least ten, and the white wyler at the centre, ripping and shaking, shredding something Ottilie didn't want to see.

Movement caught her eye. There was a footman down there, fending five off at once with a spear. It was Scoot! Ottilie dug her heels in, urging Maestro to dive, but Leo was giving him different commands. The wingerslink growled with frustration and rocked in the air.

She felt as if her throat had filled with water. 'Leo, Scoot's down there!' She could barely form the words. Her heart was pounding so hard it hurt.

Leo swore and Maestro dived so suddenly that she was thrown backwards. On landing, Maestro caught a wyler in his jaws and shook violently, chunks of rotten flesh and bone flying past them on the wind. Ottilie righted herself and aimed an arrow.

The wylers were distracted. Ottilie managed to hit one before it could dodge. Leo missed one. It scampered sideways and Scoot pierced it with his spear. There were two left, and the rest of the pack were approaching. Maestro swatted the nearest with his paw, giving Scoot a moment to dodge and grab on to the saddle.

Leo fended them off while Ottilie seized hold of Scoot's quiver strap and pulled him up. He managed to squeeze in just behind her, but there was no time to strap him in.

Hot tears scalded her icy skin. 'Hold on really tight!' she said, her throat aching from swallowed sobs.

Scoot wrapped his arms around her middle. She could feel his whole body shaking.

Maestro leapt into the air.

'Bayo,' said Scoot, with a strangled cry.

Ottilie looked down and for a moment she seemed to forget how to breathe. Then it came, short and fast. It was making her dizzy. And she could hear her own pulse, like a drum beating too loud. There was nothing … no-one left down there, and the white wyler was still, head tipped to the sky, staring after them as they fled.

➤━━━━━━━━━━━━━━━━━━➤

Ottilie, Gully and Preddy sat by Scoot's bed in the infirmary. He was bruised and scratched and he'd twisted his ankle, but he was going to be all right. Ottilie felt an unknowable pain, all over her body, and at the same time a strange numb feeling, as if she had fallen into a story, not real life. She couldn't imagine what Scoot was feeling.

'We were on our way back from patrolling,' he said, his voice choked. 'It was supposed to be an easy one. There are never any dredretches around the tarn.'

Gully nodded, his jaw tight. Beside him Preddy was bone white.

'He drew them off,' said Scoot. 'Told me to run. I shouldn't … I should've …'

'Don't think that, Scoot,' said Gully, in barely a whisper. 'There were too many of them. If Ottilie and Leo hadn't found you …' he trailed off, unable to finish.

Ottilie's eyes were fixed on Gully. He was a footman too. It could so easily have been him and Ned out there. She felt an unbearable rip, as if the invisible tether between them was being torn – she couldn't lose him, not again.

'It was an ambush,' said Scoot, tears flooding his cheeks. 'They were so organised. Like, like a hunt. Like they'd always hunted together … but that's not how they work. They're supposed to be loners. And dredretches, they don't hunt us, they just attack, they're not …'

Someone was behind this. She thought about the witch book, stolen that very morning. She knew who had it, and had seen the signs, but she had done nothing.

Ottilie couldn't just sit. It hurt too much. She had to move, had to do something. She stood up on shaking legs and headed for the door.

'Where are you going?' Gully charged after her.

She didn't know the answer until the words tumbled out. 'I'm going to find Maeve Moth.'

~ 23 ~

Witch Hunt

Ottilie and Gully were on the path through the lavender fields when the bells rang out in an unfamiliar tune.

'Which one is that?' said Gully, reaching for his knife.

'I've never heard it before,' said Ottilie, looking around frantically. Not a wyler, not again, but ... 'Those aren't the alarm bells?' It was a small comfort, just enough to keep her going.

The bells were ringing from the watchtower above the main gate. She grabbed her bow and together they ran towards the source of the sound.

Ottilie could never have imagined the scene they stumbled into. Countless huntsmen were gathered around. The air was alive with hisses and whispers. Through the crowd, she could see the gates had been raised and, walking between them, Igor Thrike was dragging someone in by the hair.

Maeve Moth was covered in mud, with leaves, twigs and feathers sticking out of her hair and clothing. Ottilie didn't know what to think.

'Thrike, what are you ... who have you got?' said Wrangler Furdles, hobbling down from the wall.

'We found her out there,' said Igor, raising his voice above the gibbering crowd.

His fledge, Dimitri Vosvolder, was following behind, his pointed face flushed.

'What d'you mean, out there?' said Furdles.

'Look where I'm coming from!' Igor barked.

Ottilie frowned. Maeve had been beyond the walls, the very day that Bayo had been attacked. Had Ottilie been right? Was Maeve really involved? But seeing her like that, dishevelled, being dragged by the hair, her icy resolve melted ... It didn't feel right.

Ramona stalked through the crowd, her face thunderous. 'Igor, let go of her!' It wasn't a shout, or even a snarl, but it was powerful, like the crack of burning wood.

The crowd fell silent, but Igor was unmoved.

'No!' said Igor, bright with righteousness. 'Bayo Amadory was murdered this morning. Someone set the wylers on him, and here, look! A girl! Out there alone. She's a witch!'

This was what Whistler had been talking about. Igor had no reason to believe Maeve was a witch, but a girl alone, in a place she was not meant to be – that was enough for him.

There were gasps and several people backed away. Wrangler Furdles spat on the ground.

'Where is your proof?' said Ramona firmly.

'Proof!' said a shrill voice from behind Ottilie. 'That girl set the tapestry on fire, right above my head!'

'Tudor, you don't know that!' said Ramona, raising her voice again.

'She was in the room!' cried Wrangler Voilies. 'She's a rebel! She signed that ... that insidious petition. And now here, look at her, a sculkie beyond the walls. An elite dead! You want more proof than that!'

'Yes, I do,' said Ramona, staring him down.

Ottilie was dizzy. She had fixated on Maeve as a distraction, because getting answers was something useful, something to help. But Ramona was right. There was not enough proof, and Ottilie remembered again that she had a very good reason to believe that Maeve was innocent. Maeve had wanted to learn to defend herself. She had wanted it badly enough that she had risked being caught conspiring with Ottilie. She had no reason to do those things if she was in control of the dredretches.

'Search her things, Furdles,' Voilies shrieked. 'We'll get you your proof! And someone alert the directorate.' He sounded feverish. 'Igor, step away from her. It's not safe. But keep her covered.'

Dimitri raised his bow, pointing an arrow at Maeve's back. Igor withdrew and did the same.

Ottilie finally felt as if she had returned to her body. Sharp with focus, she looked up. Five huntsmen on the wall had their arrows on Maeve. She felt the shift of movement as more huntsmen raised their weapons, tipping spears in her direction, holding cutlasses at the ready. Maeve was completely surrounded. Ottilie and Gully kept their weapons down.

While they waited for Wrangler Furdles to return, more people arrived. Wranglers, custodians, even Whistler had made her way from her tower and was peering over the parapet like a purple-winged vulture.

Ottilie sensed Leo move to her side, raising his bow like the others. Ned appeared on her other side and did not.

Captain Lyre was the first of the directorate to arrive. His eyebrows drawn together in an expression of deep concern, he marched swiftly to the front of the group with the hulking figure of Wrangler Morse by his side.

'Let's all remain calm,' said Captain Lyre. But he did not tell them to lower their weapons. 'Wrangler Furdles is searching her things?'

'Yes, sir,' said Wrangler Voilies.

Captain Lyre took a step towards Maeve. 'Miss Moth, what were you doing beyond the boundary wall?' His voice was firm but not accusing.

'Don't let her speak! She'll put a spell on you,' cried Wrangler Voilies.

Maeve met Captain Lyre's gaze, her eyes blazing. She looked terrified and exhausted. They all waited, but she did not answer.

Why wasn't she defending herself?

'We will need an explanation,' Captain Lyre insisted.

There were shouts from across the grounds. Wrangler Furdles was hobbling towards them, waving something in the air. He was hollering like a maniac. 'Witch!' he cried. 'She's a WITCH!'

Ottilie gasped. He was holding Whistler's book.

'She had this ... this witch book! And bones, tiny animal bones!'

Ottilie didn't know what to do. The book would condemn Maeve, but it didn't belong to her. She had only taken it that morning.

But why had she taken it? Maeve had been out beyond the wall, doing who knew what. And the strange things, the fire, the animal bones. She looked guilty. But it wasn't right.

Ottilie opened her mouth. Gully was watching her. 'Don't, Ottilie,' he pleaded.

'I have to!' she said, squaring her shoulders. She couldn't let them use the book as evidence, not until she knew why Maeve had taken it.

Ned was watching her. She sensed him piecing it together. He knew they'd stolen books from the Bone Tower.

'Don't,' he whispered. 'They're looking for any excuse to get rid of you.'

'It's not hers,' Ottilie hissed. Feeling steadier than she had in hours, she moved to step forwards but Ned grabbed her hand. The gesture caught her off-guard, just long enough.

'It's not her book!' called Gully, jumping forwards. 'It's mine!'

Ottilie wanted to claw at him, wrench him backwards. Hot panic coiled around her ribs like a cinder snake.

'Gulliver!' said Wrangler Voilies, his expression morphing into something even more unpleasant. 'There's no need for heroics. She's a pretty thing, but witchcraft is indefensible.'

Gully's mouth curved down in disgust. 'It's mine. Maeve took it off me. She said she was going to report me. That's why she had it.'

'This is your book, Gulliver?' said Captain Lyre, his eyes searching.

'Forgive me,' said Voilies. 'But I don't believe any of our fledglings brought possessions with them on their journey to the Narroway. Gulliver is simply stepping up to save the damsel in distress … very noble but –'

'I borrowed it,' said Gully, loudly.

'Borrowed?' said Captain Lyre.

'Stole it, from the bone singers. It's just, with everyone talking about witches, I wanted to learn more about them,' he said, very quickly. 'To know how to fight them … stop them. That's all.'

Sensing eyes upon her, Ottilie looked up. Whistler was watching her, an unreadable expression on her angular face.

'And I suppose the bones were yours too?' said Wrangler Voilies, trying and failing to sound amused.

'No,' said Gully, with a forced shrug. 'Just the book.'

'It doesn't matter,' Voilies sneered. 'She's a liar, a manipulator. She didn't report it, did she? She kept it for herself!'

'Enough of this,' said Captain Lyre, shifting his grip on his cane. 'We need to take her inside.'

'The burrows!' cried Wrangler Furdles with glee.

'We'll take her to my chambers, and I will discuss the next step with Conductor Edderfed,' said Captain Lyre.

Voilies gaped like a beached trout. 'But –'

'This is for the directorate to decide,' said Captain Lyre.

'I'll take her,' said Whistler, from above.

Wrangler Voilies looked aghast. 'Surely a huntsman –'

'I do not fear witchcraft,' said Whistler, sounding a
little smug. 'I'll take her.'

Whistler descended the stairs and passed through the
armed huntsmen, most still pointing their weapons at
Maeve.

'It's not about personal safety,' said Voilies, with a
sour laugh. 'It's about keeping her captive!'

'Enough, Tudor,' growled Wrangler Morse.

Whistler took Maeve gently by the arm and led her
through the crowd.

Ottilie felt bound – useless. She wanted to be angry
with Gully for taking her place, but she couldn't help
feeling grateful for his quick thinking. It was true, it
was far safer for Gully to take the blame. Ottilie would
probably have been dragged straight to the burrows if
she had spoken up.

It took her a few moments to realise Ned was still
holding her hand. She looked at him. He had turned
away from her, watching Maeve and Whistler. She
wondered if he was even aware that he had not let go.
He must have felt her gaze because he turned back.

For a moment, they looked at each other. Ned smiled
with his eyes, and Ottilie's overwrought heart shifted its
rhythm. He gave her hand a gentle squeeze and released
it. She felt lost for a moment, as if she had just dropped
something precious.

❧ 24 ❧

An Iron Coffin

'What are they going to do to her?' Ottilie asked, looking between Leo and Ned. She noticed for the first time the marks of grief. Leo, always straight-backed, was stiff as a board, unnaturally so, and she could see his eyes were red. Ned seemed heavier somehow and there was a tightness to his face that was unfamiliar to her.

'I think they'll talk to her first,' said Ned.

'They didn't talk to me,' she said. 'They just threw me in the burrows.'

'That's because they knew you were guilty,' said Leo.

'Because you told them,' Gully snapped, glaring.

Leo's eyelids flickered. Gully had never lashed out at him like that before. Ottilie's own emotions were bubbling and spitting all over the place.

'They don't know about her yet,' Leo said, ignoring Gully. 'They need answers.'

'What do you think?' Ned asked Ottilie. 'You saw that person out there, more than once. Do you think it was her? Do you think she's been' – his voice became strained – 'setting dredretches on people?'

'No,' she said, finally. She knew now that she didn't believe it. Maeve had always been horrible to Ottilie – she was certainly not a friend – but seeing her accused like that, she realised she didn't think Maeve was capable of what had happened to Bayo. 'But I do think she's a witch,' she added, surprising herself with the admission.

'What?' said Leo, with a nervous laugh.

'I got a strange feeling around her from the first time I met her, and I know I'm not the only one,' she said.

Ned nodded, but Leo looked flummoxed. 'I never did!'

'Leonard,' said Ned. 'You're too fixated on yourself to notice anything.'

Leo punched him in the arm.

Ned looked like he wanted to laugh but couldn't quite get there. 'You know it's true.'

'Strange things have been happening around her,' said Ottilie. 'The lanterns spark when she gets upset. You know, I think she did set that tapestry on fire.' She remembered the terror in Maeve's eyes as she watched the tapestry smoking. If she had caused it, she hadn't intended to.

'What about the bones?' said Leo, looking horrified. 'What are they for?'

'Do you think she's been using them for spells?' said Gully, with awe.

It was too much guesswork. Ottilie didn't like it. 'I'm going to the infirmary.' She needed to see Scoot, to tell him about Maeve, about what she was accused of doing. He was going to hear it from someone soon.

When she got there, Scoot was looking ashen, but he turned the colour of sickly marshweed when she told him what had happened. For a moment Ottilie thought he was going to throw up, but then he scrambled out of bed and she and Preddy had to physically stop him from running out the door.

'Stop it, Scoot!' She puffed as he struggled against her. 'You can't get to her anyway, they've got her. She's probably locked up somewhere by now.'

He was panting and there were tears running down his face as he slumped back on the bed.

'She did it,' he growled. 'She – sh–'

'They don't know that,' said Preddy gently. 'That's what you're saying, Ottilie? They don't know for sure that it was her?'

'Of course it was her!' Scoot snarled. 'She was out there at the same … at the same time! Why else would she go? How would she survive past the walls if she's not a witch?'

'She has been training,' said Preddy weakly.

'For two months! And she barely even came the last few weeks. She has no salt weapons, apart from that knife. It's not enough. Not out there.'

Ottilie saw the horror of the morning engulf his vision and felt her own about to go again.

'And Bayo was there, helping us train them … helping her!' Scoot was taking sharp, shallow breaths. It sounded as if every word pained him to speak.

'We have to make sure they have the right person,' said Ottilie softly.

Scoot buried his head, his shoulders shaking.

Something was wrong here, Ottilie was sure of it. If they had the wrong person, then not only would Maeve bear the ultimate punishment but the danger would still be there. She had to get to the bottom of it.

➤━━━━━━━━━━━━━━➤

The next morning, Ottilie was sitting with Gully and Preddy. Alba joined them under the pretence of wiping a spill. It was still early and the dining room was nearly empty, but they had to be cautious all the same.

'They convicted her last night,' said Alba, her face grave.

Ottilie gripped the table, wanting to hold on to something solid.

'What?' whispered Skip, appearing at the other end of the table.

Alba nodded solemnly. 'Mum told me. She heard it from Wrangler Morse. The directorate decided the evidence was enough. They're sending her to the Laklands.'

Skip paled. 'That doesn't make sense. If they think she's controlling the dredretches, why would they send her there – to a place full of them?'

'What if they're just saying that?' said Preddy, holding his own hand for comfort. 'What if they're actually taking her off to execute her?'

Ottilie swallowed. Would they really execute her? She remembered Wrangler Voilies ripping her ring from her thumb, watching her weaken … If they thought she was guilty, of course they would execute her.

'It will be the Laklands,' said Alba. 'They'll want her far away, because they don't kill witches – they'll want to bury her there.'

Skip frowned. 'But Maeve hasn't had a baby, she's only thirteen – just a kid!'

'What?' said Gully. He looked for a moment like he might laugh.

'Can someone please explain to me why people think witches eat babies!' said Ottilie.

'Witches eat their babies so they can live forever. That's all I know,' said Skip.

Preddy didn't seem to have any idea what they were talking about.

'Back in the old days,' said Alba, 'when the Roving Empire had control, they brought in a different belief system. They were scared of the witches, and rumours started circulating that if a witch consumed the flesh of their newborn child they would be granted immortality.'

Gully looked like he was about to be sick. Ottilie felt the same.

'That was when the witch purge happened,' said Alba.

Ottilie nodded. She had known that part, at least.

'They locked them in iron boxes and buried them all,' said Alba. 'Even a witch who hadn't had a child. Even the men.'

'I didn't know men could be witches,' said Gully with interest.

'That's because of the baby rumour,' said Alba. 'The idea of witchcraft has become associated with women – evil women. But the book –'

'The one that Maeve stole from you?' said Gully.

'Yes. It's different. It was written by witches – not the people who buried them. It says that no woman, especially a woman capable of channelling magic, would ever do something so against nature.'

'How come I've never heard about this before?' said Preddy.

'Because people don't like to talk about it,' said Alba.

'Particularly your kind of people, I would think,' said Skip. 'You have heard about it, though, Preddy, you just don't know it. It's in the lightning song.'

'The what?' said Preddy.

Wail, whine, dinnertime, sleeper comes for none, ' Skip chanted.

'Oh, you mean "The Sleeper Stars",' said Preddy. 'That's just an old nonsense rhyme. What's it got to do with witches?'

Everyone looked to Alba.

'It's "The Sleepless Stars", not "Sleeper". It's an old rhyme, different from the lightning song,' she said patiently. *'All in a row, the glowing guide, from sleepless stars it cannot hide …'*

'Oh, yes, that's what I was thinking of,' said Preddy, pushing his glasses higher up his nose.

Ottilie had never heard it before.

'It's lesser known,' said Alba. 'But for some reason people link them. They might have originated from the same area.'

'But the lightning song?' said Ottilie, eager to get back on topic. 'It's about witches?' Scoot had told her that once, but she hadn't wanted to believe it.

Alba nodded. 'The lightning part is about knowing where the burial sites are – *flash, smack and crackle, lightning knows the spot. Hiss, flick and sputter, three will*

mark it hot.' She shrugged. 'Then *wail, whine, dinnertime,*
sleeper comes for none. That's the eating part. Then
crunch, thud, dig deep down, pay for what you've done.
That bit's obvious. In some parts they sing it differently.
There's a line about resting or ...' She frowned, trying
to remember.

'No more rest for Mum,' said Gully, with a smile.

'That's it,' said Alba.

Ottilie and Gully looked at each other. With every
blink, Ottilie saw their old home. The sunnytree.
Longwood. The Swamp Hollows. They had been
arguing for years about the final line of the lightning
song. As it turned out, both lines belonged, but neither
were the last. They had always just thought it was about
lightning ... nothing more. Well, perhaps a superstition
that it could bring on a storm, but that was it. Never
about witches and iron coffins ... and ...

'But ... all right, like Skip said, Maeve hasn't had a
baby,' said Ottilie, twitching in her seat. 'She can't have
done that ritual. So why would they bury her in an iron
box? She's not immortal.' Ottilie had never cared for
small spaces. Being buried alive was just about the most
horrible thing she could think of.

'Sleepless,' said Skip. 'Isn't that what they called
them – not immortal, but sleepless witches?'

Alba nodded. 'I think people decided that sounded
less scary. But sleepless or not, live burials are just what

they do with witches, and iron coffins because iron supposedly repels magic — that's how they restrained the ones they caught, with iron manacles.'

Alarm bells clanged.

They all jumped. There was a moment of silence, a breath between the bells, and then Gully cried, 'Not again!'

They heard shouts.

'FLEDGES AND SCULKIES TO YOUR CHAMBERS!'

Ottilie leapt to her feet.

'WYLERS IN THE GROUNDS!'

'M-more than one?' said Preddy.

Ottilie drew the cutlass that she now always kept strapped to her back. Alba and Skip gripped their knives. Ottilie looked between the two. 'We need more weapons,' she said. 'There are some girls who don't have any.'

'There's that emergency supply down the corridor,' said Preddy, swaying as he got to his feet.

'We'll get them.' Ottilie gestured to Alba and Skip.

Preddy and Gully charged off. To their chambers, or in search of the wylers, Ottilie didn't know which.

The nearest weapon store was a hidden cupboard just down the corridor from the dining room. With sweaty palms Ottilie pressed a stone, and a chunk of the wall slid inwards.

Skip slipped through the crack in the wall. 'Argh!' she cried out, jumping back. Hot air flooded the gap.

'What, Skip?' Arms shaking, Ottilie pushed the door open further.

She gasped.

Gracie Moravec was inside. She was sitting cross-legged against the wall. Her eyes were wide open and glowing black and red, like rings of flowing lava. Her arms were stretched out over her legs, palms up, and the scar from the wyler bite cracked and sparked, a crescent of burning embers on her golden skin.

25

Moth and Moravec

Skip's face twisted with curiosity and horror. 'What's wrong with her?'

Ottilie inched into the cupboard. The stench of the hot air turned her stomach. She pressed her hand over her nose and mouth, trying to keep down her breakfast. Gracie didn't seem to know that anyone was there. Ottilie waved a hand in front of her eyes. No reaction.

'Is she hurt?' said Alba. Her face was half covered by the blue handkerchief she'd pressed over her nose. 'Did a wyler get her?'

'She's not hurt,' said Ottilie, staring down at the bite on her arm. 'She's doing something.' There were wylers in the fort again, and here was Gracie, locked in a secret store cupboard, her bite glowing. It couldn't be a coincidence.

It had been Gracie all along.

Was she the hooded figure who had stalked Ottilie through the Narroway? Was she the witch who hexed the king? Ottilie didn't know what was possible when it came to witches. Could they lengthen their lives without becoming sleepless? Could they choose the age they wished to appear? Perhaps Gracie was much older than she looked.

'Alba.' Ottilie stared at the bite on Gracie's arm. 'Have you read anything about wyler venom, about it making a … some sort of … link?'

Alba shook her head, handkerchief fluttering. 'No. I've … no.'

'You think she's controlling the wylers?' said Skip, her eyes narrowing.

'Look at her! She's doing something,' said Ottilie. 'It's like she's not here. She's in a trance, and her bite, look at it. It's glowing.' There wasn't time to figure it all out, but this did prove one thing. 'They've got the wrong person!'

'Ottilie, you don't know that! They could be working together,' said Skip.

It didn't matter. 'They're going to the Laklands now! What if it's all Gracie, and Maeve has nothing to do with it?'

'Go, Ottilie,' said Alba, lowering the handkerchief – she looked very green. 'We'll stay with Gracie. You go, get them to bring Maeve back!'

Without another word, Ottilie dashed through the corridors, down the stairs, and out into the mostly deserted grounds. The world was eerily still.

A deathly screech tore through the silence. Panicked, Ottilie whipped around and smacked into something hard.

She and Preddy both fell to the ground.

'Ottilie, what –'

'It's Gracie Moravec,' she said, barely catching her breath. 'She's controlling them. We have to get Maeve back.'

'How do you know?'

'Come on, Preddy!' She pulled him up and, both a little wobbly, they ran towards the main gate.

There were four horses tethered to a tree nearby, snorting and twitching. The huntsmen obviously hadn't had time to take them back to the stables when the alarms sounded.

'Ottilie!' Preddy panted, pointing to the horses.

She scrambled up into the saddle of a black mare. Preddy jumped onto another and they galloped frantically towards the main gate. Her heart raced. She had only galloped once before, and that was under Ramona's supervision.

Approaching the gate, she pulled back hard on the reins. Her horse skipped and stamped backwards and Ottilie nearly lost her seat. Gripping hard with her legs, she forced her breath back into her lungs and demanded, 'Let us through!'

'The fort's in lockdown. No-one leaves,' called a huntsman from above.

Ottilie clenched her fists over the reins. 'It's urgent!'

'You fledges should be in your chambers!'

'Let them through!'

It was Ned. The huntsmen on the wall froze, unsure of what to do. Ned was an elite; under normal circumstances they were supposed to defer to him.

'Open the gate,' said Ned calmly.

Slowly, the gate rose. Ottilie ground her teeth. One day she would be an elite and the other huntsmen would listen to her.

Ned looked to Ottilie, questions written all over his face.

'They've got the wrong person. It's Gracie Moravec,' she said, speaking so fast she barely understood herself.

His eyes flicked to the horse and back to Ottilie. 'How are you at riding?'

'New to it.'

'Sit back as far as you can,' said Ned.

She jerked her feet out of the stirrups and slid to the very back of the saddle. Ned clambered up in front and she hoped he couldn't feel her pulse quicken as she wrapped her arms tight around his middle.

They galloped out across the fields and through the trees. Ottilie had never ridden so fast. It was an entirely different sensation to flying. She clung on to Ned for dear life as the two horses leapt over logs and hurtled around tight bends. The ride was heavier, louder and, to her, much more frightening than flying.

They had just crossed into the Richter zone when Ottilie saw dust kicked up ahead.

'There!' she said.

The horses skirted off the path, leaping through the scrub to circle around in front of the travellers. There were two wagons pulled by mountain bucks, four mounts with them, and Ottilie heard the whoosh of wings as a russet wingerslink passed overhead. Igor Thrike was circling above.

'Eddy? Noel? What are you doing here?' said Wrangler Voilies, sticking his head out of the first wagon.

Ottilie jumped down from behind Ned. Her legs were shakier than she anticipated and she stumbled sideways, stubbing her toe hard on a rock.

Voilies ignored her. 'What is the meaning of this?'

'You've got the wrong person,' she said, shaking out her foot.

The sallow-skinned Director Yaist stepped gingerly out of the wagon. 'What are you talking about?'

'It's Gracie Moravec controlling the wylers,' said Ottilie, still catching her breath.

Yaist sniffed. 'This girl was convicted of witchcraft.'

'You don't know the whole story!' Her voice was shaking with frustration. 'You rushed to decide because you're scared. You wanted to get rid of her!'

'How dare you!' snarled Yaist, his yellowish lips pulling back from his teeth.

Whistler dropped out of the second wagon. 'Do you have proof, Ottilie?'

'Of course she doesn't!' shrieked Voilies from inside. 'She's probably colluding with the witch! This is a diversion to help her escape!'

'Pipe down, you warbling hog,' said Whistler, waving her sleeves about. 'Ottilie, from where have these wild conclusions emerged?'

'There are wylers in the fort right now,' said Ottilie feverishly, 'and Gracie's locked herself in a cupboard. She's in some sort of trance and the bite on her arm is glowing.'

'Wrong,' said a soft voice from Ottilie's left.

Ottilie jumped. Gracie Moravec stepped delicately over a fallen branch and out onto the path. Her eyes had returned to normal, but the bite on her arm still glinted.

Ottilie raised her cutlass. 'How did you get here so fast?' Her voice was thin and she knew her face betrayed her fear.

Gracie glanced at the second wagon — the one that must have held Maeve, chained up inside.

'I'm a witch,' said Gracie with a smile.

The huntsmen pointed their weapons at her.

'Careful now,' Gracie crooned.

From everywhere, all around, wylers prowled out of the trees. The white one came last. It had grown to the size of a pony. It stood at Gracie's side, black fangs bared, red eyes glowing.

Bloodbeast — that's what Captain Lyre had said. In that moment Ottilie knew: the white wyler had been eating the hearts. Perhaps not the white wyler alone. There could be more, she realised, many more. Jungle Bay … the knopoes. Her mind ticked and ticked, determined to remember. She thought that perhaps one of them, the first one, had been bigger than the others. It hadn't been white. She knew that for sure. But it might have looked different from the rest of the troop.

'No need to be frightened,' said Gracie sweetly. 'They won't attack unless I ask them to.'

'What happened to you?' said Ottilie, her tone more helpless than she liked.

'I told you, Ott. I'm the witch,' Gracie said, sounding a little bored.

Was this it, the answer she had been seeking?

'Maeve Moth is innocent,' Gracie continued, raising her eyes to Director Yaist.

'Then what was she doing past the boundary wall?' he demanded.

'She was looking for me,' said Gracie. 'She found out what I was, and she was trying to stop me. She was too late, of course.' A cruel smile twisted her face. 'Bring her out. I want to see her.'

'We do not take orders from little girls,' said Director Yaist.

Gracie's eyes flashed red and the white wyler lunged at Yaist, snapped its jaws and nipped off his left thumb.

Everything happened at once. The four mounts aimed arrows at the white wyler, but Gracie's eyes flashed again and the circle of wylers snarled, closing in so tight that the huntsmen could barely shift their weight without touching them.

'I wouldn't,' she said, reaching down to pick up Yaist's bronze ring.

A quick movement caught Ottilie's eye. Still atop his horse, Preddy was removing his own ring to toss to Yaist. But the gesture caught Gracie's attention.

'No!' snapped Gracie. 'No-one helps him.'

The white wyler turned its gaze to Preddy and braced to spring. The wylers pressed in on all sides. There were too many of them. If the huntsmen attacked, there was no guaranteeing who would survive.

No-one moved.

Ottilie was too scared to breathe, scared that anything she did might cause the enormous wyler, the bloodbeast, to leap at Preddy.

Not again, she thought desperately. *No-one else.*

In front, Director Yaist had fallen to the ground. Creamy bubbles, like sour milk, popped and dribbled out of the corners of his mouth. He clutched his head, whining in pain.

Sickened and helpless, Ottilie could not tear her eyes away. She felt a strange emptiness – surely seeing this, watching this, should have elicited pain, shrieking, tears, anything … but she felt lost, and very far away. Her mind was a kite, drifting backwards and upwards, tethered to her skeleton by one feeble string.

Distantly, she heard a sigh. Something glinted in the air and Ottilie realised Gracie had tossed Yaist's ring onto the ground. Inclining her head, she said, 'Go on, then.'

Two mounts leapt from their horses, one of them sliding the ring onto Yaist's right thumb, the other helping him to his feet. It seemed Gracie was going to let the director live, but her point had been made.

'Bring the girl out!' shrieked Wrangler Voilies, through panicked huffs.

A footman dragged Maeve from the wagon. She was bound and gagged, her eyes wild. Ottilie blinked back into her body. She wanted to help Maeve.

Gracie gently removed the gag.

'Have her! Take her. Just let us leave!' said Voilies in hysterics, his eyes darting back and forth between Gracie and the wyler pack.

'Come with me,' said Gracie.

'No,' said Maeve, her voice a mere rasping breath.

Ottilie couldn't believe what she was hearing.

Neither, it seemed, could Gracie. 'What?' she said, dangerously. 'They were going to bury you alive. They might still.'

'No,' said Maeve. 'I'm not coming with you.'

Ottilie's ribs pressed in. Would Gracie set the wylers on her?

Gracie's eyes narrowed, but they didn't flash red. She twirled and leapt onto the back of the white wyler, and in an instant, she and the whole pack turned tail and fled into the forest.

26

Sanctuary

When they arrived back at Fiory, the wylers were gone. Voilies insisted that Ned and Preddy join him in speaking to the directorate, but Ottilie's presence was apparently not required. She only hoped that it was Voilies snubbing her as usual, and not that he intended to use the meeting to get her into trouble.

In truth, she was glad. She needed time to settle, to think. So Gracie was the witch who had been controlling the wylers. Why, then, had that first wyler bitten her? Why had she been so sick? Was it all for show? And what of Maeve?

Alba and Skip were mostly unharmed, but Ramona was checking them over in Montie's kitchen all the same. The cosy room was a wonderful relief from the bracing cold. The smells of baking bread and simmering soup wrapped around Ottilie like a hug.

'She came to and pulled the knife on me,' said Skip, filling her in.

Gracie had slashed her across the ribs, but it was only a scrape. Ramona was cleaning the wound while Montie heated some pumpkin soup left over from lunch. Even after what she had just witnessed Ottilie still found it hard to picture. Gracie Moravec, attacking Skip with a knife. It didn't seem real. How could people do things like that to one another? How had Gracie's body let her do it?

'Skip tackled her,' said Alba, her eyes wide. One of her braids had come loose, and her usually smooth, straight hair was scrunched in a matted knot at the side of her head.

'I had her!' said Skip, scowling. 'But then one of the wylers came.'

'It was like she could control it!' said Alba. 'They could have killed us, the two of them, but it seemed like she was in a rush to be somewhere – obviously to reach the wagons.' She nodded her head at Ottilie, who had just finished her own account. 'So she just fled,' Alba continued, 'and the wyler held us there for a bit, and then went after her.'

'This shouldn't be happening,' said Montie, shaking her head over the pot on the coals. 'This place should be safer … safer than …'

Ottilie knew she was referring to wherever she and Alba were from.

Skip picked up on it too. 'Why did you leave the Usklers, Mrs Kit?' She winced as Ramona dabbed vinegar on her scrape. It was a question Ottilie had always been too nervous to ask.

Montie frowned. 'Because we weren't safe.'

'Why not?' said Ottilie, trying not to look at Montie's burns.

'There's a group of Laklanders who live in the north-most part of Longwood Forest. That group, they're vengeful people, filled with hate. They hate Usklerians, but more than that they hate people with Lakland blood living peacefully among Usklerians. They saw us as traitors.'

So there really were Laklander camps in Longwood. There had always been whispers but Ottilie had never believed it. Mostly because she had never believed it possible for anyone to live in that horrible forest.

Her gaze lingered on Skip and Ramona. If either of them was surprised to find out that Montie and Alba were Laklanders, they hid it well.

'Mum was attacked,' said Alba, with the casual tone that comes with time.

'We were living in Scarpy Village, by the mouth of the River Hook,' said Montie. 'Nothing like this had ever happened there before. But they must have heard about us and where we were living. One night someone broke into our house and set a fire.'

Her fingers traced the side of her face. She reached up and unwound the pink-and-gold scarf – revealing her scarred, nearly bald head. What hair she had left she kept very short.

'Alba was six years old, but she found me, and she helped put the fire out. We left as soon as I was well enough to travel. My sister still lives there, with my niece and nephew. She refused to let them drive her away. But I couldn't stay there, not after what happened ... what could have happened to Alba.' She turned her back on them. 'But here we are, in a guarded fortress, and look at what's happening. This is the world we live in.'

Ottilie, Alba and Skip exchanged looks.

'Mum ...' said Alba. 'We've been training with Ottilie.'

'You've what?' Montie dropped her ladle in the pot.

'Ottilie and some other huntsmen, and Ramona. We've been training with them at night. Just in case.'

Montie glared at Ramona. Ottilie wouldn't have been at all surprised to see steam coming from her nostrils. 'You've been training them in secret? With all this talk of witchcraft! You've been gathering them together after dark? How could you be so reckless!'

Ramona remained composed. 'I'm sorry, Montie. With Alba involved, we should have informed you.'

'Informed me? You should have asked my permission!' Baring her teeth, Montie turned to her daughter. 'How could you do this, Alba? How could you risk our position here? Risk losing our home?' Montie's dark eyes were heavy with betrayal and Ottilie felt a sick feeling in her gut.

'Because this is too important!' said Skip, louder than was probably wise.

'Don't you dare start with me, Isla! Do you know what they were going to do with Maeve Moth? You all put yourselves in terrible danger,' she growled, glaring at Alba.

Alba seemed unable to muster a breath, let alone her voice.

'And you,' said Montie, rounding on Ramona again. 'After everything that happened ... that little girl, under your care ... and you would risk this?'

Ramona's cheeks flushed and her lips became a thin line. She and Montie faced each other like two lions braced to clash. No-one dared speak and the crackling flames seemed unnaturally loud in the silence.

Finally, cautiously, Skip asked, 'What are you talking about?'

Montie didn't answer her.

Ramona drew her fiery hair back from her face, sweeping her little finger across the crocodile-skin eyepatch. She faced Skip. 'Ten years ago, the king's three-year-old daughter had an accident with a horse under my supervision.' Her eyes were fierce but her voice was calm.

She didn't say what had happened to the girl. She didn't need to. Everyone knew that Varrio Sol didn't have any daughters. Both had died, one before Ottilie was born, and another when she was very young. That must have been how Ramona ended up in the Narroway. She'd been exiled.

'Enough, Montie,' said Ramona.

Montie opened her mouth to retort but Ramona got in first, her tone still remarkably calm. 'We're all in danger, but the difference is the boys are armed and trained to meet it. If Alba and Skip hadn't been training with us, they might not have survived today. It's too dangerous not to teach them.'

Montie didn't seem to have a response. She turned back to the pot, scooped out the drowned ladle and filled five bowls in silence. Ramona tied off a bandage around Skip's ribs and Skip settled quickly into a chair, as if frightened to do anything that might set off Montie again.

Montie slid each of them a bowl and spoon. As she passed Ottilie the soup, she met her eye. Ottilie wondered if she was going to scold her, but instead she offered an infinitesimal nod, which Ottilie hoped was a gesture of forgiveness.

27

A Visitor

The wylers had been a diversion. That was Ottilie's guess. Something to keep the huntsmen occupied. Ottilie was sure that in that trance Gracie could see through their eyes. She must have guided them through, snuck them in somewhere – Ottilie still wasn't exactly sure how or where.

The rest of the pack must have been waiting beyond the boundary wall, ready to aid in her escape. But why had she wanted to escape? And why had she given herself up? It had to be about Maeve. She really had wanted to rescue her friend.

She'd known it would be too difficult inside Fiory, so she waited until the wagons were on the move, until they were far enough from the fort that they could not quickly call for aid.

Ottilie wanted to speak to Maeve. There were things that needed explaining. She was still convinced that Maeve was a witch, although, considering the fact that she had refused to go with Gracie, she was also inclined to believe that Maeve was innocent. But Ottilie wanted answers. Clear answers.

After a thorough questioning from Captain Lyre, the only one bold enough to enter the wagon, Maeve was waiting under heavy guard while the directorate held council. When it was done, Voilies strolled across the grounds, clearly in no hurry to free her.

'What are you doing here, Colter?' he asked, looking down his nose.

Ottilie was standing just far enough from the wagon to keep the nine guards happy. 'Waiting for you to let her go.'

Voilies huffed and clucked as he unlatched the back. 'You're free to leave, Miss Moth,' he said, as if forced to speak the words against his will.

The huntsmen dispersed and Wrangler Voilies leaned in, as if reaching into a snake pit. Roughly, he unlocked the iron manacles. 'We're watching you,' he said, dangerously. Turning back to Ottilie, he added, 'All of you.'

Maeve looked unsteady on her feet. Ottilie offered her hand, but she ignored it.

'Are you here for a thank you?' said Maeve.

'No,' said Ottilie, unsurprised by her coldness. 'I want you to explain everything to me. I rode out there to help you. I deserve that.'

'You rode out there because you're a good person. It had nothing to do with me.' Maeve's eyes were wild. She looked like a dog that had just been beaten. Ottilie remembered the feeling. But she'd had people to comfort her. Maeve had no-one. 'I owe you nothing.'

'Maeve!' Scoot came limping towards them, fury twisting his face.

Ottilie stepped carefully between them. 'It wasn't her, Scoot, it was Gracie.'

'Preddy told me. I don't care what you all say!' he snarled. 'I want to know ... I want to understand!' His cheeks were still wet with tears.

'I was just going to talk to her,' said Ottilie, gently. 'Come with us.'

Maeve's eyes darted around. She looked truly terrified.

'I know a safe place,' said Ottilie. She led them down to the lower grounds.

'We shouldn't be seen sneaking off together,' said Maeve, as they approached the stone stairway.

'They won't see us – most of the wranglers are scared of the wingerslinks,' said Ottilie.

They wandered down the aisles of the wingerslink

sanctuary to the sounds of inquisitive sniffing and the occasional cautionary growl, which seemed to be directed at Scoot. They stopped by some barrels of salted eel and chests full of dried marsh crab. Scoot dropped down on a chest, as far from the pens as possible. He was fidgeting violently and his jaw was twitching.

Maeve hovered uneasily. She was still wearing her dress from the day before and was painted with layers of dried mud. Ottilie could see little trails through the dirt on her cheeks, shallow creek beds forged by tears.

'You should have a drink,' said Ottilie, pumping the lever above the nearby water trough.

Maeve hurried over and cupped her hands, drinking and splashing her face, before settling down on a crate and staring at her toes.

A dark wingerslink lifted her head and regarded them with sleepy green eyes.

'What is Gracie? What happened to her?' said Ottilie. She wanted to get straight to it.

'I don't know,' said Maeve, still staring at her toes. 'When the wyler got into the sculkie chambers' – Maeve took a deep breath – 'and Gracie got bitten ... I saw it happen. I saw what she did.'

'What do you mean, you saw what she did?' said Scoot, his eyes unforgiving.

'She held out her arm to it,' said Maeve. 'She just held it out. She let it bite her.'

Ottilie frowned. So it had been intentional? Had Gracie allowed the wyler to bite her to make herself look the innocent victim? Perhaps, being a witch, she knew she could survive it and allowed herself to get sick enough to avoid suspicion. The thought made Ottilie's stomach churn.

'I didn't know why. I still don't,' continued Maeve. 'I asked her about it but she just laughed it off. And she was really sick at first, from the venom, but then she got better, and she was acting different. She would disappear, I worried that … that she was the one letting them in. I had no idea that she could control them like that.

'She never said anything about being a witch – I don't know if she really is … I think I would have been able to tell – I think she just said that so they would let me go.'

Ottilie was sure that Gracie was a witch. It was the only thing that made sense. Gracie was behind everything. Ottilie just didn't know all the details yet.

'So she was telling the truth?' she asked. 'You did go out past the walls to try to stop her? You thought she was out there setting the wylers on huntsmen?' She remembered Opal Tarn, glinting in the sun, and Bayo, drowning in a storm of orange fur, and her vision reeled. She twisted her fingers together, wishing Gully was somewhere near.

'No … that's not why I was there,' said Maeve, her voice shaking.

'Then what were you doing out there?' demanded Scoot.

Maeve got to her feet, terror in her eyes.

Ottilie jumped up and drew her cutlass and Scoot followed straight after. Something was moving above, in the dark wingerslinks' pen. Someone was in the rafters, listening to them.

'Who's there?' Ottilie demanded.

Someone crawled forwards across a beam and slowly, deftly, lowered themselves to the ground.

Ottilie's mouth fell open. It wasn't a person.

He looked confused and a little worried. His eyes flicked between Maeve and Scoot and then he removed the old leather sack from over his shoulder and held it out to her.

'I have your hair,' said Bill.

28

Maeve's Secret

Ottilie couldn't believe what she was seeing. Bill looked just the same. Two blunt horns peeked up out of his thin muddy hair. His eyes were a little too close together, the eyelashes spidery, and his nose was long and narrow. His slightly stretched-looking limbs were coated in fine pinkish-grey fur that even this far from the swamp seemed sleek with damp.

Ottilie was so glad to see him she thought she might burst. She launched herself at him in a suffocating hug. He let out a strangled gasp and stood with his arms pinned to his sides, breathing in short, wet breaths.

'Bill! How are you here?'

'Who are you?' said Maeve.

'What are you?' said Scoot.

Bill turned to Scoot. 'Not a person like you.' His eyes flicked to Maeve. 'Not a bird like her.'

'Bill, this is Maeve Moth. She's not a bird, she's a person,' said Ottilie. 'And this is Scoot.'

'I know a bird when I smell one,' said Bill.

Ottilie ignored him. 'Scoot, this is Bill, I've told you about him. He helped me get here.'

Scoot's eyes widened.

Bill turned to Ottilie. 'What is your name?'

'It's Ottilie,' she said, with a watery smile. 'Did you forget?'

'Yes,' he said, blinking.

'What are you doing here, Bill? You didn't come here to give me my hair?'

'Why does he have your hair?' said Maeve, looking disturbed.

'He cut it off for me.' Ottilie ran a hand over her head, remembering the short, uneven tufts.

'But why did he keep it?' said Scoot, with a hint of amusement.

'I've been having … I've been seeing … you were supposed to come back,' said Bill.

'I know,' she said, her smile faltering. 'I was. But things … changed. It's complicated.'

'They're going to start the pickings again soon,' said Bill, twisting his hands. 'Winter came, and I remembered. They'll take them soon, when the season changes. I remembered where you'd gone and the birds …' he glanced at Maeve. 'They told me where you were. And I wanted to come here, to warn you … warn you …'

'Warn me about what?' said Ottilie, stepping closer to him.

Bill wrapped his webbed fingers around one of his horns, tipping his head to the side. 'I can't remember,' he said.

'Convenient,' said Maeve.

'Maeve, shush, he has a … memory problem,' snapped Ottilie. 'But, Bill, how did you get here?'

'I hid in one of the food supply carts. I only got here yesterday. I hadn't found you yet and then there was clanging and fuss … so I hid.' He shivered.

'Here?' said Maeve, glancing at the rafters.

'These things seemed nice.' Bill gestured to the dark wingerslink. 'I felt safe.'

'I wouldn't exactly call them nice,' said Scoot.

There came a nettled snarl from the pen behind him. Scoot twitched and crossed to stand by Ottilie.

'Bill, you have to remember what you came to warn me about,' said Ottilie. 'You have to try.' What could it be? Something worse than Gully's kidnapping, worse than Gracie controlling the wylers? Or was it about the bloodbeasts – whatever they were?

Bill nodded, crossed his eyes and said nothing.

She sighed and turned back to Maeve. 'We weren't finished. Maeve, I don't believe that you had anything to do with all the bad things that have been happening, but I do think … I think you're a witch.' Ottilie struggled to soften the last word, to utter it as if it were neither insult nor accusation.

Maeve clenched her jaw tight.

'She's not a witch,' whispered Bill. 'She's a bird.'

'What were you doing out there?' she asked, accusation creeping in. 'How did you get past the walls with no-one stopping you?'

Bill's arm slunk into Ottilie's field of vision. One long, webbed finger stretched out and touched Maeve on the side of her head. 'She's a bird,' said Bill. 'She flew out.'

'Get off me!' said Maeve, swatting his hand away.

'He's bonkers,' said Scoot. A smile tugged at his lips but didn't quite form.

'Bill, stop it! This is serious,' said Ottilie.

He looked confused and hurt. 'She just showed me,' he said, holding the pad of his finger in front of Ottilie's left eye.

'What's on his finger?' said Scoot eagerly.

'Nothing,' she said. 'Bill, what are you talking about?'

Maeve closed her eyes. 'He's right,' she whispered. 'You both are.'

Scoot raised his eyebrows. 'He's right, is he? You're a bird. Of course! How did we not see it before! Look at you. You're a giant bird!'

Ottilie nearly laughed, but then a memory broke. The cave paintings in the Swamp Hollows. The stick figures with wide mouths and feathery crowns. Old Moss said they were fiorns. Fiory's chosen children.

'You're a ... you can turn into a ... what do you mean we're both right?' said Ottilie. Could Maeve Moth really be a fiorn? Ottilie had always imagined them as part bird, part human, or like their fearsome depictions on the cave walls. Maeve had been looking a little ragged of late, but she was by no means a monster.

'It started slowly,' whispered Maeve. 'I could make the air move ... bring sparks from nowhere ... boil water by looking at it. Then I started having dreams and losing time. I'd wake up in strange places ... I'd find dead things around me – mice, lizards ... sometimes just bones that looked like they'd been spat back up.'

Scoot screwed up his face.

'That's why they found bones with your things?' said Ottilie.

'I started keeping them. I was trying to understand where they came from. I realised ... I thought I might be a witch and so I tried to draw memories from them, because I realised I could do that with people when I touched them.'

'Is that what Bill just did to you?' Ottilie stared at Bill's finger.

'You're a witch too?' said Scoot, regarding Bill with wide eyes. 'How many witches are there in this place?'

'That was different ... I don't know what that was,' said Maeve, glaring at Bill.

Bill shrugged and patted the top of his head. 'Birds show me things. They like to talk. You're no different. Just bad-tempered.'

Scoot stood up and started waving his arms around. 'So Bill can talk to birds? The birds show him things? And you're a witch and a bird! Why am I the only one who's confused here? Am I the crazy one, or is it you three?'

'She's a fiorn,' said Ottilie. 'A witch that can turn into a bird – am I right?'

'I started remembering,' said Maeve. 'I still mostly can't control when it happens to me – I'm working on it. It's often when I'm asleep, but I started to be aware when it was happening ... and remembering things. I snatched a jivvie once, right in front of you.'

Ottilie's mouth fell open. 'You were the owl that saved Leo when we were on wall watch?'

Maeve nodded.

'And I suppose we don't owe you anything for that? You were just doing what good people do,' said Ottilie, looking her square in the eye.

'I didn't even know I was doing it,' said Maeve, looking away. 'I remembered it months later, and I'm not a good person.'

'You're a good bird,' said Bill, as if it were the answer to a riddle.

'So that's really why you were past the boundaries?' said Scoot, with narrowed eyes. 'You flew out?'

'I was trying to control it – trying to fly back and turn back into … me. But I messed it up. I changed back beyond the walls. Then Igor and his fledge found me and, well, you know the rest. I didn't know anything about what had happened that day. I didn't see any of it …' The remaining colour drained from her face.

'That's why you didn't say anything when they accused you?' said Ottilie. It was all starting to make sense.

'What could I say? That I'm a witch? That I was past the boundaries because I flew out there? It would have ended the same. It would have been an iron box either way. But then you came … and then Gracie …' Her eyes slid shut, as if she was in pain.

'Why did she protect you?'

Gracie didn't need to say Maeve was innocent. In fact, she could have declared Maeve truly a witch, which would have forced her to escape with her – but she hadn't. She'd given Maeve a choice.

'Because she's my … she was my friend,' said Maeve, her voice shaking.

Scoot cracked his knuckles.

'Why didn't you go with her when she asked?' said Ottilie, determined to understand everything.

'Because I'm not what she is. I don't want to hurt people,' said Maeve, in a hoarse whisper.

'Did you know that about her?' said Scoot, dangerously.

'No.' Maeve shook her head frantically. 'I've known her for two years. But I didn't know … I knew she could be cruel but I never knew … I liked her because she was different. I've always struggled with people. People don't like me, they leave me out.'

'Have you ever thought that if you weren't such a hideous bully they wouldn't do that?' said Scoot.

'People always treated me differently, even when I was little, like I smelled wrong or something, as if they were scared. So I guess I started scaring them off on purpose,' said Maeve, blinking away tears.

'Oh, you poor witch. You're forgiven,' said Scoot.

Ottilie shushed him. 'Scoot, that's not helpful.'

'Gracie was never like that,' continued Maeve. 'She was never scared.'

'Of course she wasn't scared of you,' said Scoot. 'She's a ranky lunatic!'

'The fact that you're both witches probably helped,' said Ottilie.

Maeve frowned. Ottilie could tell she still didn't think Gracie was a witch. But how could she not be?

'I think she and I together … we made each other worse,' said Maeve. 'But, I swear, I didn't know she could be so bad, so evil.' She looked up, her eyes pleading.

'I believe you,' said Bill.

'You're just saying that because you like birds,' said Scoot.

'I believe you too,' said Ottilie.

'Are you going to tell anyone about me?' Maeve asked, in barely a whisper.

Ottilie didn't need to consider her answer. 'We'll keep your secret.'

Bill pressed a finger to his lips, nodding. After a moment, he lowered it and said, 'What secret?'

➤ 29 ➤

Goedl

In the wake of Gracie's flight, the atmosphere had never been tenser. No-one seemed to disbelieve her story. They all considered Gracie the sole witch, and Maeve wrongfully convicted. The pair were close friends after all; their beds were next to each other. It was generally understood that the book and the bones belonged to Gracie, not Maeve.

Gully, everyone decided, had been lying to protect someone he considered to be innocent. He was punished for it too, given three weeks of singer duty – no hunts, no patrols, not even wall watch – leaving him with very little opportunity to earn points.

As a consequence, he slipped from top position in the fledgling rankings to fourth place, behind Preddy, Ross

Nest from Richter and Murphy Graves from Arko, who rose to first.

They were fast approaching the end of their fledgling year. On the final day of winter, now only two weeks away, the scores would be fixed, and the new champions named.

Ottilie remembered how important she had thought it was to earn points, to be champion, but she had barely had a second to think about it over the last few weeks. Anyway, she was proud of her performance this year. She had made a remarkable leap since they'd put her in last place at summer's end, now hovering just outside the top twenty, at twenty-third. But the level of difficulty had increased. She'd made fast progress over the underperforming fledglings, but once she reached the top thirty, her advancement slowed. The fledges around her were scoring high on every shift and Ottilie found it difficult to claw her way past them. She would have liked to crack twenty by winter's end, but she supposed it didn't matter. It wasn't going to make a difference to anything.

'You shouldn't look at it that way, Ottilie,' said Ramona, holding out a fish for Hero. She and Ottilie were preparing for that night's training session. 'Performing well might not change their minds, but underperforming hurts our cause.'

Gully and Ned would be arriving soon to help. Since the last wyler attack, their hunt shifts had increased, and

Ottilie had spent most of her limited spare time with Bill. He had done so much for her – she couldn't bear leaving him all alone down in the wingerslink sanctuary, and she lived in fear of him forgetting himself and wandering off somewhere she couldn't find him.

So she had hardly seen Gully or Ned in the past week, apart from the brief moment she'd found to introduce Gully to Bill. She still smiled at the memory of Gully hugging Bill so tight that he was pulled off his webbed feet, thanking him for helping Ottilie track the pickers.

Hero lifted her head and regarded them with a blissful expression. It rapidly changed to hungry, and dangerous, as Ramona drew out another fish. She tossed it to the leopard, who caught it easily in her jaws.

'That's the last –' Ramona froze and reached for her knife. 'Get behind me,' she said to Ottilie.

Ottilie grabbed the nearest untipped spear. 'What is it?' She hadn't sensed anything amiss. 'I can't see anything.' Ottilie looked to Hero – the leopard was happily gobbling up the fish and didn't seem to think anything was wrong.

'There's someone on the roof of the barn,' said Ramona, her eyes fixed on a shadow.

'Oh, Bill!' said Ottilie, with an amused sigh. 'What are you doing up there? I told you to stay in the lower grounds! It's not safe here.'

Bill crept forward, climbed cautiously down a splintering beam, and approached with his arms held aloft in surrender.

'This is just Bill,' she said. 'He's from the Brakkerswamp, like me. He likes to lurk.'

Ramona didn't seem to know what to make of him. 'Ottilie, he really shouldn't be here,' she said, gazing at him with interest.

'Please don't report it. He's harmless ... just think of him like any of the animals here – like the red goose that lives by the frog pond.'

'That goose is a menace,' said Ramona, with a frown. 'I won't report it. But you need to keep out of sight, Bill.' She stared at him as if she'd just discovered an entirely new species.

He nodded and Ottilie breathed a sigh of relief. 'There'll be people here any second,' she said. 'Go back to the lower grounds. I'll come visit tomorrow morning.'

'I just ... I remembered, Ottilie,' said Bill, lifting his feet one after the other, like a cat testing the ground.

'You what?' Ottilie felt the heat rising up her neck. 'You remembered the warning?' *Gracie, the bloodbeasts,* she thought, *the Withering Wood ...*

Bill nodded. 'A girl, a fair-haired girl, she's behind it all, she's doing bad things.'

Ottilie could have laughed. 'Thank you, but you're nearly a month too late.'

The trapdoor creaked open.

'Quick, Bill, hide!' Ottilie hissed, but too slow.

Her shoulders relaxed. It was just Alba and Skip. Skip had already met Bill. She had always so loved the story of Ottilie's journey to the Narroway – Bill was a legend in her eyes.

Alba approached with wonder in her gaze. 'Is this Bill? I thought he was a boy. Ottilie, you never said he was a goedl!'

'I didn't know,' she said, looking Bill up and down. 'What's a goedl?' The word was strange; it stuck in her throat.

'They're so rare!' said Alba. 'And very special.' She held out her hand to him. 'It's so nice to meet you, Bill.'

Bill didn't appear to understand a handshake. It wasn't a gesture he would have witnessed around the Swamp Hollows. Alba clasped his pale hand in hers as he stared down in interest, watching her shake it.

'Goedls are the longest-living creatures in the world,' said Alba, clearly unable to contain the information. 'They're astoundingly intelligent, and they all look different. They adapt to their environment and have amazing camouflage abilities ... see, Bill here made himself look like a person, because he was living in the Swamp Hollows, near people! And see his webbed feet ... for the swamp waters ... and you said he was good at climbing.'

'And I bend,' said Bill, helpfully.

'To fit into small crevices and tunnels around the caves!' Alba was so excited her braids were flipping and flying as she talked.

'But if they all look different, how did you know he was one?' said Skip.

'The horns. It's one of their few defining features,' said Alba. 'And it shows their age. Bill's are quite blunt. They get thinner and sharper as they get older, so he's probably only ...' She chewed her lip, thinking. 'Maybe a bit over a hundred.'

'A hundred!' said Ottilie. She couldn't believe it.

'No wonder he has trouble remembering things!' said Skip.

'No, no,' said Alba in frustration. 'No, a hundred is young. He has trouble remembering things because he's young! This is the best part!' she squeaked. 'Goedls, they're solitary – no-one knows how many there are out there. But they ... they've got a ... a collective consciousness.'

'Oh,' said Ramona, her eyes alight.

'A what?' said Skip.

Ottilie didn't understand either.

'Their minds are linked,' said Alba. 'They can share thoughts and images and memories. That's why Bill can't keep things straight – he's got countless memories swirling around in his mind. It takes them a good couple

241

of centuries to gain some control over it. Until then, their memories are a little bit scrambled. He'll get much better at hiding, too, once he gets older. That's why you've caught him a few times, when he comes close, because he's still learning. Sorry, Bill!' she said, aghast. 'I'm talking about you like you're not even here!' Her cheeks warmed.

'That's all right,' he said. 'It's very interesting. I'm glad to know it.'

Ottilie was stunned. She had no idea. She just thought Bill was a bit odd.

'This is very rare, though, Ottilie, Bill forming this bond with you, this friendship. I think it's helping his own memories stay at the forefront. You're like a tether for him, a tether to his own experience. I've only ever heard of goedls forming bonds with birds.'

'He does that too,' said Ottilie, with a smile. 'Bill, you better hide. The others will be here any second.'

Since the incident on the road, there had been no sign of Gracie Moravec. The other stations had been alerted and new rules were imposed. Footmen and mounts were no longer scheduled to hunt or patrol in groups smaller than three. Flyers were still permitted their solitary hunts, as they had the option of escaping into the air if Gracie and the wylers attacked.

While Gully was restricted to singer duty, Scoot had taken his place as Ned's fledge, but now that his sentence was over, Ned offered to be guardian to both. Considering the hunting year was almost over, the directorate permitted it. Although, taking on two fledges would not help Ned creep up from eighth position, where he currently resided.

A new duty was added to their schedule: hunting Gracie Moravec. They called the task 'witching', and the wranglers had updated their training. Now they were learning to bring down not only dredretches, but people too.

The huntsmen had always opposed each other during training, but that was to master footwork and tricky manoeuvres. Sparring had been a novelty, but now it was serious. Wrangler Morse had told them where to aim their arrows on a hundred different dredretches. Now, he was talking about where to aim on a person. Dredretches weren't natural creatures, they were soulless, evil. They couldn't be killed. They could be brought down, destroyed, felled. But Gracie was a person. It was different.

Ottilie had promised to visit Bill in the wingerslink sanctuary before breakfast. His presence was another thing to conceal, and she was beginning to feel heavy with the weight of secrets and lies. It looked as if her fledgling year would end as it had begun.

She was surprised to find Bill in the pen belonging to Igor Thrike's russet wingerslink, Malleus. Even more surprising was the image of Bill happily filing away at Malleaus's bone-cleaving claws.

'Good morning.' Bill hummed as he wandered over to fill Malleus's drinking trough.

'What are you doing?' said Ottilie, eyeing Malleus with distrust, not just because he was Igor's wingerslink, but because Maestro and Malleus didn't get on.

'I'm looking after them,' said Bill.

'We ... they're already looked after,' she said, with a laugh.

'I'm helping.'

She didn't think she had ever seen him so calm.

'Bill!' someone called.

Ottilie whipped around.

'I've had an idea.' It was Maeve's voice, and in a moment she skipped into view. 'Oh, hello, Ottilie,' she said, almost cheerfully.

Maeve had been much more civil towards her since she had confessed her secret, even bordering on friendly at times. She had assumed it was because she was keeping her mouth shut, or because deep down Maeve really was grateful that Ottilie had ridden out to free her. But now she wondered if it perhaps had something to do with Bill.

'What are you doing down here?' said Ottilie. This was shaping up to be a very odd morning.

'Visiting Bill,' said Maeve.

'Visiting … you've been visit– she's been visiting?' said Ottilie, feeling a clutch of possessiveness.

'I've had an idea,' said Maeve, her eyes bright. 'I know how we can find out – even see – what happened with Gracie and that first attack. We might even be able to find out how she let the wyler in, and how she healed herself.'

'Using magic, I thought.' Ottilie leaned against Malleus's pen, ignoring his threatening growl.

'Well, that's what I want to find out,' said Maeve eagerly. 'A bite that bad, the venom would have gone straight to her blood – she should have died. But she didn't. If she did heal herself with some sort of magic, maybe I can learn it and use it to help if there's another attack!'

Ottilie stood bolt upright. That thought had never occurred to her. 'How? How can we see what she did?'

'Because Bill can talk to birds!' said Maeve.

'So?'

'They show him things when he makes contact with them,' she said, leaping onto a crate. 'It's what he did to me.' She tapped her temple. 'Bill has this really open mind. I can sense it. There's no defences around him like people have, and birds are … like Bill says, birds are chatty. I was thinking and … my memories, when I'm changed, I see so much. Birds see everything! They're everywhere, and they talk to each other.' Maeve flung her arms around wildly as she spoke. 'What I was thinking was, maybe Bill could ask the birds if any of them saw what happened with Gracie. If they can show him, then he can show me, and then I can show you if you like. I think I could do that.'

'Do it,' said Ottilie, her pulse quickening. 'Let's do it. Bill? Can you do that? Bill? What are you doing?'

Bill was standing perfectly still with one eye closed and an arm stretched out to the side. 'They're sending the swamp harrier.'

'You already asked them?' said Ottilie, in awe. 'I didn't realise when you talked to birds you could do it inside your head. I thought you, you know, whistled at them.'

'I think all sorts of wonderful things go on inside his head,' said Maeve, stepping off the crate to stand by Bill.

Ottilie had never heard such warmth in her voice. 'Why is your arm out like that?' she asked, wondering if it was some sort of signal to the birds.

'That's just where I left it,' said Bill, lowering it. He sat down on the floor with his head under the open window. The sunlight streamed in above, dusting him with silver. Maeve sat beside him and ushered Ottilie over to sit by her.

A huge tawny swamp harrier soared in through the window, circled and settled neatly on top of Bill's head.

The beat of its wings swept cool air across Ottilie's skin. Bill didn't appear to mind the weight of the large bird, or its needle-sharp talons resting over his skull. He reached out furtively, his finger stretching towards Maeve's temple. Maeve swatted his arm away and snatched his hand in her own, offering her other hand to Ottilie.

There they sat, all in a row, under a veil of silvery winter sunlight. Ottilie glanced sideways. Maeve and Bill had both closed their eyes. She wondered if it was really safe to let Maeve Moth into her mind, but her curiosity won out and, with only a hint of apprehension, she slid her eyes closed.

First there was only soft warm light, and then an image surfaced. Gracie unconscious in the infirmary, white as the sheets that sheltered her, and a hooded figure standing above her bed.

30

Bird Tales

It was dark in the infirmary. From the window, Ottilie could see only the back of the hooded figure, bending over Gracie. Gracie lurched and spluttered. Some liquid had been forced down her throat.

Ottilie got the sense that the person was speaking, but she could only hear the low hum of a voice, no distinguishable words. Something was coming out of Gracie's mouth. Ottilie saw it twirl upwards in the dim candlelight. It was like smoke, but unnaturally black for a cloud so thin.

The figure stood up and began to turn towards the window. The image hooked and swung upwards as the swamp harrier took flight. Ottilie was about to open her eyes when the forest swam beneath her. The leaves swirled and there was a crack like a twig underfoot and a flash of light.

The swamp harrier was somewhere different now. It was morning and the stormy dawn light had a greenish tinge. Thunder rumbled far off, but it wasn't raining. Gracie was wandering through the trees beyond the boundary walls. She looked terrible. Her skin was greyish and her fair hair oily and lank.

Ottilie saw two eyes flash in the bracken. Gracie stopped and stood very still. Slowly, a wyler prowled out of the undergrowth, fangs bared. Gracie looked over its head. The hooded witch was in the shadows, watching. Gracie held out her injured arm and removed the bandages. The wound was raw, swollen and oozing. Ottilie could see little black lines zigzagging under her pallid skin.

The wyler stopped snarling and Ottilie thought she heard the hooded witch muttering a string of words like an incantation. Gracie bent down and extended her hand. She brushed the wyler's matted fur, just once with her fingertips, and, like a snowflake, a single drop of white appeared on its fur. There was another crack of thunder and the white began to spread, like milk spilling – and the orange fur, the black feet, everything turned to white.

Ottilie's eyes snapped open. Hot panic was twitching under her skin. She had been wrong. Like everyone else, she was too quick to point the finger. She had been so eager for the mystery to be solved that she had tied it all to Gracie.

But Maeve was right: Gracie wasn't a witch. She had been lying in that infirmary, dying, and the hooded witch had done something to her, saved her from the venom and bound her to the wylers. Since then, that white wyler had grown as Gracie recovered. A month ago, it had been the size of a small horse. Who knew how big it was by now.

It was different from the others – not just bigger, more alive. A bloodbeast, Ottilie was sure. She finally understood the meaning of the name. The wyler was bound to Gracie. It had become her kin – her blood.

She had wanted it to be simple, for Gracie to be the sole villain, the witch who hexed the king and raised the dredretches and appeared just before disaster struck. But Gracie was just a minor player in a bigger game, and the real villain was still out there.

Bill's eyes were squeezed shut and he was shaking his head. The swamp harrier made a distasteful shrieking sound and flew off into the sunlight.

Ottilie had the urge to call out 'Thank you!' but she restrained herself.

Bill didn't seem to have noticed the great weight lifting. 'That was her,' he said, fretfully twisting his fingers. 'The girl I came to warn you about.'

'I know, Bill,' said Ottilie. 'I told –'

Maeve wrenched her hand out of Ottilie's grip. Her eyes were still closed and Ottilie could see her pupils darting back and forth beneath her eyelids.

'Maeve?' she said.

'She can't control it,' said Bill.

Of course, Maeve said that her transformations mostly happened when she was asleep. Reading the memory, sharing it with Ottilie, she must have pulled too far away from consciousness.

Maeve's mouth began to stretch wide. Her hair stood on end. Ottilie remembered the cave paintings. This must have been what they depicted – the fiorns mid-transformation.

Maeve's eyes snapped open, twice the size they had been before. Her dress seemed to sink into her skin, feathers rolling to the surface in mesmerising ripples. There was a series of muffled cracks, like tiny bones breaking, and, with a wriggle and a snap, Maeve was gone and a great black owl swooped up to the rafters.

Ottilie's mouth was agape and her hands shook in her lap.

'I'll get her back,' said Bill calmly.

He went quiet for a moment. The owl had disappeared into a dark corner. Bill must have been communicating with her, because slowly, tentatively, she began to inch along the beam above their heads.

Ottilie, out of instinct, got to her feet and held out her hand. It made no sense, of course, Maeve didn't need helping down – she had wings – but Ottilie offered all the same.

The owl hopped twice, shook its feathers, and was gone. In its place, clinging to the beam with terror in her eyes, was Maeve. Ottilie hurriedly found a barrel.

'Bill, give me a hand,' she said, and together they pushed the barrel across the floor, positioning it underneath Maeve. Bill flung his arms out, as if to suggest he would catch her if she fell, though he would probably have bent like a green twig if she had. Maeve let her feet dangle down and jumped onto the barrel.

'Are you all right?' said Ottilie, still recovering from the shock herself.

Maeve was taking great gulps of air. 'Yes,' she managed. 'It just knocks the wind out of me. Did you see everything we saw?'

'Yes,' said Ottilie. 'Gracie's not the witch and it was a binding that saved her. That hooded witch was making a bloodbeast. But I don't understand why she – it doesn't explain why Gracie let it bite her in the first place.'

'It's just the sort of thing she did,' said Maeve blankly. 'She came from … not a nice place. She grew up in Longwood Forest, not far from the border to the Narroway.'

Ottilie gasped. 'The Laklander camps?'

She couldn't imagine living in that place. The Swamp Hollows folk had avoided even the outskirts. If Gracie had lived deep in the forest, near the Narroway border, without a ring to protect her mind – no wonder she was twisted.

Maeve nodded. 'Gracie was always different. She would do things ... swim in icy ponds, jump from high places to see what would happen. She'd talk people into doing things like that with her.

'She told me once, she knew how to fall without hurting herself. She'd done things to see what she could survive. She drank things, ate berries she knew she shouldn't ...'

'But what if it killed her?' said Ottilie, aghast. 'Any of that, that wyler bite could have killed her if that person ... that witch, hadn't done that ... hadn't bound her to the wylers.'

'She didn't care,' said Maeve, looking down at the floor. 'She wasn't scared of getting hurt. She was fearless. It was one of the things I admired about her. Or I thought I did.'

This was the most disturbing thing Ottilie had ever heard. It wasn't right. It was inhuman. 'But she tested things on other people ... she hurt other people.'

'I never saw that. She didn't do it to me. The only time I wondered was when Yosha Moses hit her head on that rock,' said Maeve, her voice weakening.

Ottilie's face ached from frowning. Something didn't add up. 'Maeve, I always got the sense that you knew things about me,' she pressed. 'That you knew I was a girl, back when I was pretending. How could you have missed so much about Gracie?'

'I didn't know,' said Maeve, paling. 'I just knew you were different and you were lying about who you were. I don't know if I sensed it, or just saw it. I can't have been the only one. But if it was a witch thing … well, Gracie never lied about who she was. There's a lot I don't know about her. But I didn't share everything from my past with her either. She would dodge, or speak in riddles, but she never lied. You were lying, and I knew it.'

⟫————————————→

'We have to be careful, the witch is still out there,' said Ottilie, climbing down from Maestro's pen later that day.

'What do you mean?' said Leo. 'We know she's out there.'

Maestro leapt over their heads to land on the slushy grass.

She opened her mouth to try to explain that Gracie was not a witch, merely a foot soldier. But she couldn't figure out a way to say it without implicating Maeve.

She regretted ever mentioning that she thought Maeve was a witch, but back then she hadn't been sure that Gracie and Maeve weren't working together. Since the directorate had released Maeve, Leo hadn't mentioned it, but Ottilie thought she caught him watching her more than he used to.

'Stop thinking about witches,' he said. 'There's a week left until the end of the hunting year. We need to focus on dredretches right now.'

Ottilie's stomach flipped. Soon she would be a second-tier, without a guardian. Leo could be a real pain but, despite everything, he was still her partner. Inside Fiory's walls she might not trust him with her secrets, but beyond the walls she trusted him with her life.

'I am focusing on dredretches!' she said, striding over to where Maestro was stretching in the sun. 'The witch is –'

'What do you want from me, Ott?' said Leo, walking beside her, kicking up twice as much mud. 'I'm helping you with your little squad. What more do you need? You want me to go and find the witch for you?' His tone was infuriatingly smug.

'My little squad?' She took a breath and calmed herself. Leo, as frustrating as he could be, cared a great deal about that squad. He loved teaching – mostly because he loved barking orders and showing off his skills. But Ottilie could tell that he really wanted them to be good. When Fawn hit the centre of the target he'd drawn on the barn wall, Leo lit up. Skip had become his favourite. She was excelling at everything, and Ottilie had heard him praise her more than once.

He was only saying this to make her mad. It was tough, but she was gradually learning not to take the bait. Ned was a master at it. He had a way of putting Leo in his place without sparking an argument. She was trying to get better at it, but she lacked Ned's patience. She also struggled with the idea that she had to do all the work to get along with him, and he didn't have to change his behaviour at all. Even more maddening was the fact that Leo definitely treated her differently. He didn't like it when she disagreed with him. Ned was allowed to have his own opinion. Ottilie, it seemed, was not.

'Are you coming?' said Leo, climbing into the front saddle.

'I want to go in front,' she said.

'What?'

'I want to take the lead today.'

'Ott, it's a week from –'

'The end of the hunting season, I know! You're two hundred points ahead of Igor Thrike. I'm ranked twenty-second. You want me to focus on scoring points – let me catch up!'

He grinned. 'You'll have more of a chance of scoring points if you let me lead. I'll give you the big ones.'

She didn't react. 'It's my last week with you and Maestro, then I'm on my own.' Ottilie had been trying not to think about it. It was bad enough worrying about the hooded witch without thinking about the new hunting year. She just wished she could be a fledgling a little longer! As of next week it wouldn't be Leo's job to teach her anymore – to watch out for her. She was going to have to learn to trust herself.

'I want to catch up,' she said. 'But I want to do it myself.'

Leo threw up his arms and slid to the back of the saddle.

They were rostered to the alpine regions. With winter's end approaching, the snowy blankets were growing patchy and pulling back higher and higher up the peaks. Ottilie could see spiky green bushes and the bright little heads of mountain flowers peeking through the shimmering white.

She was looking for learies – like mountain lions but hairless, with thick, stony skin and a poisonous barb at the end of their tails. Ottilie had never hunted them before. She had only read about them, but she was determined to find one.

Learies were tricky. They were perfectly camouflaged in rocky areas and could leap more than twenty feet in the air. But the danger was worth it. They were worth twenty-two points each, the same as a knopo.

Ottilie dismounted to hunt for a trail. Leo and Maestro covered her from the air. Learies were light of foot, but their flicking tails left clues, little scratches and marks like burns on rock.

After at least half an hour of searching, and much grumbling from Leo about wasted time, Ottilie spotted a singed scrape, and then two more. She signalled for Maestro to pick her up. They were fresh marks, all leading around the edge of a rocky escarpment. Maestro circled. Coming to a broad ledge, he dipped lower so that Ottilie could stay on the trail.

A learie leapt out from under a hanging rock.

Maestro lurched backwards in the air. The dredretch braced and bayed – a discordant, ear-splitting howl. Ottilie fired an arrow. It dodged, leaping down the steep rock face. Ottilie brought Maestro to the ground and flung herself from the saddle.

The learie beat its tail against the rock. The stone sizzled and cracked. She fired another arrow. It dodged again. Its tail lashed out like a whip. Ottilie rolled on the ground and drew her cutlass. The learie pounced. She twirled and swung her arm behind her. There was a great crunch as her cutlass pierced its side, slipping through the rib cage to meet its mark.

Ottilie pulled her blade free and watched the learie crumble to bone, the familiar hot black vapour trailing from its stinking remains.

'You didn't need to get down to do that,' said Leo, frowning from above. 'You put yourself in danger.'

'I wanted to face it,' she said, thinking of Ned – *it's more fun on foot*, he'd said, *closer to the action*.

She had wanted to feel it. This was something she'd learned from Gracie Moravec – there had to be a balance. Fearlessness was as dangerous as cowardice. Fear was important: it fed into instinct. Gracie had conquered fear, but to the point of dehumanising herself. She had offered herself to the monsters and become a creature to fear herself.

✦ 31 ✦

Champion

In the final week of the hunting year, the rankings were wiped from the walls, feeding the mood of mystery and excitement that led to the winter's end festivities.

Ottilie had been so apprehensive about becoming a second-tier that she hadn't expected to be too excited to sleep the night before. She surfaced from a dream well before dawn and spent the morning staring at the ceiling, wondering if she might finally have cracked the top twenty.

That would be an achievement that no-one could deny. She was beginning to feel that she shouldn't fear leaving the fledgling year behind. The scores would be reset after tonight. Ottilie would be back on even ground, and perhaps as a high-scoring second-tier she would finally be taken seriously.

'What happens if no-one from Fiory makes champion?' asked Gully, between messy gulps of his morning apple juice.

'Don't know,' said Ned, approaching with his breakfast plate. He nudged his head in Leo's direction. 'This one's been champion of my tier since we were recruited.'

'Kidnapped,' said Scoot, scowling down at his toast.

'Haven't you got over that yet?' said Leo, laughing. 'It only took me about a day to stop caring.'

Ottilie doubted that was entirely true.

'Nope,' said Scoot. He still wasn't himself. He was slower, sadder. He made other people laugh, but Ottilie rarely caught him laughing himself. 'They'll be bringing the new batch soon,' he added bitterly.

'Fledgling trials are at Arko this year,' said Ned. 'They'll be staying there for a while.' He settled into the empty seat on Ottilie's left. She was very aware of how close he was sitting and noticed a strange tingling up and down her left side.

She wondered when this had started. It was difficult to know; for the first half of the year, she had been nervous when anyone drew too near. Now, she was stuck in this wonderfully uncomfortable place, where all she wanted was to be near Ned but then felt unsteady and unable to meet his eye when she was. Particularly when nothing terrible was happening. At least when they were in danger Ottilie's nerves were focused elsewhere.

Her left ear feeling curiously hot, Ottilie turned away and directed her question to Leo instead. 'Will you two be going over for the trials?' She hadn't thought about it before. For their trials, the elites from every station had come to Fiory to help them train and be paired up as guardians. Would Leo be going to Arko to get a new fledge? She would never admit it to him, but she couldn't stand the thought.

'We haven't technically been named elites again yet,' said Ned.

Leo snorted. 'We will be. But we don't have to go this year. Fourth tiers get a year off from being a guardian. It's why the fourth-tier champion always has the highest score of all the champions – he doesn't have to share. That'll be me next year.' He looked sideways at Ottilie.

She smiled, knowing full well she had hogged the best shots in that last week. But Leo had been hoarding points all year, so it was only fair.

Ottilie was dressing for the champions' ceremony when there was a knock on her door.

'It's me,' said Skip's voice.

'And me,' said Gully, from a little further back. 'You ready to go down?'

Ottilie knotted the last tie on her jacket and opened the door.

'I'm here to wish you luck,' said Skip. 'Alba sent this with me.' It was a small brambleberry pie, Ottilie's favourite. 'Montie made it. Alba wanted to come but the kitchens are too busy.'

'Thank you,' she said, with a hungry smile.

'How do you think you went?' said Skip.

Ottilie shrugged. 'I guess we'll see. Argh!' She swatted a curl off her face. 'I can't keep this out of my eyes. I'm thinking of cutting it all off again.' She shook her nearly shoulder-length hair.

'Well, you don't have time for that now,' said Skip practically. 'Unless you want me to cut just that chunk.'

Ottilie laughed. 'No, thank you.'

'I'll fix it,' said Gully, climbing onto the bed. He stood above her and deftly wound the incriminating curls into a braid that sat well out of her eyes. It was a comforting feeling, having someone dealing with her hair. It reminded her of Mr Parch, cutting it with gentle hands, or Bill tentatively hacking it with a knife, or Skip, secretly trimming it in the springs before she'd been found out. Most of all, it reminded her of Freddie, those few moments in her early childhood when her mother had been there, taking care of them, brushing knots out of her hair.

'How do you know how to do that?' said Skip, with an impressed grin.

Gully shrugged.

'He used to braid our mum's hair off her face when she wasn't feeling well,' said Ottilie.

'Got a lot of practice,' said Gully.

➤━━━━━━━━━━━━━━━━➤

The Moon Court was divided in two. A long wall of stone stretched up behind the Fiory directorate, who sat facing the huntsmen. Just to the side, Ottilie spotted Whistler, sitting with a row of pale-robed bone singers. The champions' ceremony must have been important indeed to lure her into the crowd.

The excitement was palpable. Even though Ottilie knew there was no way her name could be called, her heart beat fast and, despite everything that had happened lately, she found that she was smiling a lot.

Captain Lyre stood in front of them, his blue coat swapped for a black, scaly-looking jacket, flecked with ember orange and trimmed with obsidian stones. His neat beard was twirled at the tip, and his boots were so shiny Ottilie wondered if she might see her reflection if she peered close.

'Welcome, welcome, everyone!' he said with a merry grin. 'As many of you know, today is my favourite day of the year!' He paused, his smile vanishing. 'This year … this year has been a difficult one for us here at Fiory.' His voice dropped and darkened. 'I want to start with a moment of silence for those we have lost. Please join me in honouring our fallen Fiory huntsmen, Christopher Crow, Tommy Mogue and Bayo Amadory.'

All around the courtyard the sculkies held black shades over the candles. The light dimmed, illuminating the starry sky above. Beside Ottilie, Scoot closed his eyes. On her other side, Gully leaned in and said, 'Why didn't he mention Joely?'

She shook her head. Joely was only a sculkie, that's how the Hunt saw it. But she wondered if her own name would have been mentioned. She was a huntsman, just like them, even if she wasn't supposed to be.

She closed her eyes. Were they doing the same thing at Richter and Arko right now, honouring the Fiory fallen? Or did they have casualties of their own? The Hunt didn't tell them about things like that.

'Thank you,' said Captain Lyre, and the shades were lifted. 'There are difficult times ahead. The witch responsible for this misery is still at large. We salute you on your efforts in seeking Gracie Moravec, and we have faith that she will be brought to justice soon. You have done valiant work this past year. We had an outstanding crop of fledglings join our ranks and exceptional guardians guiding their path.'

Captain Lyre went on to mention some of the brave and daring feats enacted by the huntsmen that year. He mentioned Igor Thrike's defeat of the barrogaul, and several other stories of daring deeds and impressive fells. Most, Ottilie had heard about before. Tales of heroism spread fast around the fort.

'And the kappabak ...' Captain Lyre paused.

Ottilie felt eyes upon her and looked up to find Whistler watching.

'A new dredretch ...' He continued in a carrying whisper, as if he were telling them a ghost story. 'The largest on record. A monstrous beast, discovered and defeated by our own champion of two years running, Mr Leo Darby.'

The huntsmen stamped their feet on the ground with a chorus of whistles and hoots. Ottilie did not find it particularly surprising that her name wasn't mentioned.

Captain Lyre's eyes found her in the crowd. 'This was a year of change,' he said. 'Some for the worse, some for the better. This year, we welcomed a female into the Hunt.'

The huntsmen stilled. A weighty hush fell upon the courtyard.

'Welcomed?' said Scoot.

Behind Captain Lyre, Conductor Edderfed shifted on his throne. Ottilie didn't think the directorate had known he was going to mention her. She glanced again at Whistler, who offered her a small, quite warm smile.

'Ottilie Colter started late. Beginning in last place, with only nine points, halfway through the hunting year,' said Captain Lyre. 'Over the last two seasons, she has earned well over six thousand points, clawing her way up to FIFTEENTH position! I think she deserves a round of applause!'

Ottilie couldn't believe it. She hadn't only cracked the top twenty, she'd made the top fifteen! She hadn't even thought it possible. Scoot, Gully and Preddy all leapt to their feet. Among the elites, Ottilie saw Ned rise, and Leo beside him. Several of the elites patted Leo on the back. There was a loud whistling across the room, and Ottilie saw Skip with her fingers at her lips. At the back of the courtyard Montie and Alba were beaming.

Many people remained seated and several others didn't clap, but Ottilie couldn't believe how many were cheering her. Of the wranglers, only Ramona and Wrangler Morse were clapping. Behind Captain Lyre, the directorate remained stony-faced, but just beside them Whistler tipped her head in a lopsided bow.

'He's going to be in trouble,' said Scoot, with a half-smile.

'I think he's proving a point,' said Preddy. 'He's showing them how much support you have. It's more than half the room, Ottilie.'

'I don't know if showing them that was a good thing,' she said. She couldn't help but feel that Captain Lyre had just painted a very big target on her back.

'It is a good thing,' said Gully, still clapping loudly.

'Now!' Captain Lyre cried above the clamour. 'I won't keep you waiting any longer. We'll start with our Fiory elites for the next hunting year.' He held forth a scroll and unrolled it with a flourish.

'Beginning with our new third tiers …' He called eleven third tiers and moved on to the fourth tiers. Leo and Ned were both named. He came to the end of the fifth-tier elites and said, 'Ladies, let's have the peppermead.'

The sculkies appeared at the end of each row, passing along goblets of sparkling silvery liquid, until every huntsman had one in their hand.

'What's peppermead?' said Gully.

'Pirate's drink,' said Scoot, gazing at the goblet with enthusiasm.

'Really?' said Ottilie. She had never heard of it, but then no-one really drank anything but water back at the Swamp Hollows – water, or Gurt's bramblywine.

'Triptiq pirates,' said Preddy. 'They toast their captain with it, first night at sea. It's a tradition – to honour the captain, and keep them sharp – then they get drunk on rum,' he added, with disapproval. 'But it's bad luck if they don't do the peppermead first.'

'How do you know that?' said Gully.

'My father refused to have it in the house because of the association,' said Preddy.

Ottilie sniffed it. It smelled vaguely of ginger.

'Let's have the drums!' said Captain Lyre, swinging his cane in the direction of a bone singer, who began a quick beat on an enormous drum.

'As always, fledglings first!' called Captain Lyre. 'Our fledgling champion ... by an impressive margin of thirty-eight points ... is ... GULLIVER COLTER!'

Ottilie gasped and spilled half the peppermead all down her front. She didn't care one bit. She was smiling so hard it strained her face. Gully had won!

The huntsmen stamped their feet, and it was as if thunder filled the courtyard. Slowly, the first section of the stone wall behind the directorate began to fill with names and numbers – the fledgling rankings – with Gully's name at the top.

'Come forward, Mr Colter,' said Captain Lyre, twinkling with glee.

Ottilie squeezed his hand and Gully got to his feet, a little shakily, Ottilie noticed, but no-one else would have picked it up.

Conductor Edderfed presented him with a gleaming

cutlass and said something to Gully that they could not hear. Gully raised the cutlass in the air and the huntsmen raised their goblets and then drank.

Ottilie took a gulp of what was left of the fizzing, silvery drink. It was a strange flavour and, indeed, quite peppery. Beside her, Scoot gagged and clutched his throat. Preddy had only taken a delicate sip. He was wrinkling his nose and gazing down at his goblet with interest.

Gully came back to sit beside Ottilie. He showed her the cutlass. It had a glinting silver hilt, engraved with an eagle. The bird had what she thought might be rubies for eyes, and it was surrounded by an ornate letter C. Ottilie recognised it. Leo had one almost exactly the same.

Captain Lyre announced the second-tier champion. A mount from Richter. Even though he wasn't present, they stamped their feet and toasted once more, as the second-tier rankings appeared on the wall.

'And our third-tier champion.'

The room grew very still.

'For the third year in a row –'

Leo jumped to his feet, fist in the air.

'– it's LEO DARBY!'

The room erupted into cheers and whistles. The bone singer beat the drum, peppermead slopped all over the floor and the huntsmen stamped their boots. Igor Thrike had got to his feet, but he was standing still, scowling. Ned hugged Leo, and as he patted him on the back Leo turned and grinned at Ottilie. She laughed out loud and shook her head, beaming.

Conductor Edderfed presented Leo with his cutlass and he held it in the air far longer than Gully had.

The two remaining champions were a footman and a flyer from Arko. The Fiory huntsmen toasted both, and Captain Lyre gestured to two shovelies. Ottilie hadn't noticed them there, each standing in a dark corner. On either edge of the wall, the shovelies turned what appeared to be a very heavy wheel. Slowly the wall behind the directorate slid down and disappeared beneath the floor, revealing the rest of the courtyard. Branches and leaves hung from the walls and the space was filled with candlelit tables piled high with pots and plates of glorious food.

'Well,' said Captain Lyre. 'Shall we eat?'

With a cheer of appreciation, the huntsmen made their way over to the other side of the courtyard. Ottilie lingered a moment. She watched the shovelies leaving, their only job done, and the sculkies lining the walls, ready to wait on the huntsmen.

'They get paid, Ott, they're not slaves,' said Leo, appearing at her side.

'That's not the point, Leo. It's about who's allowed to do which job,' she said, looking over at Skip, who was handing out drinks.

'So what … you're not going to eat? You'll starve pretty quick if that's your attitude.'

'Yes, Leonard, I'm going to eat.' She held her hand out. 'Let's see it?'

He passed her his cutlass. She ran her fingers over the engraving of the eagle. Below it there was a wolf with amber eyes, and below that, a mare with diamonds.

'That's the new one,' he said, pointing to the mare, grinning victoriously.

'What are they going to do if you win next year? They've run out of gods.'

Leo grinned. 'They can put a picture of me on there.'

Ottilie snorted.

'Come on,' said Leo. 'Come and eat with me.'

'I thought you didn't like eating with fledges,' she said, as they walked towards Gully and Ned.

'You're not a fledge anymore, Ott.'

That was true. She was on her own now and she wasn't sure how she felt about it. Ottilie looked around the room. She saw Gully and Ned laughing together. Nearby, Scoot was bragging that he was going to beat Preddy now that the scores were reset, even mustering a full smile or two. Ned looked over at them. Eyes bright, he jerked his head as if to say, *hurry up*.

As she approached the table, a new feeling gripped her – a sense of foreboding. This was too good, too merry … it couldn't last. She thought of Gracie and the wylers, and the mysterious witch who had bound her to them. Her mind whirled to the Withering Wood, the patches of decay, and the bloodbeasts, however many there were. Ottilie had the devastating feeling that this was probably the last night of real joy they would have in a while.

— 32 —

Wrangler Kinney's Revenge

With the beginning of spring came the order trials. The new second tiers would be tested on foot, horseback and wingerslink, and placed permanently in the order most suited to them.

On the morning of her flight trial, Ottilie found Leo waiting for her in Maestro's pen. Bill was getting better at hiding; there was no sign of him.

Ottilie's nerves were making her irritable. She was desperate to be made a flyer. If she was going to be facing witches and bloodbeasts and who knew what else, she would do it on a wingerslink. 'Why are you down here?' she asked Leo.

'Wishing you luck,' he said, helping her with Maestro's saddle.

They fastened the buckles in silence. She found herself feeling very sad. This might be the last time she rode Maestro. Even if she managed to be named a flyer, she would be assigned a different wingerslink. Maestro and Leo belonged to each other.

Once they were done, Leo leaned in and whispered to Maestro, 'Be good.' He gave Ottilie a nod and left her alone to fret. When he was halfway down the passage he called out, 'Don't blow it.'

➤──────────────➤

Ottilie had worried that Maestro would play up, as he often did when Leo was absent. But, despite having to adapt to the confines of the arena, she and Maestro dispatched the assigned dredretch – a flare – with ease.

There was only a small crowd there to watch. The order trials didn't merit the same excitement as the fledgling trials, which only came to Fiory once every three years, and pitted an essentially untrained fledgling against monsters they were facing for the very first time.

Ottilie buried her hand in Maestro's fur and whispered, 'Thank you.'

Leo clapped her on the back and flew Maestro back down to the lower grounds. Maestro was considered a difficult steed, so no other fledglings would be trialling on him.

Ottilie took Leo's place in the stands, next to Ned, to watch the rest of the trials. Gully had gone just before her, and she hadn't been able to watch.

'How did you go?' she asked.

'They gave me a flare too. I got it with a knife, but it wasn't deep enough so the wingerslink finished it off for me. I think it still counts, though,' he said sheepishly.

Ned laughed, his shoulder brushing against hers. 'It counts.'

Ottilie fixed her stare on the back of Jobe Yord's head, just a few rows down, her heart beating a little harder.

The next day, she rode Billow for her mounted trial. She struggled a great deal with the swarm of stingers. She was really only a beginner at riding, and Billow moved very differently to Maestro. After a minor fall, a slight sting and some helpful stamping and kicking from Billow, Ottilie finally felled the entire swarm, cutting all six down with her cutlass.

The following day, she dealt with a grieve on foot. It was tricky, and it took a while, but she rolled and tripped it up with her boot, successfully pinning it with a knife.

At the fall of that final day, they gathered in the centre of the arena. A few spectators were scattered throughout the stands to hear the results. Most were guardians, interested to see if their former fledges would be joining their order.

'We'll be starting with mounts,' said Wrangler Morse. 'If I call your name, you can come and get your pin' – he shook a little red bucket, the bronze pins clinking inside – 'and then head over to Wrangler Ritgrivvian and she'll introduce you to your assigned horse.'

Ottilie's nerves were terrible. She liked riding, and she adored Ramona, but she didn't want to give up flying.

Preddy's name was called, and nine others, but that was it.

'Flyers next,' said Wrangler Morse. 'Once you've got your pin, go over and see Wrangler Kinney for your instructions.'

Ottilie's breaths grew shorter with every name he called. She glanced over at the mean, balding little man with the gold tooth and nasty smile. How much sway did Wrangler Kinney have? Could he keep her from being a flyer? Who made these decisions? Her thoughts spiralled out of control. She had forgotten to listen. What did Wrangler Morse say? Was he still calling flyers? She looked up at him, heat flooding her face.

His eyes crinkled kindly. 'Ottilie Colter,' he said, his braided beard twitching.

She breathed a huge sigh of relief, and hurried forwards to take her bronze raptor pin. She remembered her first day in the Narroway – remembered noticing the pins on Leo, Ned and the other huntsmen who had come to collect them from the guard tower.

She could never have known, back then, just how it would feel to have a pin of her own, a badge that named her a Fiory flyer. She could never have fore-seen the pride, or the strange feeling of belonging, that the little bird-shaped pin instilled. Attaching it to her uniform, she grinned up at Leo and found him beaming back. Giddy with relief, she wandered over to stand by Wrangler Kinney.

'Stuck with you, am I?' he said with a sneer.

Ottilie ignored him. Her elation was like a shield.

The new flyers didn't wait around, but Gully and Scoot hadn't been called yet, so there was no doubt they would be footmen. Gully would be happy. She knew that, like Ned, he preferred to be on the ground, in the thick of it.

Wrangler Kinney led the new flyers down to the lower grounds, where six wingerslinks were waiting in the paddock. He assigned one wingerslink to each flyer, leaving Ottilie for last.

The only remaining wingerslink was small, far smaller than Maestro. She looked like she might once have had black fur, but it had dulled to a grizzled charcoal, and where it might have been thick and shiny, it was now coarse and clumped in odd tufts.

'Colter, this is Nox,' said Kinney, with a smirk. 'She's been retired for years, but we keep her around for training. We were going to send her away this year, but I decided she's the one for you.' His tone was gleeful. 'Careful around her mouth, she's lost a few teeth, but she's a mean-tempered old harpy, and she loves to bite.'

Ottilie could imagine his scathing smile, gold tooth glinting, but she didn't look. Instead, she approached Nox and held out her hand for the old wingerslink to sniff. Nox looked into Ottilie's face. There was strength in her pale green eyes. Ottilie took a step closer, and Nox bared her teeth in a snarl.

— 33 —

Nox

The footmen and mounts only had one day before things moved forward, but the flyers were granted a little more time, and Ottilie was thankful for it. She headed for the wingerslink sanctuary at dawn. The end of winter had not brought the end of frost. Ottilie's breath puffed into mist as she carefully descended the icy steps to the lower grounds.

The first time she tried to climb into the saddle, Nox growled and pitched into a brutal roll. Ottilie had to scramble out of the way on her stomach to avoid being flattened like dough under a rolling pin.

When she finally managed to clamber onto her back and ask Nox simply to walk forwards, the wingerslink bent her legs, tucked in her wings, and gripped the ground with her claws. Frustrated, Ottilie dug her heels in, and Nox responded to the pressure by leaping into the air and launching into a dangerously tight circle. Ottilie was caught off-guard, and flung sideways onto the grass.

She could hear cackling in the distance, and looked over to see Wrangler Kinney laughing like a madman.

'Kept her for training,' Ottilie muttered under her breath. It was obvious that Nox hadn't been ridden by anyone for a very long time.

The next day, refusing to give in, she looked for a fresh angle. She marched into the sanctuary to get Nox's brush, but it was missing from the hook in her pen. She checked the sanctuary was empty before whispering, 'Bill.'

'In here,' said Bill's voice from nearby.

Ottilie found him around the corner, gently brushing a golden wingerslink called Glory. She was lying on her side, emitting rumbling purrs as Bill tended to her coat.

'You're spoiling them,' she said, with a smile. 'I need Nox's brush.'

Bill stopped brushing Glory and held it out to her. The golden wingerslink growled, rolled abruptly into a more upright position, and beheld Ottilie with accusing eyes.

'Eel is her favourite,' said Bill, reaching back to offer Glory a consoling pat.

'Eel?'

'Nox. You should give her some dried eel. She loves it.'

'Thanks, Bill.' Ottilie grabbed three crusting eels from the nearest barrel. She was willing to try anything at this point.

By midday, Nox allowed Ottilie to climb onto her back again, but still refused to move. By mid-afternoon, she would walk and run but not fly. By dusk, she finally stretched her scraggy wings, and beat them unevenly in the air. Ottilie dug in with her heels. Nox was doing this on purpose. The old wingerslink was perfectly capable of flying.

On the third day, when Ottilie reached to greet her, Nox lashed out, her fangs snapping over the thin air where Ottilie's hand had been only seconds before. Ottilie responded by baring her own far less impressive teeth and shoving the wingerslink with her elbow. For a little while, it seemed they were even, until Ottilie tried to saddle her and Nox swung sideways, pinning her to the wall of the pen.

That set the tone for the entire day's work. It was as if they had never worked together before and Nox simply locked her bones and refused to move. She was running out of time. Tomorrow Ottilie would be hunting alone and if Nox didn't behave she would doom them both.

'You'll be fine, Ottilie, don't worry,' said Gully.

He was splayed on the end of her bed, one leg hanging over the side, too tired to move.

'It's not like the footmen,' said Ottilie. 'I'll be on my own. What if we get out there and she flies off over the ocean, or just dumps me into a gorge? She doesn't listen to me at all! She just does what she wants.'

Gully laughed. 'Maybe you should let her take you somewhere else. Anywhere would be safer than here, with Gracie and that witch running around, making packs and bloodbeasts and everything.'

Ottilie sat up. She always kept Gully filled in, but he had never talked about leaving before, not since before Christopher Crow. 'That's not funny.' She would never leave him behind. She grabbed his arm. 'Unless you came too? We could just take some glow sticks and go. Right now.'

Gully smiled sleepily and closed his eyes. It was strange remembering how much they had wanted to run away; now neither of them would think of it. Not seriously.

'How was it out there without Ned?' she asked.

Gully had just finished his first proper hunt as a second-tier footman. He'd been rostered on with three others – fourth and fifth tiers who Ottilie didn't know. He lifted his arms and let them flop beside him, his eyes still closed. 'Not as fun,' he huffed.

'Could he ask to be rostered with you? They might let him.'

'Maybe,' said Gully with a loud yawn.

She wanted to keep asking questions, to keep Ned in the conversation, but she couldn't think of anything else and Gully was being unhelpful.

When sleep came to claim him, Ottilie nudged him awake and sent him off to his own room. After he left, she stared at the arched ceiling, her thoughts divided. One part of her was fretting over Nox, worrying that tomorrow would be even worse than today. The other part was still thinking about Ned. Would she ever see him now that he was no longer Gully's guardian, and Leo wasn't hers? She hated the thought.

She rolled over and buried her head in the pillow. What a strange thing to be worrying over. She would stop: that was what she decided. She would stop thinking about it.

But that didn't work, and Ottilie lay awake far longer than made any sense.

***

Her last day with Nox started better. Bill greeted her at the sanctuary by holding out a dried eel. With a tired laugh, Ottilie took his offering and marched into Nox's pen. The wingerslink greeted her with a snort rather than a snarl. It was a definite improvement.

Once in the air, Nox would occasionally dive with no

warning, or swing her head around and snap at Ottilie's ankle, but Ottilie refused to give in. They worked well into the night, until finally the stubborn wingerslink seemed to accept her. She circled and dived, sped and slowed, leapt and rolled, almost always at Ottilie's command.

She trekked back to the upper grounds feeling worn out but pleased with herself. She had finished just in time to catch the end of training in the haunted stables, and tell Leo of her triumph.

Ottilie was halfway there when she saw activity at the boundary wall ahead. Tensing, she rushed over, frightened of what she'd see. The gate was thrown open and three horses galloped in. Ottilie's stomach twisted into knots. Preddy was on one of them.

There were two riders, each holding an injured huntsman slumped in front of him. Ottilie was swimming with guilty relief: Preddy was not one of the injured. She hurried over as they were helped down. The third horse, with no rider, moved timidly towards one of the injured boys, and began sniffing at his face.

One of the boys was able to walk with some assistance, but the other remained motionless, hanging over Preddy's horse like a lumpy blanket.

'He's all right, I think,' she heard one of them say. 'Just unconscious. We lost his horse – the wylers ... t-tore it all up.' The speaker was very white.

'That's not all they did,' said the other boy shakily. 'That white one, the big one … it … it ate the heart. I saw it!'

Ottilie stood frozen, her heart beating hard. There it was – proof. The white wyler was doing what no dredretch was supposed to do. It was eating, consuming … the wyler was a bloodbeast, bound to Gracie, bound to the living world.

'She was there,' said the first boy. 'That little sculkie witch! She had knives!'

So they were back. After her escape, Gracie had lain low. But the wylers were on the prowl again, seemingly intent on picking off the huntsmen one by one, and, united under Gracie's command, they were more dangerous than ever.

Preddy moved over to Ottilie's side. 'There was someone else,' he whispered. His voice was steady. She recalled his reaction to the first wyler attack. How changed he was. She didn't know if that was good or bad. 'I don't think they saw,' he added, tipping his head towards the other boys, who were already making their way to the infirmary. 'But there was someone in a hood, watching from far off.'

Ottilie swallowed. 'If they think there's a second witch they'll start suspecting us all again. They'll start building iron coffins right now.' She didn't even want to think about what might happen to Maeve.

'Do you want me not to tell them?' said Preddy.

Ottilie shook her head. 'They need to know.'

Last time, Whistler's prediction had come true. But there was no avoiding it; the Hunt needed to know that there was someone worse than Gracie out there, a true witch. Everyone needed to be on guard.

❧ 34 ❧

Bill's Warning

Ottilie had spent the night in Gully's room. She had that horrible fear again, the fear of separation. Seeing those boys injured reminded her just how dangerous it was out there, and today she would be facing it alone.

She didn't care if people thought she was weak or afraid. She was afraid and she wasn't the only one. Word had spread quickly about the attack, and that morning Ottilie saw a notice on the dining room door, informing the huntsmen that their schedules would be revised to include fewer general patrols and more witching shifts.

Preddy had informed the directorate about his sighting of the hooded witch, and Ottilie was awaiting the ramifications. She had found Maeve late the night before and warned her to be on guard. Thankfully, Maeve said she had gained some control over her transformations, and was doing better at keeping her magic in check.

But Ottilie was still worried. The Hunt had been willing to lock Maeve up solely on the evidence of bones and a shaky accusation about a flaming tapestry. With everyone so on edge, the directorate might condemn any girl who didn't act in the way they expected. Ottilie herself could easily be accused and carted off to the Laklands.

She was considering paying Whistler a visit, to ask more questions. Things had changed since they'd been caught in her tower: she couldn't help feeling that Whistler was on her side. She'd never reported their break-in or spoken up about the witch book. And it was Whistler who had warned her not to talk about witches in the first place.

Ottilie couldn't spend another night in the dark. She resolved to visit Whistler after her hunt that afternoon — if she made it to the afternoon. Her insides knotted, she reached for the dining room door.

'HEY!'

It was Scoot.

Heart in her throat, Ottilie opened the door just in time to see Skip punching Igor Thrike in the face.

'Skip!' She hurried over.

Scoot was pulling Skip away, pinning her arms to her sides, and Leo was helping someone off the floor. Igor's nose was bleeding. For a moment he was preoccupied with wiping the blood away, but he quickly recovered. His face beetroot red, he advanced upon Skip, who was still struggling against Scoot.

Just in time, Ottilie stuck out her foot, tripping Igor. He looked up at her from the floor, rage warping his features, but before he could do anything Montie Kit bellowed, 'ENOUGH!'

Everyone froze. Montie stormed out of the kitchen stairway to stand between Igor and Ottilie.

Igor scrambled to his feet. 'SHE –'

'I saw it, Igor.'

He raised his blood-covered hand and pointed at Skip. 'Then you saw she –'

'I saw it all! Come with me,' snapped Montie. 'Isla, report to the custodian chieftess. You tell her what happened and mind you be truthful. I'll meet you in her chambers when I'm done here.'

Skip finally stopped struggling against Scoot. She glared at Igor one last time and then turned for the door.

'Take her to the infirmary, would you, Ottilie,' said Montie, gesturing to someone behind her. Ottilie turned and saw Maeve, held up between Leo and Scoot. Her eyes were half closed and her head was drooping.

Montie grabbed Igor and pulled him bodily out of the room. As she passed, Ottilie heard her say, 'Wrangler Morse can decide what to do with you.'

She hurried over to Maeve. 'What happened?'

Leo was pale, regarding Maeve with deep concern. On her other side, Scoot was fuming, his jaw jutting out.

'Are you right to walk?' said Leo.

Maeve managed a dazed nod, but Scoot and Leo helped her across the room. Ottilie hurried along with them as Scoot explained what she had missed.

'Thrike was the first one in there,' he seethed. 'She was alone. I came in and he had her by the throat. He was holding her there, talking in her ear. She couldn't move.'

'Calling me a witch ...' mumbled Maeve.

'They called all the elites in for a meeting late last night,' Leo explained. 'Told us there's another witch.'

Ottilie ground her teeth. She had been worried about what the directorate would do. It hadn't even occurred to her that they needed to fear the huntsmen too!

'I yelled out,' said Scoot. 'And at the same time Skip and Mrs Kit and a bunch of sculkies came in with the food. He let her go, but shoved her, and her head hit the wall and she fell.'

'Then Skip punched him in the face,' added Leo, with a slight smile.

'I saw that bit,' said Ottilie. 'Are you all right, Maeve?'

'Just dizzy,' she said. But Ottilie could see red marks on her neck from Igor's large hands.

'Will Skip get in trouble?' asked Scoot.

'A bit,' said Leo. 'Would have been worse if Voilies saw it, but I think Mrs Kit will help.'

As soon as the patchies declared Maeve well, Ottilie and Leo had to leave her in the infirmary. The Hunt didn't consider sitting with a shaken sculkie a good enough reason to be late for a shift. Maeve looked so distressed that Ottilie was reluctant to go, but Scoot promised he would stay as long as he could.

When they reached the sanctuary, Ottilie and Leo went to their separate pens. Then, meeting in the field, their wingerslinks stood a short distance from each other. Both dominant felines, they weren't the best of friends. Nox took every opportunity to swipe at Maestro with her claws, and Maestro had a nasty habit of butting into her side.

Leo and Ottilie looked across at each other. He was off to patrol the alpine regions, and she would be heading north-west to hunt along Flaming River. She had never been beyond the wall without Leo before. Even when she first arrived in the Narroway, Leo had been there, leading the pickings from the guard tower at the Uskler border. The bells tolled. Leo flashed her a grin, and they took off, soaring over the wall in opposite directions.

It was different, flying Nox beyond the boundary walls. Practising in the grounds was one thing but hunting in the Narroway was quite another. Nox was far better behaved. Although she did seem to consider Ottilie's commands more suggestions, the wingerslink wasn't stupid – she knew this was no place for games.

When they reached Flaming River, Ottilie had to ask three times before Nox finally slowed. Ottilie closed her eyes and listened, ears probing for anything disturbing the natural sounds of the forest below. She heard it immediately, the jarring call of cleavers not far off.

Before she had time to ask, Nox descended, skimming the trees, which thinned into a clearing. Cleavers always moved in pairs and, sure enough, she spotted two below. They looked like drawings she had seen of rock sloths of the north, only the cleavers' elongated arms spread into thin, flesh-like wings, with long claws of yellow bone at the ends, and curved spikes protruding from the joints. Like rock sloths, they had a mask of black fur across their eyes – but they had no eyes, only red gashes, as if their skin had been sliced and their eyeballs had fallen out.

The cleavers spotted Nox and hooted their piercing call. Leaping from the ground, they flapped their wings and flew at the wingerslink, like a pair of lanky bats, gnashing their teeth as they rose.

Nox was smaller than Maestro, and Ottilie could feel her movements were less powerful. She was undeniably slower, but something was soon apparent – Nox was exceptionally clever. The shrewd wingerslink knew exactly how to handle these cleavers. Not wholly by choice, Ottilie pulled back and let her take the lead.

Nox kicked out at the first cleaver. It dodged her and she seemed to know just where it would duck. She tilted to the side, dipping her wing, which smacked into the cleaver, sending it plummeting towards the ground. Nox righted herself in the air in time for Ottilie to shoot the second cleaver down with an arrow. As it fell to pieces, the first recovered itself and shot up like a stone from a slingshot. Nox rolled almost lazily, and before the cleaver had even begun to change its trajectory, Ottilie shot it down.

Giddy with victory, Ottilie threw herself forwards and hugged Nox. The wingerslink dived into a great looping spiral. She laughed out loud and held on tight. Nox was celebrating. Ottilie could feel her elation as she pulled out of the spiral, throwing her wings wide and drifting with the breeze.

After the cleavers, Ottilie tracked a scorver to where the river weakened at the base of the Red Canyon. The trail turned east and she was just about to change direction when she spotted something that stilled her breath.

Wylers hadn't been seen around the canyon since Gracie's escape. It was the first place they had looked for her, considering the pack had been sighted there in the past. After nearly two months of no signs, the Hunt had been focusing elsewhere. But Ottilie had seen it, an unmistakable flash of white. Stubbornly urging Nox forwards, they dipped between the cliffs, searching.

There was no sign of the white wyler, but she spotted an orange one, slipping into a gap shaped like a bolt of lightning, halfway up the cliff. Gracie must have waited until they stopped looking there, and then doubled back to set up camp in the canyon caves. It was clever. Ottilie didn't know how they were going to get to her; the huntsmen couldn't follow her in. There were hundreds of tunnels and caves in there, and no doubt countless wylers, just waiting for someone stupid enough to go in.

'Better go, Nox,' said Ottilie.

Nox made a disappointed rumbling noise as they headed for home. She would have to report it immediately. She didn't know if the wyler had seen her, but if it had, if Gracie knew that her position was discovered, she might be gone before the Hunt had a chance to act.

Ottilie went straight to Captain Lyre. He thanked her and dismissed her immediately, so Ottilie headed to the infirmary to see how Maeve was faring.

She was on a bed in the corner of the room. They had erected partitions around her so she could get some rest. Ottilie found Bill perched like a watchful gargoyle on the end of her bed. Maeve was lying on her back, staring at the ceiling.

'She's sad,' whispered Bill, the moment Ottilie stepped behind the partition. His mouth was drooping at the sides.

'How are you feeling?' Ottilie asked her.

'Fine,' said Maeve blankly.

Ottilie didn't quite know what to say next, but before she had a chance to consider it, the door to the infirmary creaked open and she heard Whistler's voice, saying something about a director. She didn't quite catch it but, whatever it was, the patchie left the infirmary in a hurry.

Bill slipped beneath the bed as Whistler's footsteps approached. Whistler had been kind to Maeve when she had been suspected of being the witch. Perhaps she wanted to check in. Ottilie was glad – now she wouldn't have to seek her out.

The moment Whistler stepped behind the partition, Bill's clammy hand wrapped around Ottilie's ankle. She nearly jumped. What had got into him? He was going to get caught! She shook him off, pretending to scratch her other ankle with her foot.

'I heard about what happened,' said Whistler. Her eyes darkened and she looked quite angry. 'Are you injured?' Her gaze flicked up and down.

Had Ottilie imagined it or did Whistler know someone was under the bed?

Bill reached out again, grabbing Ottilie's ankle with his hand. This time Ottilie didn't move. She didn't want to draw any attention to the bed, but something was wrong.

'Just a bump and some bruises,' said Maeve, still staring at the ceiling.

'You can come out,' said Whistler abruptly.

Ottilie froze. Bill's hand shook as he released her ankle and slipped out from under the bed. He stood on the other side of it, looking more terrified than Ottilie had ever seen him.

A strange smile crept onto Whistler's face. 'A goedl. Always a pleasure.' She ducked into a lopsided bow, her stormy eyes fixed on Bill.

Ottilie didn't know what to do. What was going to happen to Bill? Would Whistler report this?

Bill's gaze was set on Ottilie. He seemed to be trying to communicate with her. What was happening? Was he terrified because he had been caught?

'Go ahead and speak, will you,' said Whistler, still staring at Bill. 'We all want to hear it.'

'That's her,' mumbled Bill.

'What?' said Ottilie, her veins frosting over.

'That's the girl,' he said in a strangled whisper, titling his head in Whistler's direction.

'The girl?' It took her a moment, but she got there. The girl! He was trying to say that Whistler was the girl he had come to warn her about. Ottilie could hear her own heartbeat. Her shoulders rose up towards her ears. All of her instincts told her to run, to get away from Whistler.

'Go on,' said Whistler, dangerously.

'Dreams …' said Bill. 'I've been seeing, or remembering, a girl, sometimes younger, sometimes older –'

'It was Gracie, Bill,' said Ottilie. 'You said, after the bird showed us, you said that was the girl.'

Bill shook his head. 'The girl in the room. I meant the one standing above. I meant the one doing the binding … that was the girl and this … this is her.'

Whistler's eyes flashed with an impossible midnight light, and across the room Ottilie heard the scrape of the bolt sliding across the door.

✦ 35 ✦

The Witch

Ottilie drew her cutlass. Maeve scrambled out of bed. She was unarmed but positioned herself in front of Bill all the same. Whistler was the witch. She had been inside the grounds all this time. Now that she was unveiled, what would she do? Ottilie's thoughts flew to Gully. Where was he? If Whistler went on a rampage, would he be in danger? She thought he might be on a hunt, but she couldn't remember.

'Bill, is it?' said Whistler with a birdlike croon.

No-one answered her.

'What do you know?' she asked, cocking her head.

'A girl with a bent hand … a witch … when you were very young, you used to scare people. And hurt them,' said Bill, as if the words scraped his throat.

'Hardly fair, Bill.' Whistler flicked back her sleeve to reveal a gnarled hand, bent out of shape, with a thumb significantly smaller than its left twin. 'How much of the story do you know?'

'Pieces, all jumbled up,' said Bill.

Whistler caught Ottilie staring at her hand. 'It wasn't always this bad. My wrist was bent and my thumb was too small, but my father tried to have it fixed. Now it's a claw.'

'Unlock the door,' Ottilie said in response.

'I gave you a clue, you know,' Whistler said, flinging her sleeve back over her hand. 'The night you stole my book. I gave you his name.'

'What do you mean, his name? Whose name?' Ottilie tried to calm herself, struggling to think.

'You wanted to know what all this is about.' Whistler waved her arms in the air. 'Why everything's happening. Where they all came from.'

'A witch,' said Ottilie. 'We figured that out without your clue.'

Whistler laughed. 'A witch! Yes, yes, a witch! A horrible, terrible, wicked witch setting the dredretches upon you, very good. Fairly obvious, though, piglet.'

'Piglet?'

'Pigs are smart. Pigs are tough. Take a compliment when it's given. Now prove me right, clever girl. What name did I give you?'

Ottilie strained her mind. Whistler had only given them one thing, a book … 'Sol,' said Ottilie. 'The name of the royal family.'

'Fennix Sol,' said Bill, dizzily, as if he had just remembered something.

'Indeed,' said Whistler.

'Who …' said Ottilie.

'My name,' said Whistler. 'When I was a girl. That was my name.'

'You're of the royal line?' said Maeve, her eyes darting to the window.

'I am,' said Whistler, her mouth tipping down, as if the answer tasted bad. 'But that's not why I gave it. You wanted to know why the dredretches are here? Who made up the rule of innocence? I gave you a clue. When I say the name Sol, who do you think of?'

Ottilie ran through the royals she knew. Seika Devil-Slayer, the princess who felled the fendevil, and Viago the Vanquisher, who broke the promise – both long dead – and Varrio Sol, the current king, the creator of the Narroway Hunt.

'The king,' said Maeve, simply.

Ottilie shook her head. 'The king didn't raise the dredretches. He doesn't control them. He's not a witch.' Whistler was talking nonsense.

'How do you know?' said Whistler.

For a second Ottilie didn't have an answer. But

finally, she said, 'Because Bill wanted to warn me about you. We saw you binding Gracie to the wylers. You turned that wyler into her bloodbeast. And I saw you the day the kappabak nearly killed me and Leo, and the day the yickers attacked in Floodwood.'

'I was testing you,' she said.

Ottilie choked on air. 'Testing me? Why?'

'Because I knew you were a potential candidate from the first. You're a fascinating little hatchling. You snuck in here, fooling everyone – not me, of course, but I was eager to see how it would play out, and I am thorough in my research. Did I set some nasty obstacles for you? Yes. But they made you stronger. They made you stay.'

All Ottilie could see was Floodwood – Christopher Crow sprawled on the ground, Leo resting a hand over the hole in his chest. 'What do you mean, a candidate? Why did you want me to stay?'

'I just told you. You're fascinating. I wanted to see what you're made of. I'm a champion of fascinating people. That's why I chose Gracie.'

'Gracie's not fascinating, she's evil,' spat Ottilie. 'I'm nothing like her.'

'Of course not. Everyone's different. But you can come with me if you like.'

'What?' said Ottilie, genuinely surprised.

'Well, the jig is up. I'll be leaving in a moment. It's about time, too. I told him thirty years – three decades that battle-happy buffoon couldn't send out his men. It's time to give the king back his toy soldiers. He'll be over the moon. War is his favourite thing, and what a war we'll have.'

'What do you mean, war?' said Ottilie, her voice thinning with every word.

'As I said. You can come. Maeve as well.' Her bird-like eyes fixed on Maeve. 'You're an intriguing thing. Gracie already offered, of course. We were hoping you would say yes, but look, another chance – best take it.' She snatched at the air with her sleeve.

'We're not going anywhere with you,' said Maeve.

'Pity.' Whistler cocked her head. 'But I'm afraid I can't let you keep the goedl. I like to be in control of the clues, see, and goedls tend to know just a bit too much.'

Ottilie fired an arrow at Whistler without a thought. Whistler waved her hand and turned it to ash. She didn't have time to marvel at it, because Whistler grabbed Bill by the wrist. Ottilie and Maeve both lunged at her, but Whistler flicked her sleeve and knocked them down with a gust of wind.

The bolted door flew open and Whistler marched Bill out into the lavender fields. Ottilie and Maeve stumbled to their feet and scrambled after her but it was too late. There was a terrible shriek, which seemed to be coming from somewhere inside Whistler. Her hair stood on end, mouth stretched wide, and she transformed into a great winged creature. She was like a dredretch, but not quite. Her beak was hooked and needle sharp. Her grey eyes darkened to thundercloud black and her feathers were all the colours of a storm.

She launched into the air, Bill's long pale arm clasped firmly in her talons, and soared out over the boundary wall, rolling and sweeping, dodging arrows from the wall and disappearing into the Narroway.

36

Hostage

'Tell someone!' Ottilie cried as she spun and sprinted in the other direction.

'What?' Maeve called. 'Where are you going?'

'I'm going after them!'

Ottilie had never run so fast in her life. She tore down to the lower grounds, through the wingerslink sanctuary, where she saddled Nox and leapt out into the field.

'Ott?' It was Leo, who had finished his morning hunt but was still astride Maestro.

'Help!' she cried, gasping for breath. 'Come with me, Leo. The witch, she's got Bill – she's got my friend. Come with me!'

'What? Who's Bill?'

'Please.' There was no time to explain.

Leo blinked. 'I'll follow you.'

The two wingerslinks cleared the wall. There was no sign. Nothing. Ottilie didn't even know where to begin. Tears streamed down her face as she shouted, 'BILL!'

That was when she remembered the canyon. Whistler had recruited Gracie. She might be taking Bill to the canyon caves.

Nox seemed to know that this was serious. Ottilie threw herself forwards and Nox shot over the tops of the trees. They were still a way off the canyon when she heard a cry from below.

'BILL!' she called, pushing Nox into a dive.

Beside her, Maestro copied.

Ottilie felt as if a clawed thing was trying to tear out of her chest. It wasn't Bill. She could just make them out, from flashes beneath the thick canopy. It was Scoot, Ned and Gully, crowded into a dense patch of forest, surrounded by the wyler pack.

Leo had gone deathly pale, his eyes fixed on Ned, who was warding off a wyler with a spear. The wyler leapt. Ned lunged and impaled it. That seemed to set them off. Every wyler attacked at once.

Her heart hammering, Ottilie, still in the air, tried to shoot them down from above, but the branches were too tangled and everyone was moving too fast. She couldn't risk hitting one of her friends.

The towering webwood trees were like spindly giants, their many arms intertwined, making it impossible to land. Ottilie and Leo had to touch down nearby, in a glade at the edge of Flaming River. Together, they charged on foot to join the fray.

Gully rolled beneath a pouncing wyler. His head snapped up and their eyes locked, but Ottilie couldn't focus on him or Bill or anything else. If she did, she would get someone killed. She dodged and swung, injuring one wyler and felling another. There was a growl from behind her. The white wyler prowled through the trees, Gracie Moravec on its back.

'Where is he?' Ottilie bellowed. She gasped and stumbled. Leo had grabbed her shirt and wrenched her back, just before a wyler could sink its teeth into her side.

Gracie simply tilted her head and continued her slow approach. Ottilie fired an arrow. The white wyler dodged it. She fired another, and it dodged again. Gracie was clutching its fur for dear life, but still her face remained smooth.

She shook her head at Ottilie, as if to say, *bad girl*. She slid off the white wyler, drawing the knife that Leo had given her, and another one Ottilie didn't recognise. Hearing Scoot's strangled cry, she knew immediately where it had come from. It was Bayo's knife.

'Take her brother,' Gracie said quietly.

Ottilie's heart cracked open. Her vision swung. It was so wrong. It didn't seem real, like it was a game of make-believe and this ordinary girl was pretending to be a villain.

Gracie's eyes flashed red.

Ottilie found her balance and whirled around as every wyler turned to Gully. Three pounced at once. He ducked and dodged, fighting them off, but one got through, severing his thumb.

'NO!' she cried, running towards him. She couldn't breathe. It felt as if the ground were breaking apart.

Leo took the opportunity to shoot one down. Gracie's eyes flashed again and the white wyler lunged at Leo. Scoot ran to help him and Ottilie could hear the clashing of metal behind her. Ned must have been fighting Gracie.

Gully was still upright. He was bleeding badly, but all right. Ottilie breathed again. He was wearing it out of habit; Gully didn't need his ring anymore. But warding off the sickness would only get him so far. Surrounded by the advancing wylers, his spear pointed at them, all he could do was back away.

Gracie cried out behind Ottilie. Ned must have struck her.

Ottilie fired an arrow, felling one of the wylers advancing on Gully. She needed to get to him. She had to bandage his hand, stop it bleeding.

'Ott!' cried Scoot.

Ottilie looked around just in time to roll out of the way of the enormous white wyler. From the ground, she could see Ned with his cutlass, fighting Gracie and her knives. Ottilie had never seen blades moving so fast. Whatever the truth was about Gracie's history, she had learned to use a knife long before Leo put one in her hand.

For one chilling moment, it looked like Gracie was going to win. But Ottilie couldn't watch; the white wyler was coming at her. From the ground, she fired an arrow. It dodged, but the arrow scraped the side of its face. It screeched, and Gracie cried out with it. Of course, it was her bloodbeast – they were bound! Ottilie aimed another arrow.

'I'll make them kill him!' Gracie shrieked, her voice harsher than Ottilie had ever heard it.

She believed it, without a doubt. Gracie wasn't really human anymore. She wasn't a thirteen-year-old girl. She was bound to a dredretch, a dredretch that had become a giant, heart-eating bloodbeast. Gracie was every bit the monster that the white wyler was.

Her eyes flashed and Ottilie saw the wylers bend to spring at Gully. Ottilie lowered her bow without a thought. Her hands shook as she released it. She clenched them into trembling fists and grounded her feet.

Ned was about to strike.

'Only I can stop them!' Gracie trilled as the wylers leapt at Gully.

Ottilie's heart stopped.

Ned dropped his cutlass.

Gracie's eyes flashed and the wylers pulled back.

'No-one moves or I tell them to attack again,' said Gracie, the airiness returning to her tone. 'They can't get all of you, but they can certainly get one of you.'

None of them moved. Gracie looked down at the blood dribbling from a gash on her upper arm, caused by Ned's blade.

'You're coming with me,' she said venomously.

'I'm not going anywhere,' said Ned.

'Yes, you are,' she said. 'Otherwise he dies.' She pointed at Gully, still surrounded by wylers.

'Ned, don't,' said Gully.

'What do you want him for?' spat Scoot.

'Security,' said Gracie, calmly. 'You tell the Hunt to stop searching for me.' She pointed her blade at Ned. 'He'll be fine as long as I'm left alone.' Gracie climbed back onto the white wyler and held her hand out to Ned.

'Ned,' said Leo warningly.

Ottilie was frozen in place, her instincts a mess.

'Ned!' said Gully and Leo at the same time.

In that moment Ned looked very young and utterly lost. Ottilie could see him shift to step forward, away from Gracie, to safety. But she sensed him steel himself. He looked to Leo and then to Ottilie. She felt as if her ribs were cracking, pressing in, as he took Gracie's hand and swung up behind her.

Leo let out a noise like a wounded dog and lunged towards them.

'No-one moves,' Gracie repeated, flinging out her arm and pointing her knife in Gully's direction.

'Leo,' Ottilie pleaded.

He froze.

'I can be in their eyes. I'll know if you do. No-one moves until I tell them to leave you. That includes the cats,' she added, waving gently at the sky, where Ottilie caught glimpses of the wingerslinks circling above the treetops.

They stood, motionless: Gully, blood leaking from his hand, surrounded by the wylers, and Scoot, Leo and Ottilie, like statues, as Ned disappeared with Gracie and the white wyler.

There were shrieks from the sky. Ottilie risked a glance and saw that, high above the webwood trees, jivvies had begun to swarm.

✦ 37 ✦

Missing

Ottilie was slumped on a chair in Gully's bedchamber. The patchies had fixed his hand as best they could and given him something to help him sleep. Ottilie couldn't bring herself to leave his side, not after everything that had happened. Not now that Bill and Ned had both been taken prisoner.

The jivvies' bloodlust had been their undoing. Almost half of the flock had been torn apart in the manic fray. The wingerslinks had helped keep the rest of them at bay until the wylers withdrew and Ottilie, Leo, Gully and Scoot dared to move.

Leo and Scoot had talked to the directorate, and a distraught Maeve had visited the infirmary to tell her that the directorate now knew what had happened with Whistler. Ottilie hadn't seen any of them since. She didn't know where Leo was. Under normal circumstances she thought he would have gone after Gracie, but it was too big a risk. If anyone came looking for her, she would hurt Ned.

Ottilie couldn't stop reliving the moment he had taken Gracie's hand. Where was he now? What was happening to him?

Gracie hadn't seemed to know about Whistler revealing herself, but she must by now. Ottilie hoped Ned and Bill were in the same place; at least then they wouldn't be alone. Of course, there was no guarantee that Bill was all right. Ottilie's head fell into her shaking hands. She didn't know what to do.

There was a small knock at the door, and Preddy slipped into the room. 'How is he?' he said softly.

'They say he'll be fine,' she whispered, her throat swollen. 'At least it was his left hand, not his right.' She glanced sadly at her sleeping brother. 'How's Scoot? Have you seen him? Or Leo?'

'Leo's over at the training yards,' said Preddy. 'Scoot's gone to his room. He's not … not doing very well. First Bayo, and now …'

Ottilie sniffed, a painful lump rising in her throat. 'Does he blame me?'

'What? Why would he? If you and Leo hadn't come they might all three be dead,' said Preddy.

'Because I said we should stay.' Her voice cracked. 'If we'd run away last year like we'd planned, none of this would have happened.'

'This would still be happening, Ottilie, we just wouldn't be involved,' said Preddy gently.

'I, well … that's what I mean,' said Ottilie, her eyes filling with tears.

'I know. But that's the point, isn't it. We can't walk away. They need us. It's too important.'

'What does she want?' said Ottilie sharply.

Gully sighed and rolled over in his sleep.

'Whistler?' said Preddy.

'She said something about giving the king back his toys, and the beginning of a war. She's going to start a war. Why? What's it all for?' Ottilie clenched her fists. 'And her army … her army is the dredretches. That's what she's been doing here, building her army. But we've been cutting them down … and if she wants the dredretches to attack the Usklers, they have to get past us, past the Hunt.'

'She'll be planning a big move against us, then,' said Preddy, thoughtfully.

Ottilie's heart thudded. 'Do you think they'll attack here? At Fiory?'

'I don't think that would make much sense. We're in the middle here. With Richter and Arko on either side and nowhere to retreat because south and north of us is ocean – and the dredretches won't go near it.'

'Most of them,' said Ottilie, thinking of the knopoes.

Preddy nodded gravely. 'I think, to take control of the Narroway, she'd have to start from the west.'

Ottilie frowned, thinking hard. 'Richter backs right onto the Laklands, doesn't it?' she said.

'Yes,' said Preddy. 'Part of our job over there was to man the border wall between the Narroway and the Laklands. The coast cuts in a fair way on either side, so it's not a huge infestation near the border.'

'It makes sense, though,' said Ottilie. 'If I were her, I would try to take Fort Richter, then knock down that west border wall and bring in more dredretches from the Laklands. If she has some control over them, like Gracie does the wylers, I bet she can make them pass through coastal areas that they wouldn't normally ...' Ottilie's mind drifted back to the knopoes, living near the coast.

'Someone was controlling them ...' she muttered. Out of the way, in an unexpected place – it was as if someone had been testing them, testing their limits.

'What?' said Preddy.

'I think someone was controlling the knopo troop at Jungle Bay.' She frowned – was it Whistler? Or someone else? She had thought that one of them might have been a bloodbeast like the white wyler – so perhaps Gracie wasn't the only one bound to a dredretch. Perhaps there were others like her. Or many more like her – just what, exactly, were they up against?

Ottilie found Leo in the training yards at dawn. His face was pale and puffy and his eyes drooped with the weight of the night hours. He was slumped against the fence, digging his knife into the dirt.

She approached him silently, unsure of what to say.

'It's quiet,' he said, without looking at her.

'It's dawn,' she said. The birds were singing.

'No. Listen.'

He was right. Something was different. Sounds were missing. Not just sounds: a presence was missing.

'They're gone,' he said.

'What do you mean?'

'I went up there.' He pointed his muddy knife at the boundary wall. 'I walked it over and over last night. I didn't see a single one. They've gone somewhere.'

'The dredretches?'

He nodded.

Ottilie had been so caught up in her own thoughts and fears she hadn't even noticed the absence. Any prickling of nerves or tight feeling of foreboding she had attributed to losing Ned and Bill, or Gully's injury.

Where had they gone? Were they all gathered together? They must have been. It all lined up.

'We think Whistler might attack Fort Richter,' said Ottilie, breathing through the rolling, burning sensation in her chest.

Leo nodded again. 'The directorate thinks so too, but they don't want to send us down there in case they actually circle round and go to Arko. They're deciding what to do about it.' He looked at her. 'We have to get him back, Ott.'

'We have to get them both back,' she said.

She told him the story from the beginning: how Bill had helped her catch up to the pickers, how he had cut her hair and stolen the pickings list, how he had come here to warn her about Whistler, and how Whistler had taken him captive, just like Gracie had taken Ned.

Leo didn't say anything for quite a while. Finally he said, 'I thought you were done keeping secrets from me.'

'I know. I'm sorry,' said Ottilie, without guilt.

'Do you trust me?' he asked, with fresh pain in his eyes.

She didn't answer.

'I'm so sorry for all of it,' he burst out. 'For what I did, and for saying all those terrible things.'

Weak little witch played again in her memory.

'I didn't mean a word of it,' he said firmly. 'I was just in a rage, because I felt stupid for not seeing that you were a girl. I know it's my fault!'

'What is?' She frowned.

'That you don't trust me. But, Ott, I promise you can. You can tell me anything, I won't ev–' His voice shook and he swallowed. 'I won't ever betray you again.'

'I know,' she said. And that was the truth. She realised it then, in that moment. She knew he would never betray her, or anyone under her protection. 'I should probably tell you something about Maeve ...'

The message came just after sunrise. The directorate were still in their chamber, deliberating, planning, but it was all too late. The dredretches were attacking Fort Richter.

'This will be different from anything you have ever faced,' said Captain Lyre.

They were gathered in the Moon Court, armed, ready to travel. There was one notable absence – Conductor Edderfed's throne was empty. He was at Arko for the fledgling trials. They would have just finished. Ottilie wondered what those freshly picked fledges would be thinking, watching the huntsmen march west for battle.

She remembered her own sense of purpose, once she had realised the enormity of the threat that the dredretches posed. Would those fledges feel the same? Or would they be panicking, terrified, desperate to go home?

'Under the influence of the witch, Whistler, the dredretches are attacking en masse,' Captain Lyre continued. 'This is not a flock of jivvies, or a trick of flares. This is worse than a pack of lycoats or a swarm of stingers. This is every dredretch. Cleavers, oxies, giffersnaks, wylers, barrogauls, kappabaks. All together. All at once. If the witches take Fort Richter they will move eastward to us, to Fiory, then to Arko, and finally there will be nothing left standing between the dredretches and the Usklers. Boys. This is your duty. Defend the Narroway. Defend the Usklers!'

A bone singer beat the drum and the huntsmen stamped their feet.

'Gully, what are you doing here?' Ottilie muttered as he appeared at her side.

'I'm coming!' said Gully, outraged.

'You are not!' she said, unable to contain her panic.

Around them the courtyard echoed with the sound of drums and stamping feet. It was powerful, like hail and rain and thunder cracking. Ottilie felt it in her bones, and it gave her courage.

'You're recovering, Gully, you can't,' said Preddy.

'You can't stop me!' His voice was shrill.

'You're not coming,' Scoot said roughly.

'Scoo—'

'I'll chain you to a tree and guard it myself if I have to. You're not coming,' he said, his voice shaking. 'No-one else is dying.'

'Ned's not —'

'No-one else!' said Scoot so violently that Preddy actually jumped. 'You're injured, Gully. You're not coming!'

Gully looked into Scoot's anguished face and nodded. 'Be careful,' he said, to all of them, taking Ottilie's hand in his good one and squeezing it tight. He blinked at her. 'Don't get … don't …'

'I'll be all right,' she said, her voice firm. She would be all right. She had to be all right. Because she was going to get Bill and Ned back.

38

The Cave

Ottilie and Leo had a plan. Word from the west was that Gracie and Whistler were both in the Richter zone. Ottilie had no doubt that they had left Ned and Bill well-guarded, but it was now or never.

Keeping their distance from the horses, the winger-slinks and their flyers lined up facing the boundary wall. Wrangler Morse raised an orange flag and one by one they shot out over the wall and soared westward, to Richter's aid.

Ottilie and Leo flew side by side. Behind them a scattering of huntsmen remained with the shepherds to guard Fiory, and she would be forever grateful to Scoot that Gully was among them.

Far below, she could see the mounts disappearing into the trees, their horses the size of mice. A little further back were carriages pulled by mountain bucks, carrying several wranglers and directors, flanked by the steadily marching footmen.

Ottilie and Leo stayed on course for as long as they could manage it, but once they reached Flaming River, Maestro and Nox swept northward.

'Where do you think you're going?' called Igor Thrike.

Neither responded. No-one would come after them. Everyone was needed at Richter, and if all went to plan, Ottilie and Leo would be there only a little later than the rest.

They reached the Red Canyon and dismounted on a ledge by the lightning-shaped gap.

'Anything?' Leo muttered to Maestro, who was sniffing the air, his tail flicking back and forth. Beside him, Nox was still, tense, ready for a fight.

Leo trailed Ottilie through the opening in the cliff. The passageway wasn't wide enough for Maestro and Nox to follow along. She felt uneasy leaving them behind, but they didn't have a choice. This was the only place she could think to look and there was no time to seek a wider gap.

They kept their weapons drawn, but after several twists and turns, they still hadn't encountered anything.

Finally, the tunnel opened up and Ottilie could barely believe what was in front of her. A great cavern stretched out, and built into the walls of the cave were what appeared to be the ruins of ancient buildings. Or the ruins of one great building, it was difficult to be sure. There were crumbling statues and broken archways and, over by the far wall, what looked like the skeleton of an old well. Something was slumped against it. Drawing nearer, Ottilie saw the bent shadow of a boy.

'Ned,' Leo breathed, and they hurried towards him.

Ned looked up very slowly. It was clear he had not been kept comfortably. One of his eyes was bruised and swollen, he had a great gash on his cheek, and Ottilie could see a string of strange, almost star-shaped burns up one of his arms.

He looked at her with unfocused eyes and something to the left of him caught her gaze. Carved into the stone was an ancient engraving of a duck. What was this place?

She looked around. There was no sign of Bill. But she spotted something else that made her blood drain all the way to her toes. High on a crumbling ledge was a bone singer.

Ottilie gasped. She knew him. She had worked with him when she was a shovelie. His name was Nicolai. Recognisable in his pale grey robes, he sat cross-legged with gleaming eyes, and beside him, as if standing guard, was a shank.

She should have known! So much had happened after Whistler's unveiling, Ottilie hadn't pieced it together. The bone singers were working with her! Nicolai was here guarding Ned, and the shank …

Shanks were usually small, like stretched rats covered in yellow spines. But this one was the size of a large house cat. Its scaly face was chestnut brown and its spines were like rusted blades. Ottilie knew immediately what she was seeing. The shank was another bloodbeast, and she would have bet her ring that it was bound to Nicolai.

'The bone singers,' she whispered.

Leo whipped around and aimed an arrow at Nicolai, but he hesitated. His uncertainty mirrored her own. That was a boy up there, a boy she knew. Leo lowered his bow.

Ottilie's thoughts whirled. She remembered Bayo telling her a bone singer had been taken ill after she and Leo had felled the knopoes. She had never thought to find out if he recovered … but, remembering Gracie's shriek when the white wyler had been grazed by her arrow, she suspected that if the bloodbeast died, the person bound to it died, too. The thought made her feel sick. She couldn't for the life of her remember who had felled the biggest knopo – it could have been her or Leo.

Ottilie had so many questions. All this time Whistler and her bone singers had been pretending to help, when really … really they had been controlling the dredretches, maybe even raising them from the ground. Their rituals with bones and salt … was it all a ruse, just for show?

That must have been how the wylers were getting in. The bone singers probably had secret doors through the boundary walls, and uncanny ways of concealing them. But was every bone singer bad? Ottilie remembered Bonnie, the bone singer who had hated the Withering Wood — surely she couldn't be one of Whistler's minions, could she?

Ned gripped Ottilie's hand. She turned to him. He opened his mouth, but it took him a moment to make words. 'Watch out,' he croaked, staring behind them.

Ottilie whipped around. Prowling out of the shadows, from every corner of the cavern, were dredretches.

'Trap,' Ned muttered.

Ottilie nocked an arrow. Beside her, Leo drew his cutlass. On the ground, Ned pulled a knife from Leo's boot.

'Ned, where's Bill?' said Ottilie quickly. 'There was another captive, did they bring him here?'

'Took him away,' he said. 'Didn't want you to get him. She knew you'd come. I think they hoped there would be more of you.'

They were surrounded. Trapped. There were wylers and lycoats, morgies and learies. Nicolai and the shank didn't move. He was doing something in that trance and the shank was guarding him, but there was no time to dwell on murky predictions.

The lycoats pounced first. Ottilie shot one down and Leo struck out, taking another. From above, a giffersnak dropped. Ottilie and Leo scattered, and Ned managed a clumsy roll out of the way. It was chaos. In twos and threes, they attacked. Ottilie couldn't count how many she knocked back.

Then the little ones came, scurrying down the walls and up out of cracks in the ground. The shanks led them in, controlled by Nicolai. Then came yickers, spike mites, barbed toads, and countless more that Ottilie had never seen before. They could beat back the big ones, wave after wave, but the little monsters slipped between the others, the shanks a synchronised unit under Nicolai's control.

Ottilie spun and pierced a yicker with an arrow just a second before it landed on Ned's face. Another yicker zoomed towards him; Ottilie aimed again and while she was distracted, a dark-scaled morgie leapt off the well, right at her head. Ottilie lunged sideways, and a searing pain sliced her ear. She reached up and felt hot blood trickle through her fingers. Dizzily, she realised the very top of her ear had been torn clean off. She swayed on her feet.

There was a screech from the tunnels beyond, a live screech, an owl's screech.

'What is that?' Leo shouted above the clamour.

Soaring into the cavern came a shining black owl.

'That's Maeve!' Ottilie cried, clutching her ear, trying to slow the bleeding. She couldn't feel it – she couldn't feel anything.

The two wingerslinks were behind Maeve. She must have found them a tunnel wide enough. The owl circled and dived, plucking a barbed toad off the ground and flinging it into the cave wall. Nox pounced on a lycoat, tearing it in two. Leo whistled and pointed – Maestro curled around Ned, shielding him from harm.

'We have to get out of here!' said Leo.

Blood streaming down her neck, Ottilie fought her way over to Nox and clambered onto her back. Across the cavern, Leo was pulling Ned up into Maestro's saddle. A wyler leapt at Nox and Maeve dived again, piercing its eyes with her talons.

Ottilie turned to Nicolai and aimed an arrow. She took a breath, thinking of Bayo Amadory, and drew back the string, but something stopped her. Shifting her aim left, she focused on the bloodbeast. She still couldn't do it.

Nox seemed to sense where Ottilie's focus lay. The wingerslink leapt from the ground and rose, beat by beat, into the air. The bronze shank dashed to stand in front of Nicolai, its spines flaring so that it doubled in size.

Ottilie felt Nox bracing to dive, but she couldn't let her do it. Nox had to listen to her. Tipping her toes down, she dug in hard and threw her weight back, commanding the wingerslink to stay where she was. Nox let out a roar of frustration that echoed off the cave walls. Maestro roared in response and Maeve let out a shrieking battle cry.

Ottilie's heart raced and Nox changed direction, diving not at the bloodbeast but at the mass of dredretches that were closing in on Maestro. Swiping with her blade-like claws and gnashing her teeth, Nox sent bits of dredretch flying in all directions like leaves in the wind.

'Maeve, show us the way out!' called Ottilie, aiming an arrow at a learie that was zigzagging up the rock wall, preparing to pounce from above.

Maeve turned to face her and screeched. Ottilie didn't speak bird but she knew what she meant.

'He's not here!' she said. Bill. Maeve was looking for Bill.

Maeve screeched again and soared out through the tunnel. The wingerslinks bounded behind, following her around every twist and turn, finally leaping out of a wide opening in the cliff, into the air.

They settled on a shelf high above the canyon.

'We have to take Ned to Fiory,' said Ottilie. 'He's hurt.' Her ear throbbed, and she felt unsteady in the saddle. She had never thought such a small part of her could bleed this much. Free of the danger for just a moment, Ottilie felt the shock of it: a tiny part of her had been cut away. It was just her ear, only the very tip, but it was a piece of her and it was gone.

She felt a wave of panic and reached down to grip Nox's fur hard, fighting the urge to spiral into terror and tears. If the wingerslink was bothered by Ottilie's firm grip, she didn't show it. She thought she felt Nox push up against her hands, an offer of support.

There was no time to go to pieces. She took a sharp breath and released Nox's fur. With her knife, she began to cut away a strip of her shirt to tie around her head. For now, it was the best she could do.

'Not Fiory,' croaked Ned. 'They went to Richter, we have to help!'

'You can't help anyone like this,' said Leo.

'There's no time,' said Ned.

Leo looked westward. Ottilie couldn't argue. He was right. They had to go.

39

Fort Richter

Black clouds were gathering in the south and an emerald glow sharpened the sun. From the air, Ottilie could see where the land thinned and the ocean cut in on either side. Richter was perched on a cliff on the north-facing shore. Preddy had told Ottilie that its coastal location made it more peaceful than Fiory, the fort safeguarded by sea air. She had an image of Richter in her mind, shaped by stories from Preddy's time there. That picture would be forever replaced by the scene that awaited them below.

What was left of Richter's boundary wall stretched in honeycombed fragments. Dredretches barrelled, clambered, slithered and swept through the gaps. Ottilie could see Gracie on the back of the white wyler, cutting through huntsmen, knocking them aside and slashing with her knives. Whistler's winged form was perched on a turret, screeching into the cloud-threatened sky.

She wondered if there were more bone singers with bloodbeasts. Gracie could control the wylers, and Nicolai the shanks. What other dredretches roaming this battlefield were being controlled by one of Whistler's minions? Perhaps they were tucked away safely somewhere, in trances. Not Gracie, though. Gracie wanted to play.

There was no time to get Ned somewhere safe. He simply clung to Leo, pale but determined. Fiory's mounts were just beginning to fight their way through the field below the Fort. Richter's shepherd pack dashed here and there. It didn't look as if the footmen had arrived yet. Ottilie could see flyers from all three stations, dipping and diving, picking up injured huntsmen from within the battered walls and flying them to safer ground.

With a whistle and a spark, a flare spiralled out of the sky. Nox rolled and Ottilie swung her cutlass, slicing it in half. Swinging upside down, she saw a streak of white. It was Gracie, her knives flashing in the stormy light. Fury blazed at the sight of her. Nox soared in a wide circle, sweeping down to cut across her path. The white wyler tossed its head high and shrieked. Nox met it with a roar so powerful Ottilie felt as if she were roaring too.

The wyler's white fur was caked with mud and blood, both red and black. Gracie looked tired, but very alive. Her pale eyes shone with excitement as she flashed Ottilie her first true smile.

The wyler bent and lunged at Nox, but Nox leapt overhead. Swatting with her claws, she knocked the white wyler down, and Gracie was unseated. Scrambling back up onto its back, she threw a knife. Ottilie reeled backwards and Nox tucked in her wing, the blade passing by without contact.

The wyler changed direction faster than Ottilie's eyes could catch. Before she knew what was happening, Gracie and the wyler were fleeing northward.

Nox leapt into the air, catching the wind, and soon cut in front once more. Gracie was panting. She had mud smeared on her face from the fall.

Neither moved. They had broken free of the fighting, and the crashing of waves against rock half-drowned any sound. A cool salty breeze brushed across Ottilie's face, clearing her head. They were perilously close to the cliff's edge and Gracie had the higher ground. She saw Bayo's knife, clutched in Gracie's right hand, and spat, 'What happened to you?'

Gracie didn't respond. The white wyler snarled.

'You're from Longwood, aren't you?' Ottilie pressed, vying for time, trying to think of a way out. 'The camps near the Narroway border?'

The wyler leapt and Gracie lashed out with a knife. Ottilie flattened herself against Nox, just missing the blade. Nox swiped out with her claws and the wyler dodged, losing its prime position.

'How long have you been like this?' She wanted to know, to understand. She didn't want to believe that Gracie was just bad.

Nox had the wyler right up against the edge. Ottilie remembered the rumour that Gracie had pushed someone off a cliff near Scarpy Village. She should end it right here. Gracie was dangerous, too dangerous. She could let Nox do it. She could feel the wingerslink's energy flowing forwards, wanting to attack. Even if Ottilie tried to stop her, Nox wouldn't necessarily listen. She could just allow it.

Gracie couldn't hide her unease, but a knowing look mingled with the doubt. 'You can't do it, can you?' she said, glancing backwards, towards the drop. 'How long have I been like this?' She offered a slight shrug. 'I could tell you the first thing I remember, if you like.' Her lips twitched. She knew Ottilie couldn't end it.

'I remember when my parents set a fire,' said Gracie. 'I remember the building lighting up. It looked like the end of the world.'

'A fire? Where?' said Ottilie. Her stomach dropped. She didn't want to hear Gracie say it.

'I think it was Scarpy Village,' said Gracie, innocently.

She loved this – taunting Ottilie, knowing she wouldn't do anything about it.

'The villagers were very upset. It turns out there was a mother and her young daughter inside. The woman got badly burnt and the villagers attacked our camp. We all got separated after that,' said Gracie, almost lazily. 'Still nothing?' She cocked her head. 'I don't know why she's so interested in you.'

Ottilie could hear the bitterness in her voice.

'You don't have it in you,' said Gracie. 'Though after the binding, that won't matter anymore, everything darkens once you're bound.'

'What are you talking about?' Ottilie spat.

'She wanted to give you a really good one, too,' said Gracie. 'She had the kappabak all lined up. She's not like me.' She patted the white wyler. 'She can control any of them. She dropped it in your path to see what would happen. All you need is a mortal wound from a dredretch to get it started, but you and Leo destroyed the poor thing before it could harm you. Though she only found that more impressive.'

Ottilie was sickened, her senses slack. The sound of the waves faded into a fold of her mind. Whistler had intended to bind her to the kappabak?

'She said you were wasting away as a shovelie,' said Gracie. 'But then you became a huntsman, the first girl ever … she wanted to see how that would play out.'

Ottilie wanted to tell Gracie to shut up, but couldn't find the words. Her curiosity had the reins and refused to let her move.

'Why can she control them? What is she?' said Ottilie.

Gracie smiled. 'Interested, are you? She's like Maeve. She's a fiorn, or she was one. She's a little different now that she sings to them.'

'Sings to them?' said Ottilie. 'What are you talking about?'

Gracie looked like she was dangling a bit of eel above a hungry wingerslink. 'She can make it so they won't hurt you at all.' She pulled a delicate chain out from beneath her shirt, something sharp dangling from the end. 'Of course, I don't need the protection anymore, but it's useful for other things –'

'What do you mean she sings to them?'

'She summons them,' said Gracie, as if Ottilie was too thick to comprehend it. 'Viago the Vanquisher was her father. He broke the promise and the dredretches came. That was the Laklands, of course, a hundred years ago – but that's where she got the idea.'

Viago the Vanquisher's daughter – the one they called the clawed witch. Whistler had told them that story herself. Ottilie could remember it as if it were yesterday. In the Bone Tower, she hadn't said the dredretches came from the Laklands – she'd said they were here because of the Laklands, because that was where she got the idea. Her father had broken a promise and doomed a kingdom, and now she was doing the same, in her own way, for her own reasons …

'Why,' said Ottilie. 'Why is she doing this?'

Gracie merely smiled. 'Vengeance.'

'Why? What happened to her?'

'I didn't say it was vengeance for herself,' said Gracie. 'Enough of this.' She bared her teeth. The white wyler lunged and Nox skirted to the side, catching its flesh with her claws. She heard Gracie yowl in pain as Nox rose into the sky.

Ottilie looked to the ocean and felt a change in the wind.

For a little while the world seemed clean, the dredretch stench not yet poisoning the southerly breeze. The air felt thicker, warmer, not with the sickness but with a storm. Nox rose higher and higher. Ottilie knew she had to go back down, but she just needed a few moments to breathe.

Below, she saw Gracie pause and stare up at the sky. Thunder rumbled overhead. That was what they needed. They needed rain! Whistler had chosen a poor day for a battle. Her bone singers were supposed to be able to predict the weather, but perhaps the sky kept secrets too.

Perched on a crumbling parapet of the boundary wall, the monstrous bird screeched, her eyes flashing with an impossible black light that Ottilie seemed to feel rather than see. The dredretches shrieked in response, and a flock of jivvies billowed like a ghastly, tumbling cloud. Under Whistler's control, they didn't turn on each other. They moved as one, engulfing the huntsmen in a vast shroud of shadow and feathers.

40

Varrio's Hex

There were hundreds of jivvies, sweeping and winding, herding the huntsmen in like sheep. The swirl of black wings gathered Nox along with them. There was no escape. They could only move where Whistler wanted them to go. Nox was forced to land, and people pressed into her on all sides. Finally, the jivvies slowed, and the huntsmen were squashed together inside the broken boundary wall.

Whistler plunged from her perch and, with a shriek and a piercing flash, returned to her natural form.

'Better,' she said, wiggling one ear with her good hand. 'Such a ruckus is war.'

Gracie, astride the white wyler, moved to her side.

'While I've got you here,' said Whistler, playfully, 'I'd like to give you a choice.' The way she spoke the word made it clear that there would be no choice at all. 'Your cowardly leaders are still hiding inside,' she continued. 'But it's you I want to talk to. I want to tell you why you're here, and when I'm done, you will have a decision to make.'

Ottilie held her breath. She could feel Nox tense beneath her, muscles coiling to spring, but there was nowhere to go. The jivvies were above, with hundreds of other dredretches surrounding them.

'Thirty years ago, almost to the day, I told your king that I had placed a hex on him,' said Whistler.

Ottilie couldn't believe what she was hearing. After all this time, all her wondering, Whistler was going to tell them about the hex.

'I told him that for three decades he could send no man to fight to defend his lands.' She smiled madly to herself. Still proud, three decades later, Ottilie thought.

'Any external threat to his kingdom had to be resolved by other means,' Whistler continued. 'I told him that if he broke the rules I had set for him, he would die.'

There was something strange about Whistler's wording. She was making it sound as if the hex wasn't real.

'My nephew, Varrio Sol, is a violent, power-hungry man. But you know none of that. You were only children, after all, when you were ripped from your homes,' she said. 'I turned one of the most violent kings in Uskler history into the most peaceable king in Uskler history.' She paused. She found Ottilie in the crowd and looked her squarely in the eye. 'But what does this have to do with you? Well, you're the exception.

'When your great king heard about this threat' – she flapped her sleeves, gesturing at the dredretches – 'this western invasion, he had several paths available to him. He could have given his life for his kingdom and sent an army to defend his people. Of course, coward that he is, he did not take that road.' Whistler laughed. 'No Usklerian army can operate outside the king's command. If he told his people the truth, he would have been dethroned. He could have chosen that path – stepped down and given the crown to his heir, who could have freely sent armies to meet the monsters. Or he could have kept his crown, and armed women instead. But you know the choice he made.'

It was everything Ottilie had suspected. She and Alba had been right about all of it.

'He kidnapped young boys from all across the kingdom,' said Whistler. 'He had them trained to hunt these monsters. He spread the lie of the rule of innocence among your leaders and trainers, to scare them into hiding behind your scrawny, still-growing bodies.

'He created the Narroway Hunt and, in so doing, gave me thirty years to experiment and amass this army.'

She waved her arms, sleeves swinging. 'An army that will be the ruination of his precious kingdom.' Whistler leaned towards them, her voice rasping with derisive glee. 'But here it is, here is the truth: there is no hex.'

Ottilie was frozen, listening hard. For so long she had wanted to know, to understand.

'Magic is not so simple, so specific,' said Whistler. 'But in his ignorance and cowardice, he believed my lie, not daring to risk his life, to question, to test. I will allow him this, I made a convincing show of it ... but, all the same, it is my great pleasure to reveal to you what a fool and coward is the man who wears the crown.'

Ottilie could see it on her face, the elation, the release.

'This is just the beginning,' said Whistler, raising her voice. 'I said I would give you a choice and here it is.'

Ottilie tensed.

'Now: join me.'

High on the parapets of Fort Richter, against the backdrop of dark cloud, Ottilie saw bone singers emerge, their grey robes rippling in the wind.

'You will become immune to the dredretch sickness, to run wild through the Narroway without fear. Live freely and safely in my new world. Please me, and I'll give you a guardian, a partner, a pet.' She waved at Gracie. 'You will gain power over them, learn to see through their eyes. Accept my gifts. Join me. Or fight for a king who sacrificed you for the sake of his own power.'

No-one moved. Not a twitch.

Whistler waited.

There was only silence, and then, in the silence, the beat of bodies. Weight falling. Running. The pounding of hooves. The rattle of wagons. Ottilie stood up in the saddle and craned her neck to look through a gap in the wall.

The Fiory footmen had arrived.

They charged up the field towards the trapped huntsmen. Ottilie saw Hero bounding, a streak of white, and Billow thundering just behind with Ramona on his back. At least fifty Fiory girls sprinted in her wake. Skip was at the head, her cutlass raised to the sky. Somewhere in the throng Ottilie saw Alba's braids flying as she ran. Soaring above them was a black owl. Maeve.

The canopy of jivvies lifted and tore down to meet the reinforcements. The dredretches surrounding the trapped huntsmen followed.

Nox leapt. Ottilie gripped her fur tight as she scaled the chunk of wall behind them. Reaching the top, she launched into the air and soared out over the field, ready to defend the new arrivals. Below, a wagon burst open and Captain Lyre jumped out.

'What are you doing?' Ottilie heard Wrangler Voilies shriek. 'Don't stop here, take us in to safety!'

Ottilie landed beside the wagon and yelled inside. 'You can hurt them. It was all a lie. You can help!'

Captain Lyre nodded darkly, and drew the sword sheathed within his cane. Wrangler Morse burst from the wagon, picked up a fallen spear and bounded into the fray. Behind him, Wrangler Voilies slammed the door shut and locked the bolt.

Ottilie circled above the girls, taking down any flying dredretch she could see. Below her, Skip and Alba tackled a cleaver and Fawn shot an arrow through the skull of a pobe.

Scoot took a great running leap, diving on top of a giffersnak and pinning it with his spear. Something drew his gaze up. Ottilie knew what it was. Maestro flew overhead, casting him in shadow. When the light returned, Ottilie could see Scoot smiling. He'd seen Ned, rescued, flying with Leo.

Time moved strangely.

The black clouds swallowed the sky but were yet to yield a drop of rain. For what might have been hours, it felt like nothing had changed. The mounts from Arko arrived but, still, for every dredretch they felled, there was always another. Ottilie would have welcomed a storm, but there had been no thunder since the first crack.

Then, something shifted. Ottilie could smell it. Nox spiralled into the sky and, above the blood and horror and festering dredretch flesh, she could smell rain. She looked down and for the first time realised they were winning.

Nox circled low. A scorver was barrelling through the footmen; Ottilie shot it without blinking. A great reddish shape zoomed past. It was unfamiliar, and too fast to distinguish, but she could sense it straight away – another bloodbeast.

Preddy was nearby. He had come off his horse and was fighting a lycoat on foot. A fat raindrop landed on Ottilie's cheek, but it almost didn't matter anymore. The huntsmen were beating them back. They were going to win!

'PREDDY!' cried Scoot.

Ottilie's head whipped around so fast her neck burned. She watched in horror as a learie pounced at Preddy, but he was grappling with the lycoat. There was no escaping it. Scoot leapt and, knocking Preddy sideways, disappeared beneath the learie.

Nox dived. Grasping the learie in her jaws, the wingerslink tossed it aside. From above, Leo shot down the lycoat. Preddy lay panting, staring in panic at Scoot, who was sprawled, unmoving, on the grass.

Ottilie jumped from the saddle while Nox was still in the air, landing hard on the ground. Her knees throbbed as she crawled to where Scoot lay.

'Scoot?'

He saw her. She ran her hands over his wounds, trying to close them, trying to help. Scoot was deathly pale. Preddy was beside her, gripping his hand. Ottilie didn't know what to do. She had to get him inside, to safety. She had to find Richter's healers.

Wings flapped and air beat across her face. The world darkened and Whistler appeared. 'Oh dear,' she clucked.

Ottilie jumped to her feet and pointed her cutlass at Whistler. Her mind was set on a single purpose. 'Fix him!' she demanded, her arm shaking. 'You can do magic. Fix him!'

'Now why would I do that?'

Ottilie took a step closer, without a lick of fear. Whistler waved her hand and the cutlass burned so hot Ottilie cried out and dropped it.

'Fix him, please. Just fix him!' she begged.

Whistler sighed. 'Well, why not?' she said with a lazy wave of her sleeve.

Ottilie couldn't believe what she was seeing. The wounds were glowing with a pale light; the flesh was knitting together. Scoot's breathing eased. He looked merely asleep.

'You just remember this, Ottilie,' said Whistler, reaching out to grip Ottilie's chin, her fingers like claws beneath the sleeve. 'You remember this mercy.'

She didn't know what to think. What had just happened? Why would Whistler do that? She opened her mouth to thank her. To say thank you to the witch who had caused all this misery. But before she could speak, a cruel smile twisted Whistler's face.

'Oh, I'm not finished yet,' she said and, dropping her hand, she muttered something under her breath.

Ottilie whipped back to Scoot and cried out in horror. From the top of his head, grey flint started creeping across his skin. He was turning to stone!

'Stop!' Ottilie cried. 'Please stop! STOP!'

But it was done.

'WHY?' she shrieked with more malice than she had ever conjured.

'I fixed him for you, dear – where's the gratitude?' said Whistler.

'He's stone! Turn him back!' She flung herself at Whistler, begging, clutching at her clothes.

'He'd be no use to me if I turned him back,' she said, prising Ottilie's fingers from her jacket. 'But heartstone. That's very useful.' She stepped towards him, but Ottilie shoved her aside and flung herself over the statue that was Scoot. 'Don't you dare touch him!' she growled, the words cutting up her throat.

Around her, she felt others emerge, encircling Scoot, pointing their weapons at Whistler. The witch could have shifted them with a mere blink, Ottilie could sense it, but instead she just smiled. 'You can keep him for now. But don't forget, Ottilie, you're in my debt.'

With a flash, the monstrous bird launched into the air. She felt the wind from her beating wings but didn't watch where she flew. She was searching Scoot, looking for any tiny part of him that was still flesh.

Hours might have passed. Days even. Someone took her hand, pulling her gently back. Ned was there. He pulled his shirt loose and pressed it carefully over her hands, wiping away the blood.

'It's not mine,' she said, in a daze.

'I know,' he said gently.

Ottilie looked down and saw Preddy rocking back and forth in Skip's arms. Alba was beside him, holding his hand, tears streaming down her face.

Leo dismounted and stood by her side. Ottilie looked up and around in a panic. The dredretches! Gracie! Where were they?

As if hearing her thoughts, Leo looked at her.

'They fled,' he said blankly.

— 41 —

Victory

Ottilie stared at the ceiling. She had a bandage wrapped around her head, covering the severed tip of her ear, which had been cleaned and stitched up by the patchies. Gully was beside her, curled into a ball. He had barely moved from that position over the last two days. Preddy was sitting by the window, staring at the closed shutters, and Ned was on the floor at the end of the bed, knees bent, his head resting on his arms.

Scoot was in the infirmary. No-one knew what to do; the healers were flummoxed. Only magic would save him, Ottilie knew. Maeve had vowed to try, but she was still getting her bearings, with no-one to teach her.

Ottilie refused to believe that he was gone. She would find a way. If Maeve couldn't do it, she would make Whistler fix him. Somehow. Some day.

Whistler and Gracie had disappeared and so, it seemed, had most of the bone singers. The few that remained at Fiory insisted on their innocence, but were locked up in the burrows for the time being. The directorate wanted information from them. Ottilie, too, wanted to understand more about them. There was so much she wanted to know. And she would find out soon enough, she didn't doubt that. The battle of Fort Richter was not the end.

Richter was already in the process of restoration. Things were settling, but everything was different. They knew now. Word had spread. Everyone knew that the rule of innocence was a lie. They didn't have to do this anymore; the king's army could do it. That was the logic. But no-one offered it. Conductor Edderfed didn't suggest it when he welcomed them back and congratulated them on their victory. Because he knew, they all knew, that no-one would take up the offer to leave. No-one who had lived through that battle, who got a taste of what Whistler had in store for the Usklers, could walk away now. No-one who had stood around the funeral pyres and mourned their fallen brothers and sisters wanted to be anywhere else. They wanted to be in the thick of it, on the frontlines. They wanted justice to be served. They wanted Whistler vanquished and Gracie Moravec to pay for her crimes.

The king could send his soldiers – Ottilie assumed he would – but they were trained to fight men, and out of practice at even that. The huntsmen knew how to handle dredretches. They were still the best hope for the Usklers.

Leo entered the room without knocking, and without looking at her. Ever since they had returned, whenever Ottilie's tears fell, his were triggered within seconds. And since the battle her eyes were rarely dry. So he had developed a habit of staring at her good ear and nowhere else.

Ottilie was glad of it. She couldn't look into his face without drowning in memories of the funerals. She remembered the pyre flames reflected in his eyes and the unfamiliar look of uncertainty, of fear. Leo usually shone with confidence, so sure of everything. Now that it was gone, Ottilie realised it was this quality that had helped make her feel safe in this dangerous world. As they said goodbye to the fallen, Leo had looked like a lost little boy, and Ottilie's rock had crumbled to dust.

She remembered Preddy with his arm across Gully's shoulders, so racked with grief he was barely able to stand. She had felt it herself. There was a hollowness, as if she had no bones anymore, only flesh and no way to prop it up, just strangled breath, trapped inside. Alba's face had been buried in her mother's arms. Skip was statuesque and dry-eyed, moving only to twitch when Captain Lyre spoke each name.

Ottilie could still see the smoke spiralling up from the pyre, and the bright flames dancing beneath. She saw it when the lights dimmed, when she closed her eyes, sometimes just when she breathed.

Leo moved out of the doorway to sit beside Ned at the end of her bed, and there they waited.

The door banged open. Skip was standing there, her eyes alight. 'Why is it so dark in here?'

'We were waiting to hear –' said Ottilie.

Skip snorted, as if unable to muster a real laugh. 'Why do you need to do that in the dark?'

There was a scrape of flint and Skip lit the lantern by the doorway. Ottilie pulled herself off the bed and lit another. Everyone was staring at Skip.

'What did they say?' said Gully, unfurling his limbs.

'They gathered us all. Everyone here who's not already a huntsman. Custodians, shovelies, even the adults – the cooks, wagoners, blacksmiths … Captain Lyre did the talking. He said we here in the Narroway are the first defence, all of us, that the huntsmen will be Whistler's downfall, and that regardless of Usklerian law, and the names on the wall, anyone in the Narroway who wants to bring Whistler down will be trained to help do it.'

Leo turned to Ottilie, lantern light flickering in his eyes and a small smile on his face. She met his gaze and felt her own face lift. This little thing, which should have been so easy but had been so hard, this tiny step that had grown to the size of a mountain … they were going to train the girls. They were going to let them fight! There would be no more hiding, sneaking or lying. This was too important. Defeating Whistler was the only thing that mattered, and they had to do it together.

'He's not hurt,' said Maeve.

Ottilie whirled around. Maeve was walking up the empty corridor behind her, not far from where she had pulled Ottilie and Scoot into the cupboard, months ago. Her chest hurt to think of Scoot hammering on the door.

'Bill?' said Ottilie, breathlessly.

'I tried calling out to him in my head,' said Maeve, 'like he does with other birds sometimes, and I found him.'

'You talked to him?'

Maeve shook her head sadly. 'Just a sense, that he's not hurt, and he's not too frightened. I think they're looking after him. They must need him for something.'

'Like what?' said Ottilie, her voice rough.

'I couldn't make the connection strong enough to get more. I'm still learning – trying to teach myself. I can choose to turn now, but it still happens when I'm sleeping, and the other things, the witch stuff, I can sort of squash it, but I can't make anything happen on purpose. I've tried, for Scoot … and I wanted to at the battle, but I was most use as a bird,' said Maeve, the memories dimming her bright eyes.

'What is that thing Whistler can turn into?' Ottilie asked, remembering the monstrous bird clinging to the turrets. 'Gracie said she's a fiorn, like you, but that thing is a monster.'

'Do you know, I've been thinking about it,' said Maeve. 'I think, when she started meddling with dredretches, she corrupted herself, corrupted her form. I don't think she chooses to become that thing. I think she wishes she could still be a bird.'

'How do you know?' said Ottilie.

'Because, really, everyone wants to be good, don't they? They must … Even Gracie, she still saved me, remember? Even after the binding she still came to rescue me and gave me a choice.

'And Whistler, it's hard to explain, but turning – apart from being really scary – it feels so right, like you've found a part of yourself that was missing. I think she hates herself. Hates what she's become. I've felt that before, not on the same scale, but I've felt it. You can get to a point where you hate yourself so much, you think there's no turning back. She's old, Whistler. I read up on her after Bill said her name. I asked Alba for the book. Fennix Sol is the daughter of Viago the Vanquisher.'

Ottilie nodded. Gracie had told her that.

'That makes her King Varrio's aunt,' said Maeve. 'Clearly, she's found a way to look younger. But that's what I mean. She's been around a long time, and she's obsessed with this game with the king and, by the sounds of it, he's not going to give up his power for anything. Between them, they're going to turn the kingdom to ash.'

What was it, Ottilie wondered – why did she hate him so much? Ottilie had no love for the king herself. Villain though she was, Whistler didn't seem like she was lying about his character. The existence of the Narroway Hunt proved him a selfish coward. Gracie had said all of this was about vengeance: vengeance not for Whistler, but for someone else. But who?

'We're going to stop it,' said Ottilie. 'We're going to rescue Bill and we're going to end this.' She twisted the ring on her thumb.

Something had happened two days ago. Every ring-wearer had felt something, everyone but Ottilie. Her friends described an icy prickling on the skin beneath the ring. Sitting in the infirmary beside Scoot, she had looked over to see Alba cringe and scratch at her thumb. Across the room, the patchies had done the same. Alba had removed her ring to examine it under the light. Ottilie could still hear her tiny gasp as she beheld the new words scratched on the inside.

Ottilie had pulled hers off immediately, seeing as always: *sleeper comes for none*.

But Alba's ring and, it appeared, everyone else's now read: *pay for what you've done*.

❧ 42 ❧

Bone and Heartstone

It was early morning when the idea occurred to her – a way to help Scoot. She felt so stupid for not thinking of it before. Without even bothering to change from her nightclothes, Ottilie pulled on her boots and hurried to find Alba.

Outside the communal springs, behind a statue of three sea eagles, Alba showed her the hidden passage that led to a dark corner of the burrows. There were no dredretches down there anymore. Not since the bone singers had revealed themselves as Whistler's allies. Even though the guilty had fled, and those who claimed innocence were being closely monitored, the

Hunt decided that keeping any dredretches within the boundary walls was too risky.

Wall watches had tripled, much to Leo's displeasure. Huntsmen now patrolled every inch of the boundary, day and night. From the interrogations they discovered the bone singers had secret entrances to the grounds. This, the bone singers suggested, was how the wylers got in. The first, Ottilie assumed, had been guided by Whistler, perhaps with the particular purpose of wounding Gracie, preparing her for the binding. The others, Ottilie knew, Gracie herself had let in.

She still didn't like to think about the night she had spent down in the burrows, all alone with the dredretches. But the Hunt had made things more comfortable for the bone singers, providing them with straw beds and meals twice a day.

She stepped into the flickering torchlight. There were rustlings of straw as the bone singers peeked through the bars to see who had disturbed their miserable silence. They still insisted they knew nothing of what Whistler was really up to, but Ottilie couldn't believe it. They had been performing rituals on the bones of the dredretches, under Whistler's instruction. How ignorant could they have been?

Ottilie and Alba hopped over a dark puddle in the centre of the floor, no doubt some foul fluid the dredretches had left behind. Peering into a cell on her left, Ottilie found Bonnie. The bone singer's dark hair was braided neatly to one side. She supposed she didn't have much else to occupy her hands. The straw, too, was knotted and braided into patterns here and there, or arranged into letters.

Bonnie's pale eyebrows pressed together. 'What are you doing down here?' Her voice was just above a whisper.

'I want to talk to you,' said Ottilie.

'We told them everything,' Bonnie said, with a shiver.

'The directorate doesn't keep us in the know,' said Ottilie. 'Will you answer our questions?'

Bonnie shrugged. 'It doesn't matter what you do. She'll win. She rigged the game. As soon as the king starts playing, she'll end it all. She's been waiting.'

Ottilie felt Alba twitch beside her. Captain Lyre had set out for All Kings' Hill to speak with the king in person, arranging for his armies to join them in the Narroway. They needed them, she knew that. They needed all the help they could get. But Bonnie was right – as soon as the king entered the arena, Whistler would show her true strength.

'I know as much as you,' said Bonnie. 'If you think we're lying, why bother talking to me?'

'Because you don't like the Withering Wood,' said Ottilie. 'I saw it months ago. The day the kappabak appeared. I don't think you're guilty. I just think you know more than you're saying.' She spoke quickly, eager to get to the point.

Bonnie's shoulders settled. Ottilie must have been the first person to suggest she might be innocent. Alba moved a little closer and held out a fat pumpkin scone through the bars. Bonnie shuffled forwards and snatched it. Clearly, the two meals a day were not substantial, or at least not very enjoyable.

'Whistler turned our friend to stone,' said Ottilie, her lips trembling as she spoke. 'Heartstone, that's what she said. Do you know how to turn him back?' Her heart beat fast, desperate for a yes.

Bonnie just shook her head, ripping the scone into small chunks and laying them out in her dress. She pressed one piece into her mouth and closed her eyes.

Ottilie swallowed the lump in her throat. 'She said heartstone was useful to her – do you know why? What is it?' She was desperate for anything, any scrap of information that could help Scoot.

Bonnie looked up at her, her eyes heavy. 'Heartstone is just that – people turned to stone. I don't know what she would need it for. Truly. She didn't tell us her plans. And I can't fix your friend. Only a witch could do that. I don't – we don't have any magic. Not really.'

Ottilie closed her eyes. The ground seemed to reach up and grip her, drawing her down. This had been her great hope, that one of these bone singers could fix Scoot.

'Tell me about the bone singers,' she said, fending off tears. 'Who are you all? Where did you come from? What sort of magic do you use?'

Bonnie finished her mouthful before answering. 'Whistler recruited us, all of us. She took me from Rupimoon Rock.'

Ottilie knew of it. It was the largest town on the north island.

'She likes to think of herself as a saviour of unwanted children,' said Bonnie. 'She found me curled up with the goats one night when my father was in a rage.'

Ottilie was surprised. She had always assumed the bone singers were special somehow.

'She said she was a mystic,' she continued, 'employed by the Crown, and that she would share her gifts with me — that she was building a family.'

The way Ottilie understood it, mystics were glorified priests and, like the faulty peddlers who sold potions and amulets on the side of the road to Market Town, mostly frauds.

'Does the king do that?' Ottilie turned to Alba. 'Employ mystics?'

She nodded. 'There's always at least one royal mystic.'

'But why are mystics trusted enough to work for the king, when everyone hates witches so much?' said Ottilie.

'Because the mystics don't have any power, really,' said Alba. 'There weren't even any mystics in the Usklers originally; they came with the Roving Empire. Lots of tinkerers and inventers call themselves mystics because people will pay a higher price for something that's spell'd.

'Some texts say that the Roving mystics were jealous of our Usklerian witches, and scared that a demonstration of real magic would expose them as fakes. They say the mystics were responsible for spreading the rumour about the sleepless ritual that led to the witch purge.'

'The baby-eating ritual?' Ottilie screwed up her face. Alba nodded.

'She used "mystic" to get people to trust her,' said Bonnie. 'She couldn't very well admit to being a witch, and she never showed any of her real power in front of us, or anyone. Just small things, marking the ranking walls, reading the weather, a bit of healing …'

'So if none of you are magical at all, what did you do, then?' said Ottilie. 'What were all the rituals? How did you know when we felled dredretches for the scores?'

'She gave us all one of these …' Bonnie crawled to the back of her cell and dug around beneath the straw pallet. Moving back into the light, she held out what looked like a sharp tooth hanging from a chain.

Ottilie recognised it. It was the same thing Gracie had shown her at Richter.

'I took it off. I didn't want to feel it anymore,' said Bonnie, holding it far from her body.

'Feel what?' said Alba.

Ottilie stared at the tiny white shard. It wasn't a tooth, she realised, it was a chip of bone.

'I think it's dredretch bone,' said Bonnie, as if reading Ottilie's mind. 'She never told us, but I think we all guessed.' Turning to Alba, she added, 'It linked us together. All of us, with her, and we sense the dredretches – we hear it like a song … it's hard to explain, it's like a code that we can all understand. But it's all Whistler, it's all through her. None of us have any power on our own – nothing once we take these off.' She jiggled the chain, eyeing it fearfully.

'I was told that when you wear them, the dredretches don't attack you,' said Ottilie.

Bonnie shrugged. 'She didn't tell us that. We had a chant to keep them at bay. That's all I knew.' Her eyes flicked to the side. 'We didn't ask questions.'

Ottilie was sure she was lying about something. She remembered Bonnie and Nicolai turning in circles, chanting when dredretches attacked, months and months ago. It was all for show. It had to have been. No-one could know that Whistler was so linked with the dredretches, and that a simple shard of bone could keep them from attacking – it would have given her away, and given the Hunt the upper hand.

But she had given them the rings. Why? To even the odds? Whistler wanted the Narroway Hunt to exist. She wanted it as evidence of the king's character, and to keep the dredretches out of the Usklers while she summoned more, built her army, experimented … and recruited. She had wanted to recruit them. In her twisted mind she had believed that when they found out the truth about their king, they would want to join her – to punish him.

Ottilie held out her hand. 'Can I try it?'

'Ottilie, I don't think you should!' Alba grabbed her sleeve.

Bonnie dropped the chain onto Ottilie's palm. It was heavier than she expected, but there was nothing else unusual about it, until she placed it over her head. Then she heard it. The song. It was otherworldly, high and low at the same time, like a beating drum and the shrillest tin whistle. There was something wrong, a scraping and a hypnotic beat, air shrieking, but not wind – air trapped, fleeing some unnatural place. Then she felt eyes upon her: stormy, birdlike eyes.

'Hello, hatchling,' said a voice in her head. Whistler's voice.

Run, Ottilie thought. It was all she could think. *Run*.

Distantly, she felt fingernails scraping her neck. Alba ripped the chain back over her head and Ottilie gasped for air.

'Are you all right? Ottilie? Ottilie!'

Alba's wide, dark eyes came into focus.

'Sorry,' Ottilie rasped.

'You stopped breathing!' said Alba. She rounded on Bonnie. 'Did you know that would happen?'

'It takes practice,' said Bonnie, with a shiver.

'Can I keep it?' said Ottilie.

'What?' Alba snapped her fingers in front of her face. 'Are you hypnotised?'

'I'm not going to put it on again, I just think it might be useful,' she said, thinking hard. 'And I want to show it to Maeve.' She turned back to Bonnie. There was so much more she wanted to know. 'Tell me about the rituals, with the bones ... what were you doing?'

'We were making sure that the dredretches didn't rise again,' said Bonnie blankly. 'We had special salt and a song.'

'But that's not really what you were doing,' said Alba. 'It can't have been.'

'That's what she told us.' Bonnie's eyes welled up, guilt washing her face.

'You were doing the opposite, weren't you?' said Ottilie. 'It wasn't salt – it was something else. You were singing to them, making them come back?'

'We didn't know,' she said, her voice cracking. 'It was Whistler, through that.' She pointed shakily to the necklace in Alba's hand. 'They wouldn't come back straight away; it took time, we never saw. I don't know anything.'

'You do,' said Ottilie, growing angry. 'What about the bone singers with bloodbeasts? What happened to the boy who was bound to a knopo?'

Bonnie seemed to slip backwards, disappearing behind blank eyes. 'We were told that he got sick and didn't recover. I never knew anything about the binding.'

'I don't believe you!' said Ottilie. 'How can some of you have been slipping into trances and controlling dredretches and others of you not known a thing? You live together, work together, sleep and eat together – there's no way!'

Bonnie shuffled back, away from the light.

Ottilie clenched her hands around the bars. If Bonnie really did know something … she had either chosen not to go with Whistler or been left behind. What good would it do her to confess what she had concealed? But she could help. It was the right thing to do. Surely, she could understand that.

'Bonnie,' she said, trying to soften her voice. 'The more we know about her and the bone singers, the better chance we have of defeating them. Do you know anything that could help us?'

'He told me – Nicolai,' Bonnie said, in barely a whisper. 'Once it was out, just before they fled Fiory.'

Ottilie had to lean closer to hear.

'He told me about the bound ones and the blood-beasts,' she breathed. 'They have to be near death, then she weaves a link between them and a dredretch, then they become as one and the person is able to control any dredretch of that species. He, Nicolai, he is one. I don't know what kind –'

'Shank,' said Ottilie.

Bonnie looked at her questioningly, pain pulling at her face.

'He's alive,' said Ottilie.

'He said the bound ones are special – her true family,' whispered Bonnie. 'A family found. Not a family born. He said they'll be the leaders of the new world. Her world.'

Ottilie's fingers turned white on the bars. Whistler's world. A world overrun with monsters. Whistler had wanted her to be a part of it, to bind her to the kappabak. Her eyes found her left thumb, the bronze ring still wrapped around it.

'Why did the rings change?' she asked, unsure that she wanted the answer.

'Because she offered everyone a chance to join her,' said Bonnie. 'And no-one came to her. It means ... it means she's going to punish us.'

Ottilie's chest tightened. 'But ... mine ... mine didn't change.'

Bonnie met her gaze, her eyes widening, showing a strip of white. 'If yours didn't change,' she said, 'it means she hasn't given up on you yet.'

☛ 43 ☚

Restless

A ruthless wind beat against Ottilie's window shutters, knocking her in and out of nightmares. Eyes snapping open, she felt shivery and adrift. She must have kicked her covers off. She yanked the blankets off the floor and threw them over her head. She curled her hands into fists, wrapping the sheets around her icy fingers and trying to block out the relentless knocking and thumping that stirred up her nerves.

Unable to stand it any longer, she abandoned any attempts at sleep and knocked on Gully's door just after eleventh bell.

'Hungry?'

'Starving,' said Gully, scrambling out of bed.

Together they crept down to Montie's kitchen. The lanterns were lit and Montie was inside with Alba, getting things in order for the morning.

'What are you two doing out of bed?' said Montie.

'Hungry,' Ottilie lied. She didn't know how to tell anyone the truth, that she hadn't had a solid sleep since talking with Bonnie three nights ago. That when she wasn't lying awake thinking about Scoot and how to save him, she was woken by nightmares and visions of Whistler appearing above her, binding her against her will.

'What's new?' said Montie, with a smile. 'Here, you can have a bit of this.' She pulled a large loaf of bread baked with brakkernuts and waterfigs from the cupboard. 'But then you need to sleep. You're both falling to pieces in front of my eyes. I can't stand it.' She cupped her hand gently over Ottilie's torn ear. It felt like magic. As if her motherly touch could heal a wound. If only it could. If only Montie could rest her hand on Scoot and turn him back to flesh and bone.

Alba sat down beside Ottilie and tore a chunk of the bread for herself.

'You too, Noel?' said Montie, turning to the doorway. 'And Isla – this is a party.'

Skip and Preddy sat opposite them at the table. He cut off a piece of bread and nibbled at it quietly.

'I saw you from the end of the corridor,' said Skip.

'And woke Preddy, by the looks of it,' said Gully, nudging Preddy, who seemed to have forgotten to keep chewing. He yawned and choked a little.

The outside door swung open with a bang.

Ottilie jumped in her seat and twisted to face a very windswept Leo.

'Where was our invite?' he said, pressing his weight against the door so it didn't slam shut in the gale.

Ned was beside him, bruised but recovering well. He'd wanted to go straight back into hunting after the battle. Ottilie understood why; she felt it too, the need for distraction and, if she was completely honest with herself, vengeance. But the wranglers only allowed him to take on wall-watch shifts, and only with other elites.

'Finished on the wall?' She cringed as a biting gust breached the doorway. 'Here for your treat, Leo?'

Leo was too busy easing the door closed to answer.

Ned flashed a grin and slid in beside her, his hand brushing against hers. He wore a bandage, but Ottilie knew that beneath it three nasty burns, shaped like stars, trailed up his arm.

Despite the violent night, a warm calm settled in the kitchen. Beside her, Gully rested his head on the table, closing his eyes. Opposite, Skip, as always, looked alert and ready for action, and across the room Alba stared thoughtfully at the water she was boiling for tea. Ottilie watched the lively flames flickering and dancing beneath the pot, and for some reason she thought of laughter, and she thought of Scoot. He would be back, she just knew it. She was going to rescue Bill and bring Scoot back. Whatever it took, she would find a way.

Preddy got up to gather some cups and began pulling them down from the shelf, one at a time, careful not to chip them. Montie had dragged Leo over to the light to inspect a scrape across his jaw and he was bragging about how he nabbed the dredretch that did it to him. Ned was laughing along, his eyes brighter than they had been in weeks.

It was a sense of family that Ottilie had seldom experienced. She felt in that moment that everything really would turn out all right. It wasn't a burst of determination or a stubborn willing. It was just a feeling of comfort and warmth. If that feeling could exist in a world plagued by monsters, after everything they had been through – horror and injury and terrible loss – Ottilie felt unshakeably that there would always be hope.

☛ THE END ☚

COMING SOON

BOOK THREE
of
~ THE NARROWAY TRILOGY ~

Ottilie Colter
AND THE
Withering World

The Narroway Huntsmen are under attack — by something far worse than dredretches. A witch is cursing them one by one, making them unwilling participants in a vengeful scheme. But what, exactly, is she planning — and can Ottilie stop her before it's too late?

Don't miss the thrilling finale of

RHIANNON WILLIAMS'

groundbreaking trilogy!

AVAILABLE IN 2020

Acknowledgements

Thank you to everyone at Hardie Grant Egmont for giving this series wings, especially Marisa Pintado, Luna Soo, Haylee Collins and Penelope White for looking after Ottilie so very well.

A huge thank you to the outrageously talented Maike Plenzke and Jess Cruickshank for another magnificent cover, and to Emma Schwarcz for helping this story shine.

To my whole family, thank you for cheering so loudly.

Trish, I am ever grateful for the life rafts. Thank you for spreading the story far and wide.

A special thank you to both of my wonderful grandparents – your encouragement means everything.

I have the most supportive parents on the planet. Mum and Dad, I don't deserve you and I can't ever thank you enough.

Catrin, thank you for passing out books at the pub and fizzing with enthusiasm, even when I'm being a monosyllabic ghoul.

I have to thank my extraordinary friends, Zoe and Holly, for shouting support across this maddening distance, and Oran, for brightening my days and handing out books like candy.

Lastly, Lu, your brilliance never ceases to inspire me. Thank you for holding me up when my bones go bendy.

About the Author

Rhiannon Williams is a Sydney-based writer. Originally from Taradale, Victoria, Rhiannon has a background in theatre and hopes to tell stories until the end of her days. She studied Creative Arts at Flinders University, has climbed Mt Kilimanjaro, and once accidentally set fire to her hair on stage. Her Ampersand Prize–winning debut novel, *Ottilie Colter and the Narroway Hunt*, was published in 2018 and will soon be released in Germany and the Netherlands.